THE RAG QUILT
Alex Bischoff

Table of Contents

Author's Note 2
Chapter 1 3
Chapter 2 8
Chapter 3 20
Chapter 4 31
Chapter 5 42
Chapter 6 52
Chapter 7 63
Chapter 8 77
Chapter 9 89
Chapter 10 103
Chapter 11 120
Chapter 12 133
Chapter 13 146
Chapter 14 160
Chapter 15 181
Chapter 16 196
Chapter 17 211
Chapter 18 224
Chapter 19 240
Chapter 20 255
Epilogue 268

Author's Note

While the main events of this novel are real, the characters are not. The only characters who have direct participation in the story who were real people are Col. Bouquet and the Conestoga tribe member, Will Sock, all others are figments of the author's imagination. Any similarities to people, living or dead, is purely coincidental. This was largely done out of respect for the dead. I did heavily rely on historical sources but there were some which contradicted others and when that occurred, I chose to use information that was agreed on by more than one source though I did try to acknowledge the other source.

Chapter 1

Bam! Bam! Bam!

"Anna! Are you in?"

Lydia recognized the booming voice of Brother Jacob. She sprang to the door and tore it open revealing a large man with broad shoulders, black hair, and a long black beard. She was quickly joined by her three sisters and her little brother who was too small to work in the fields.

"Lydia," Brother Jacob panted, "Is your mother home?"

Lydia's mother, Anna Fischer, pulled the door open further, revealing her pale features. Though the day was warm, despite it being early in the spring, she wore a quilt wrapped around her shoulders like a shawl, her children gathered around her. She coughed slightly. "Yes, Brother Jacob, I am here. What is it?"

"There's been an accident. One of the oxen caught his foot in a groundhog hole. The plow went over, it fell onto Elias's leg. It's badly broken. Michael and Elder Weber will be here with him soon."

"Oh no!" Lydia gasped. Her younger sister, Deborah, began to cry, clinging tightly to her mother.

Little Peter tugged on Lydia's dress. "What happened?"

"Da's broken his leg."

Anna's wan visage grew stoic, her chin lifted slightly. "Yes, my dears. We must make ready for your father when he comes home. Deborah, dry your tears. Father will not want to see sad faces when he arrives. Lydia, make up the bed, good and soft"

Lydia ran to the chest and grabbed armfuls of thick, down-filled blankets.

"Will Da be well?" Lydia heard her youngest sister ask.

"Of course, little mouse," Lydia's mother stroked Esther's flaxen hair, "God is the great physician, He will heal your father."

As Lydia was folding the final blanket on the bed to form a little hill for her father's leg to rest upon, she heard a great commotion from the other room.

"Amos! Take him to the bedroom," Brother Jacob said.

In a moment, Lydia's brother, Michael, came in with Elder Amos Weber on his right side, the broad shoulders of her father, Elias Fischer, between them as a yoke, his legs trailing behind.

Lydia shrank back in horror as she saw the torn trouser leg, the blood, the way the lower part of the leg seemed to move on its own accord. She had hoped there would be no blood. Blood meant death. It meant the break would become infected. A finger might be survived, but she had seen many fine men, younger and stronger than her father, succumb to a broken leg when there had been blood.

"Michael! Bring him over here!" she ordered.

Her brother and the elder moved her father to the bed where he lay, his brow ruddy, his breathing shallow. Her father's leg lay on the cushion she had made for it, the lower part lying almost beside itself.

"Lydia, fetch water. We need to clean the break," Elder Weber said.

Lydia did as she was told.

When the doctor arrived she was ordered to draw more water and boil it with white oak bark to make a bitter smelling tea. She cut onions and garlic. She gathered the large leaves of the broadleaf plantain and watched as the doctor crushed these together with the tea into a poultice and wrapped them around the leg. She was glad she had been outside scouring the ground for plantain leaves when the doctor set it. In truth, she had fled the room the moment the doctor told her father to bite on a leather strap. She knew what was coming and she could not bear to see it.

Now her father lay in the bed, his leg bound in a splint. His breathing had returned to normal though he winced whenever he turned. Seeing no more danger for the time being, the doctor left with orders that he should be contacted if anything were to change for the worse.

Michael sat in a chair across from the bed wringing his hands. Her mother knelt beside Father, dipping a cloth in the bowl of water and wiping his brow while Lydia sat with her back against the door, listening to her mother's soothing voice. Though she was eighteen years old, and such things were certainly childish, she found, in this moment, she desperately needed to hear the soft, whispery words of her mother answered by her father's own strong tones.

"What of the ox?" Anna asked.

Father turned his head away. "He broke his leg in the hole. Brother Jacob did what was needed quickly."

"How will we finish the harvest with but one ox and one man?"

"Brother Jacob will fetch Cousin Egon when he goes to Reading tomorrow. He will help. The others will help, too, once their work is done. Michael can manage until then."

"For now, but Old Dan is a cart horse, not a plow horse," Michael said. "We'll need an ox."

"We do not have the money for an ox and mother's medicine," her father said, grimly.

"I can go without," mother said. "We need an ox."

"No." Elias said, "Without that medicine you will only become sicker and die."

"Without an ox to finish the planting, we will all die."

Lydia raced to her room, fighting back the hot tears that stung her eyes. She ran to the cedar chest at the foot of her bed. Throwing open the heavy lid, she thrust both her hands in and pulled out a stack of thick, colorful blankets. Lydia pressed her face into the soft linen, breathing in the scent of the goose down. She lifted her head from the flying birds spiraling around the carefully stitched square, two wet spots were left where her eyes had been.

She took a deep breath and rushed from the room and down the stairs. She burst through the doorway to her parent's bedroom. "Sell my quilts!" she panted. "We will be able to make more than enough from them to pay for mother's medicine. Then we can buy the ox as well."

"But those are your wedding quilts!" her mother cried. "We cannot sell them. You've spent years sewing them."

Lydia's heart sank as she recalled every hour she spent stitching the fine quilts while her father read from the Good Book. Every stitch of thread a hope set in the Word of the Lord. She had sewn her very heart into the soft fabric of the quilts; chosen each pattern to bless her and her future family. She had glowed with pride as her friends adored them, tracing the patterns with their fingers, rubbing the soft fabric against their cheeks. Special fabric, woven by her grandmother before she died for Lydia to use, the finest in their town, now almost all in these quilts.

Lydia set her jaw. "I made these; I can make others."

Her father sighed, then winced in pain. "It matters not. There is no one to go to the market in Lancaster. Michael must finish the planting and your mother is too ill."

"Perhaps Jacob could take them to Reading and see if he might find a buyer?" Anna suggested.

"I could not impose on him like that. He has enough worries of his own without ours."

"What about me?" Lydia asked. "I could go. I've been many times with you and Michael and mother."

"It is a fair bit different to go with family than to go alone."

"I won't be alone, though. Uncle Zeke and Aunt Sarah are there with the cousins. They will let me share their stall. Brother Jacob can leave me off with them."

"If you are certain," her father said, with no small waiver in his voice.

"I am. Send me with all our wares and, God willing, I will have them sold by the time Cousin Egon arrives."

"Come here," he said. She did as she was asked. He stroked her hair, then placed a hand on her forehead. "My brave child. Go with God's blessing. And be careful of those strange to you, do not speak to them except to sell them something. There are many who will see a face as pretty as yours and wish to do you harm." He sighed. "And who knows, perhaps God has been preparing you for such a time as this."

"Da, you are thinking of Esther," Lydia managed to smile through her tears.

Her father grimaced as he pulled himself up to kiss her brow. "You are correct, as always," he forced a pained smile which did not travel to his eyes where his smiles usual sat in miniature shelves beside them, "Lydia was a successful cloth merchant, and so too will you be, for you do it out of sacrifice and love. If there is one thing our Lord understands, it is that."

Chapter 2

Lydia's friends, Agatha, Gretel, and Evony, came to see her off early that morning, with Seth Garten and his cousin Ald, behind.

"You are so fortunate to be going to Lancaster!" Agatha cried.

"I would hardly call it good fortune," Evony scolded, her ebony brows knit above her straight, little nose.

"You'll bring us back something?" Agatha asked.

"Your aunt does make the best oat cookies," Gretel added, her twin golden braids carelessly peeking out from under her bonnet.

Ald nodded his head in agreement.

"I am certain she would be happy to bake cookies for all of you," Lydia said, eager to help her aunt in that endeavor. She loved making cookies for her friends - sometimes slipping in a special one for each, such as a cookie shaped like a lamb for Agatha, or one with slices of apple on top for Seth. She was planning to bake a special batch just for him.

"Ald and I will help Michael while you're away," Seth said.

"I would hate to put your fathers out."

"It is no trouble; father has my brothers to help him. Between the five of them, he won't miss me. I asked him when I heard your father had been hurt and the plow broken."

Lydia beamed up into his face. "Thank you!"

Seth glanced down at the ground, his cheeks like two radishes beneath his blue eyes, the shadow cast by the wide brim of his hat not enough to conceal the bright shade.

"My father told me to help, too!" Ald said, pushing in front of Seth.

"Thank you, Ald," Lydia said. "And thank your father as well."

Ald was neither as tall nor as handsome as his cousin. If she had not known they were related, Lydia would never have believed it for they held not a feature in common. While Seth was a whole head taller than her and owned blonde hair and blue eyes, Ald had hair of the same chestnut tone as the Fischer's horse, hazel eyes that met Lydia's when they stood, and a spare frame that belied his strength. In many ways, Seth seemed older than his cousin despite being the same age. He was more responsible, though that had been a relatively new turn for him.

When she was younger, she could not tolerate them. They were the same age as her, Gretel, and Evony and fond of nothing more than teasing the girls and playing sports. But last year, Seth had gone to Reading to help his cousin with her farm after her husband passed and stayed until she'd remarried. The Garten family were able to spare him, seeing as they had been blessed with six boys and he the youngest among them.

He'd returned quite changed. He still enjoyed riding sports with his black horse, Schwartz, but he was more responsible, more serious. Perhaps it had been the experience of running his own household and farm that had altered him so. He talked of little else than wanting to finish his own house and start his own family.

Ald had changed as well, without the presence of his closest friend. He had become more eager to be of help around the village. Many of the girls were quite fond of him for he was always giving them thoughtful gifts, though he was not especially inclined toward work.

Her dearest friend, Gretel, often told her Seth had already chosen Lydia to be his future bride and she prayed it was truth her friend spoke. She found herself picturing him as her husband in her mind. He was tall and handsome with skin of the swarthy tint of the sun, hair as fair as straw, and deep blue eyes that spoke of many thoughts his lips would not.

"It is time to be going," Brother Jacob called from the driver's seat of the buggy.

Seth leaned in so his warm breath tickled the edge of her bonnet. "Be careful of Indians," he whispered. "People say they're joining with Pontiac's rebellion. I wouldn't want you to be hurt. Safe travels." He pulled away and joined the others.

Ald gave him an elbow to the ribs and Gretel covered her mouth with her hands, a braid shaking free from her silent giggling. Lydia was glad for the shade, though she was certain he could tell how red her face was. She quickly stepped up into the other seat and let out a deep breath, her hands on her burning cheeks to cool them.

"Goodbye, Lydia!" her friends called as the horse pulled them away. "Take care!" She heard Seth's voice above the group. A thrill shot through her. She grinned and turned to wave as her friends slowly disappeared into the distance, watching until, finally, she could see not even the faintest guess of Seth anymore.

Lydia sat at the back of the buggy watching as the dirt road passed by, counting the stone mile markers as they passed, taking her further from the little town of Birch Run. The sunlight streamed through the leaves of the trees casting dappled shadows upon her bonnet and face. Next to her were her quilts, as well as eggs, butter, cheese, pickles, jam, and the finest cuts of meat from the ox they lost yesterday, smoked overnight, and a cut of bacon for Uncle Zeke as thanks for taking care of her.

Ten mile markers to Lancaster. She and her sisters loved to count them on the way to market. Her aunt would be waiting for them with open arms and a piece of molasses pie for each of them. In the evening, she would set them to making cookies or cutting vegetables to pickle or plucking the ends off of long beans. Lydia had many fond memories of their visits. Aunt Sarah was kind and warm, she always understood. She was looking forward to telling her aunt about how Seth Garten had come out early that morning to wish her a safe journey.

She squirmed with delight at the memory of those words, not so much the warning, but that he cared enough for her to give it in such a tender way. Perhaps Gretel was correct, though she could not believe it. But the words still held a chill to them.

Lydia had met few Indians in her life and, like many of her people, she was frightened of them with their fearsome looks and savage ways. They sometimes came to market with packs of pelts, dead animals, and tomahawks, half-naked and painted, their heads mostly bald but for a long patch of black hair twisted and tied with feathers and quills, their earlobes separated and stretched so that they dangled, wide open, with jewelry of all sorts hanging from them.

One had approached her two years ago, and said something in stilted Dutch. She'd just stood there terrified, neither understanding his words nor being able to reply as she only spoke the Swiss-German dialect of her people and some English. In her memory, the man's skin grew redder and his face larger, those earlobes dangling close as he repeated himself.

That was when Da stepped in, pointed to the butter, and told the Indian he would trade it for a rabbit, but no less. The Indian raised his voice and appeared angry, he held out two squirrels, but Da shook his head and said, "A rabbit or nothing." The Indian walked away, disgruntled.

Later, her father told her the Indian felt the price was too high for butter and admitted it was, but that he'd neither wanted to trade for game nor had he wanted to encourage other Indians to try to trade at his stall. "Once they know you will trade with them, they will insist that you do. It is better to turn away one than to face their wrath later."

She didn't want to face another Indian again, but then, seeing one was unlikely. She rarely saw Indians in the market, mostly only their women selling baskets and brooms, if any. The men preferred to go on to one of the larger port cities like Philadelphia or Baltimore. They had little use for the Amish Anabaptists who cared little for their pelts and game.

Besides, Aunt Sarah and her cousins would be with her. There was nothing to fear except that she might get so caught up in her needlework that she burned the pie. She contented herself to think of the many wonderful things she would do with Aunt Sarah and the girls when she arrived.

"You may leave me off here," Lydia said to Brother Jacob as they came to the marketplace. Already, it was bustling with activity. "They'll be at their stall by now. Don't trouble yourself driving by the house. I know you are eager to continue on."

Brother Jacob nodded. "As you say."

Lydia jumped from the buggy and began piling her wares beside her, bundling them in one of her quilts. She waved farewell to Brother Jacob. "May God bless your journey," she said.

"And may He bless you with good fortune as well. Brother Egon should arrive sometime this evening. He'll bring you home tomorrow." He shook the reins and was off.

Lydia stood on the balls of her feet as she surveyed the crowd, giddy with the number of people. And it wasn't even noon! She would have no trouble selling her quilts. She picked up her makeshift sack and walked toward where Uncle Zeke's booth was.

When she arrived at the place she recalled, her uncle was not there, nor was her aunt. There was only a young man, turned from her, wearing very plain English clothing. Perhaps she had been mistaken? She walked further this way and then the other, but no. She walked up to a man dressed in the garb of the Brethren. "Brother, do you happen to know where Hezekiah Fischer's booth might be? He is my uncle."

"It is over there," he pointed to where she had just been, where the young man stood. "But you'll not find him there today."

"Why not?" Lydia was greatly troubled.

"The whole house has the yellow fever. Been sick with it all week."

"Then who is that stranger, Brother, at their booth?"

The man she was speaking to squinted toward the booth. "I don't rightly know; I've not met him before. Just some trader come into town. I believe Brother Hezekiah is renting the space to him."

The trader turned, putting down a bundle of furs upon the wooden ledge. Now Lydia could see the dusky brown of the man's face underneath his wide-brimmed black hat. "He's an Indian!"

The other man nodded. "I suppose he is."

"Aren't you afraid?"

"Brother Hezekiah attests Will Sock has spoken for him. Will is a good Indian. I have known him for years and trust him. He'd never give his word for one that was trouble. Should I send word for your uncle that you've come? My son, Wendell, can take you by if you would like." He indicated toward a young man with a cart. The young man was fine to look at, but certainly no Seth Garten and clearly unspoken for if his father was so keen to offer his aid.

She'd been receiving such offers ever since she turned fifteen. She knew why: she was pretty. That was always why. Her mother had been a beauty in her day and Lydia had taken only the best from both parents, granting her mink-colored hair, large brown eyes, a complexion as fair as milk, and a sturdy frame that was neither too thin nor too large. Though it was from her grandmother she gained her freckles, and those she treasured the most.

Agatha and Gretel would often lament how they were not even remotely as beautiful as she and Evony, for all were second to Evony in beauty. Lydia thought rarely on such things, for she was not inclined towards vanity, but was neither ignorant to the advantages her beauty gained her nor the trials it brought.

"You need not trouble yourself on my account," she said. "I am here today to sell. But I thank you."

"Good day to you, then. If you should require aid in anything, do not hesitate to call upon me or my family. My daughter, Birgitta, and son will be here until evening."

"I am very much obliged to you for the offer."

The man left Lydia standing with her wares in a large bundle beside her. She glanced around for a free booth, or, at least, one that was being run by someone she knew that they might allow her to sell beside them. But, alas, the crowd made every face a stranger, she recognized none though she was certain she must know someone.

All the selling stalls were full. Pigs grunted and sheep bleated, adding to the din. The Indian's horse reared and whistled. He rushed over and grabbed it by the reins, pulling it down and, gently laying a hand on its velvety nose, he looked it directly in the eye and spoke words lost in the noise.

Why did he have to be here? If he were not, she could sell her quilts properly - even without her uncle and aunt. She knew well how to. She'd been selling at her uncle's booth for years. He'd often joked he should just go home and let her handle things.

She glared at the Indian for the offense he was committing against her.

"Fine." she said. She gripped her bundle by the knot, walked over to the empty space next to the stall, and spread out her blanket, stacking her wares in front and kneeling behind them, the quilts prominently displayed so their best patterns showed to any passerby.

"Hey! Hey!" the Indian called.

Lydia smoothed her skirt as though she had not heard him.

"Hey! You! Hey! Girl!"

How crude! You? *Girl?* Had no one taught him any manners? Likely not. She raised the point of her chin haughtily to make clear to the man she heard him perfectly well, she simply did not deign his attempts worthy of response.

"Hey girl! What? Are you just going to sit there? Doesn't your family have a stall?"

He was persistent. But at least he spoke the language well. Though the syllables were slurred together at points, it was not so different from the way they spoke in Philadelphia. Lydia refused to even glance over at him. He had already taken her space and now he was speaking to her in the rudest of manners, he did not deserve her attention.

"Fine, don't talk to me then." He went back to laying out his skins.

Hours passed and, though she called out, few people looked down to notice her, dazzled by those things that lay in front of them in the booths. As noon approached, she had only sold one quilt and a few cookies to the children of the English who were the only ones low enough to give her any notice. Even then, she gave away more sweets than she sold, for she could not resist breaking off a piece of cookie when a child stared with want shining in their eyes.

She glanced over at the Indian who was happily displaying a fox fur for a well-dressed Englishman and discussing how he might have it turned into a muff for his wife, and perhaps, for a discount, he might also purchase some rabbit skins to line the inside that her fingers might luxuriate in the warm fur for these were by far the softest, having been caught over the winter when their fur was the thickest. He held up the rabbit skin for the Englishman to stroke. The man quickly agreed and emptied out a handful of coins to the Indian as Lydia watched. Her eyes burned with tears at the injustice of it all.

She tried to remind herself that God was kind, that perhaps this was merely a test of her faith, or perhaps to teach her to rely on Him and be patient of His timing, to not compare her lot to others. The latter was a difficult lesson to teach, for He had blessed her so much she rarely saw the need to notice what others had, let alone to covet it. At this moment, she could feel envy growing in her heart.

Yes, that was surely God's plan. And He, being merciful and kind, once she had borne her trial and learned the lesson, would surely grant her success in abundance. God would never let one of His children come to failure when she was making this sacrifice all for the sake of her family.

The Indian man looked her over. "Why don't you go set up shop with your family? You look like King Thrushbeard's wife on the ground like that."

"I would if you were not occupying their stall," Lydia answered, turning her nose up from him again.

"Oh." He went back to reorganizing his furs, glancing over at Lydia every now and again.

She found herself stealing covert glances as well. Eyes darting back quickly when the Indian's look caught hers. He was different from the Indians she had seen in the past. His face was rounder, his nose slightly wider, he had no tattoos or piercings like the others. In his plain deerskin breeches and cotton shirt covered by a loose-hanging leather waistcoat and shaded by the wide-brimmed black hat, altogether his appearance was rather pleasant. The only vestige of the Indian he wore were a pair of worn deerskin moccasins and even those lacked the common decoration of beads and porcupine quills.

Wait, had he not just said she resembled King Thrushbeard's wife? She barely knew that old German tale; how did an Indian?

"Hey, I'm sorry. I didn't know. Look, why don't you take half the space? See, I don't need it all. There's enough for you." Lydia glanced up to see the Indian had moved all his things over to one side, leaving almost half the booth empty.

"No. You rented it, it's yours."

"Now don't be stubborn, it's more than I need."

Lydia didn't answer, only smoothed her quilts.

He threw up his hands. "Fine, then. Do as you like."

Another hour passed and still Lydia had not made any sales. People didn't even notice her to ignore her and all the while the Indian continued to have a steady stream of people examining his wares. Lydia couldn't bear how God was testing her! She was so lost in her ruminations that she didn't even hear the cry of, "Catch that pig!"

Suddenly, she was thrown into a whirlwind of hooves, coarse hair, and desperate squeals. Something slammed into her, knocking her over with its bucking body, large head hammering against her chin.

"Hey! Git off her!" As suddenly as it happened, the thing disappeared. "Here! Take it!"

She looked up to see the face of the Indian.

"Are you alright?" he asked.

Lydia propped herself onto her elbows.

The Indian moved to help steady her. "Woah there! Don't try to get up too fast." The sound of loud squeals nearly drowned out his voice.

"Yes, I think so." She looked toward the commotion to see a man struggling to hold a forcefully writhing pig. She felt something wet on her apron. Pulling up her fingers to her face she saw they were covered in a dark blue glop. She looked back at the pig and saw his entire rear, from trotters to tail, was covered in the same indigo splotched with red. Lydia was confused a moment.

Wait.

"The pies!"

She scrambled forward, her hand landing in the half full remains of a cherry pie and sliding forward.

"Watch yourself!" The Indian grabbed her by the waist, keeping her from falling.

She found herself surrounded by the remains of a dozen pies and crushed cookies. "My quilts!" Lydia sifted through the ruins of her makeshift shop desperately, throwing over pies and jars without even looking to see if they were damaged.

"Here. Here's two of them." The Indian held out two and placed them on the corner furthest from the disaster. "And here's another. Just a little mud. Let it dry and you can brush it right off. It's not so bad. And oh..."

Lydia's eyes landed where the Indian stopped. There was her fourth quilt, the final she'd made. It was covered in a stew of baked cherries and blueberries, the fabric torn from the sharp pig hooves. It was more than Lydia could take. She burst into tears, rubbing the wrecked fabric between her fingers.

"Hey, hey," the Indian said as soothingly as his rough voice allowed. "It'll be alright, you still have three."

"But mama's medicine... the ox... three quilts isn't enough to buy both! And I've lost the pies!" She gulped back sodden sobs before they overtook her again. "How could God do this to me?"

And in that moment, she truly felt it. All she had done, all she had been willing to sacrifice - why would God not only abandon her but crush her and her family? What had they done to earn His wrath? Had they not always lived according to His principles? And He had seen fit to cripple her mother with illness, strike down her father, curse her aunt and uncle and cousins with the fever, and now this!

"Hey… hey, it's not so bad. How much are you selling the quilts for?"

Lydia was too upset to recall her disdain, she named the price.

He reached into his leather money pouch. "Here, I'll buy it. I could use a warm quilt like that come winter." He offered her his hand and helped Lydia up. Still, she could not face him.

"No. I can't accept your charity," she said, her eyes directed to the ground.

"You can. And it's not charity. I need a warm blanket and I'd never be able to convince myself to take something as fine as these into the backwoods. I'd feel badly if they got dirty or ripped. But this one already is so I won't feel so bad. Doesn't change that it's still a fine quilt, so I should still pay the price in full. But if truly bothers you, you can wash and mend it before you give it to me. Just don't try to take those stains out - if you do, I'll never use it. Now, do we have a deal?"

She glanced up into his smiling face. It was warm. The brown of his skin and the twinkle in his dark eyes no longer felt threatening. "Yes, I suppose we do."

Chapter 3

"That's good. Now then, my name's Sam." He offered his hand.

"Sam?" That wasn't an Indian name.

"Just Sam."

"What is your family name?"

"If I have one I don't know it. Sam is what the Jesuits decided to call me, never gave me a last name."

"Jesuits?"

"It's a long story. I might tell it to you someday. So what's your name?"

"Lydia..." she hesitated, considering whether she should give her family name, but then, would it not be better to do so? She did not want this veritable stranger referring to her so familiarly as to call her by her Christian name, especially an Indian. People would certainly talk. "Lydia Fischer."

"Well then, Miss Fischer, how about we move your things up here into the booth before another pig comes by? What do you say?"

"I suppose we could."

"Good, I could use a partner." He picked up the remaining quilts. "Bring in more of the ladies."

Lydia suspected he was only using this as an excuse for his kindness so that she would not feel she was imposing on him, still, it put her at greater ease.

Soon she was set up beside the Indian, what was left of her foodstuffs framing the three remaining quilts. "Thank you, Sam," Lydia said.

"You've got nothing to thank me for."

"But you have been so kind to me, when I was so rude to you."

"Miss Fischer, most people are rude to me. I'm used to it. Besides, the way I see it, you would not have come to such trouble had I not been here."

"It doesn't make it right for me, even so. It was really the fault of the yellow fever. My uncle needed to rent the booth to make up for the lost income."

"Still, I can't ignore my part in it. But that's no matter, you're where you belong now and we can thank God for that."

"You believe in God?" Lydia was surprised. She'd been told most Indians were heathens.

"Don't see why I wouldn't."

"Oh yes, you are a Jesuit you said?"

He laughed. "No. I couldn't stand them. I'm a Quaker."

A Quaker! Lydia had met Quakers before, they were a fairly common sight in Pennsylvania, the colony itself having been named for one, but it surprised her that the Indian would be one. Taking a better look at him she could now see in his dress he was telling the truth.

"How did you come to be a Quaker? Don't you have a tribe?" she asked.

He smiled, though this time there seemed something behind it. Lydia could not tell whether it was sadness or if he was hiding something. "That's a long story for another time."

Another time? She did not anticipate ever seeing this man again! It seemed he didn't want to talk about his past, whatever it might be.

"It appears you have a customer," Sam said.

Lydia was startled to see an elderly woman running her fingers over the quilts. She smiled and greeted the woman warmly.

Within the following hour, she sold two of her quilts, the remaining pies, the meat, and three rolls of butter. She was surprised how well she worked with Sam; if she did not know better she would have thought they'd worked together for years.

"How much are you asking for that quilt?" An Englishwoman asked, pointing to the last of her blankets.

Lydia could see from the woman's fine clothing she was exceedingly wealthy. Lydia named the price without hesitation.

"You see, this is why I adore the Amish market! So much less expensive than in Philadelphia," the wealthy woman said to her companion as though Lydia had been suddenly struck deaf. "Oh, and have your slave bring over those gloves," she pointed to a pair of rabbit fur lined gloves not more than two feet from where she stood, within easy reaching distance.

Lydia simply stared, confounded. Had she heard right? Her *slave*?

"Well, hurry up. I don't wish to purchase them until I've had a proper look. Come now, boy, bring them here."

"He's not... he's not..." Lydia protested.

Sam held up a hand. "It's fine." He picked up the gloves and handed them to the woman. "Here you are ma'am, the finest gloves in town."

"That's better. It's nice to see evidence that these savages can be taught manners and be useful to society, just as I was telling you," she said the last part to her companion, an Englishman in a long, silver-gilded coat and silk waistcoat that had all the colors of a peacock's plume, as she pulled the gloves onto her hands. She held them up in admiration. "Such fine stitching. I really must compliment you, dear."

"I'm sorry, madam, but I did not sew them."

"Oh, did your mother?"

"No," Lydia said, coldly. "He did."

"Oh how generous of you to teach him to sew like a civilized person! You see, this is just what I was talking about, this is why we needn't kill the savages. If we remove them from their stick huts when they are young and put them in schools, we can teach them to be almost as good as white servants. Why should we bring in from Africa when the good Lord has provided for us here? Isn't that right, dear?"

Lydia was seething. "How dare you-"

Sam tugged her over. "Don't. I'm used to it. Just make the sale," he whispered.

Lydia took a deep breath. No. Such speech could not be condoned. It was monstrous! Was it not bad enough what they did to the Africans? And to suggest that God had placed the Indians specifically to be slaves, as well, was simply disgusting! And, beyond that, to treat such a kind man so horribly! No, this was beyond her tolerance. "This man is not my slave nor my servant, he is my partner. It is by his generosity that I am able to sell at his booth. And while he may allow your poor manners and sell you those gloves, I would not sell you my quilt even for ten times the price!"

The woman was taken aback. "Oh! You rude child! You shame your parents speaking to a lady so."

"On the contrary, I believe my father would be quite proud. He would sooner die working in the fields than enslave another to do his work. I have spoken my peace, and I shall say no more. Good day to you."

The woman stared, mouth agape. Finally, she threw down the gloves and turned around. "These Amish are hardly better than the savages. To allow a mere girl to run a market stall, and with an Indian man no less! Perhaps they may not mind the shade of their grandchildren - but the disgrace of it to all who see!" She marched off in a huff.

Lydia felt her cheeks burning at the woman's scandalous suggestion.

"I told you to just make the sale," Sam said. "You need the money."

"I couldn't. Not with the way she spoke to you. The very thought of my quilt, my grandmother's finest weaving, wrapped around such a cruel and hateful person! I simply couldn't allow it."

"You know you might not find another to purchase it?"

"I don't care. I would sooner eat gruel, I would sooner starve, than sell to such a horrible person! Just because you are used to being spoken to in such a way doesn't make it right." She turned to see Sam beaming.

"That's good of you to say. Hey, why don't we eat lunch? Seems to be what everyone else is doing, we won't have too many people coming by until it's over."

Lydia flushed. She had expected to lunch with her aunt and uncle. "I didn't bring anything."

"Don't worry, I have enough for both of us. So long as you don't mind rabbit."

Lydia loved rabbit, but she so rarely had it. Not since Seth's last birthday when his grandmother made the dish. "If you're certain..."

"Of course. And my horse would love to meet you," he said. "Follow me."

Lydia suddenly felt nervous. As kind as he seemed, this was still a man, alone, and she couldn't pretend she had not heard warnings from her mother and many of the other women about what might happen to a girl who went off alone with a man. That horrible woman's comment about the shade of her children sent a thrill of fear through her. "Is it far?"

"You tell me." He pointed to an area not more than ten feet behind the stall where a red roan horse stood tied to a post, pulling up shreds of grass next to a small black kettle that hung above the glowing coals of a fire just across from a log that was meant to serve as a bench. Lydia felt quite silly being so afraid.

Sam drug over a second log. "Have a seat."

Lydia sat down and Sam filled a wooden bowl with rabbit stew. Then he went and retrieved a tin cup and a small loaf of bread from the pack on his horse.

He patted the animal's shoulder. "This is Wa'ya."

"What does that mean?" Lydia asked.

"I don't know. It's just the only word I remember. I think it might be wolf, which is a strange name for a horse. But he doesn't seem to mind." The horse nickered and nosed Sam's hand for a nibble of bread. "Sorry, he doesn't have any manners. Came to me this way. But he's as good a trail horse as you'll find, even if he does chew up every corral he's in." Sam took a small shaping knife from his belt and cut two thick slices from the loaf, then he filled his cup with stew.

Lydia laughed.

"What's so funny?" Sam asked.

"All the boys I know simply dip their cups to fill them. I realize that is not with soup, but still, I've not seen someone fill a cup with a ladle."

Sam chuckled, sitting on the other log and handing Lydia a piece of bread. "All the meat and potatoes settle at the bottom, if I dipped my cup in, I'd only get the broth and the side of the cup would be dripping. I suppose with the bread that second thing isn't so bad, but I made the stew so I could eat it, not just drink the broth. Now, tell me how it is."

Lydia dipped her bread into the soup, letting it soak in the simple stew of rabbit, potato, yam, onion, and flour. Taking a bite she felt the warmth of it flow through her insides all the way to her fingers. She shivered. "It's very good!"

"If you need another slice of bread, just ask."

They ate in silence for a while, only the occasional involuntary grunts of approval as they ate broke the reverie. Finally, Sam spoke, "So, you said you needed to buy an ox?"

"Yes. Ours broke its leg in a gopher hole; we had to butcher it."

"That's terrible! I take it that was your only ox?"

Lydia nodded.

"Do they expect you to purchase it as well?" Sam asked.

"Yes. Well, I'm certain they expected my uncle to help with the purchase."

"But why send you alone? Was there no one else who could come with you?"

"No. My father's leg was broken when the plow fell on top of it."

Sam winced.

Lydia continued, "Mother is too ill and my older brother must plow the fields as best he can with the cart horse. My younger sister, Hannah, needs to tend to my parents and the little ones. It is not as though I was to be alone, though. We had every reason to believe my aunt and uncle would be able to help."

"Will you be staying with them for the night?"

"As much as I would love to help them recover, my parents would never allow me to risk catching the fever. My cousin, Egon, will be coming through from Reading this evening; I am certain he will be able to bring me home. It is only ten miles from here."

Sam thought for a moment. "So, that means we'll need to find you an ox before he comes."

"I suppose so."

"Will Sock has a few friends who might be able to help out. I'll ask him if you like."

"Yes. But who is Will Sock?"

"He's an Indian man like me. A good old man. He's pretty well known around these parts."

"He spoke for you, one of the men said."

"Yes. I've known him a few years. I always try to make his wife a new pair of moccasins for the winter. She's getting too old to do it herself, but she always makes certain to remind me that she could but doesn't because she knows how important it is for me to give her a pair."

"She sounds much like my grandmother. Even when her fingers were so stiff she couldn't hold the shuttle she would insist she was merely allowing us to do the work so we would learn."

Lydia and Sam continued to talk for some time, even after their soup had been long eaten. She could not remember a time conversation had flowed so easily for her; perhaps it was because she had no expectation of ever seeing this man again nor any pretense to the prescribed respect to be shown to members of her own community. Speaking to Sam was much the same as speaking to Gretel or her own family. "And then Seth jumped from the upper window of the barn into a pile of hay. Ald said he would have done it as well if Seth's father hadn't seen what they were doing, but I don't think he would have, not even to impress Evony. He's not especially brave, at least, not in that way."

"Sounds like he's not especially reckless."

"That might be a more charitable way to say it. Perhaps you would say Seth is quite reckless, but it is impressive the things he has done. All the girls like him very much." Her cheeks reddened.

Sam put his hands on his knees and pushed himself up. "Well, I'd best see if I can find Will. In the meantime, you do your best to sell that last quilt, I don't want to go to the trouble of arranging the sale to find you don't have the money to purchase."

It took less than an hour for the quilt to find a proper home with her aunt's neighbor who wanted it as a wedding gift for her own daughter, who, she claimed in confidence, could not sew a straight stitch. Lydia laughed and told the woman her sister, Hannah, was the same way and threw herself into spinning to make up for the deficiency, though she was not much better at that.

It wasn't long after the sale Sam returned with a young, snow-white ox. "I didn't mean for you to buy me the ox!" Lydia cried.

"He was more likely to give a better deal to me than you. I had faith you'd have the last one sold before I returned. Don't tell me my faith was misplaced?"

"No, but it's too fine. You would have spent a good deal on it."

"The cost of four quilts, no more, no less," Sam said, proudly.

"You must drive a hard bargain."

"Well, it did help he has a striped hoof, you'll have to watch that. They say that makes them weaker than the others. I think that's nonsense, but it doesn't matter what I think, just what the seller thinks. Plus he's young and untried, but he's well-formed, has a good musculature to him, I think he'll do you well."

Lydia knelt down in front of the young ox, really not much older than a calf, and stroked its nose. It nudged her hard. She took its large head in her arms. The ox licked her face, causing her bonnet to go askance. Sam laughed with her as she straightened it.

"I can't thank you enough, Sam, for all you've done for me today."

"It made the day more interesting."

"Still, it meant a lot to me."

"If it wasn't for me, you wouldn't have had any of the troubles you did."

Lydia smiled. "You just can't accept gratitude, can you?"

Sam managed something of a laugh. "I suppose I'm not used to it."

As the sun began to set, the grey horse belonging to Egon Fischer came into view. Egon dismounted and, tying the reins of his horse to the hitching post, he approached the market. He raised a hand of greeting as he spotted Lydia from across the square.

Egon was almost two decades older than she, yet still unmarried. He was a cattleman by trade and his long, leathery face and sun-bleached hair bore witness to the hours he spent outside. Lydia and her siblings liked him rather a lot. He had a plain, sensible nature that seemed unaffected by the same need to act in the expected way of most of the other Brethren Lydia had met.

She turned to Sam. "That's my cousin."

Sam shaded his eyes from the sunset. "I suppose it is. Well, it's been a pleasure working with you today."

"Thank you for all your help."

Egon sauntered up to the booth. "Is this the ox Brother Jacob said you hoped to purchase?"

Lydia smiled. "Yes."

Egon knelt, feeling the legs and shoulders of the beast. "He's a bit young, but he looks sound." He stood. "Who's this?" Lydia noted Egon did not say gentleman when he asked, as was his way.

"This is Sam. He's renting the booth from Uncle Zeke."

"Where is Zeke?"

"He and Aunt Sarah are sick with the yellow fever."

"That's no good. I suppose we'll have to make the rest of the journey tonight. I'll not have you staying at an inn, your parents would never forgive me. Best make a start of it, then."

Sam handed the ox's halter to Lydia. "It was nice to meet you, Miss Fischer. I hope to see you again, soon. I'll be here until November."

"It was nice to meet you as well, Sam." Lydia followed her cousin to his horse, the ox plodding along behind, fully certain that she would never see Sam again and half-convinced he had been Christ in disguise as He'd said He'd do.

Chapter 4

It was well into the wee hours of the night before Lydia and Cousin Egon arrived at the edge of town where the Fischer's house was. Even for an Amish house it was modest, so small it could barely hold the town for church without people having to stand on the porch. A light burned in the window of her parents' room. Lydia was uneasy.

Egon stopped the horse they were riding. "What is it?" he asked.

It was always a surprise to her how her cousin could simply sense when something was amiss with anyone. She could hide secrets from her sisters, her friends, even her own mother, but never Cousin Egon, he always found her out.

"They should be asleep at this hour."

"Perhaps they wanted to leave a light on for us?" Egon didn't even sound convinced of this, himself.

Lydia shook her head. "No. They believed we would not be coming home until tomorrow morning at the earliest. Something must be wrong."

Egon nodded and flicked the reins, giving his horse a squeeze with his heels, barely a tap, but the creature understood. The ox grunted his displeasure at suddenly being asked to run, but followed along as they cantered up to the house. They opened the door to the reeking stench of boiling onions and sassafras. Lydia's mother was stirring the pot, her face drawn. Hannah, long sandy hair loose and without covering, entered from her parents' room with a white cloth.

She emptied the cool onions and held the cloth open for mother to ladle new ones in.

Feeling the cold air enter the stifling room, Lydia's mother turned. "Oh! Lydia, Egon, you're home. Praise God!" She rose to kiss them both on the cheek.

"Yes. We brought the new ox." Lydia said. "What has happened? Is Da alright?"

"He's ill with a fever."

"A fever? Is it bad?"

"He took ill this morning and it's gotten worse through the evening. The doctor said to keep him warm, to do onion poultices and give him cinchona bark powder and sassafras tea to drink."

Egon strode into his uncle's room, Lydia following behind. Her father lay in bed, naked from the waist up; his skin waxy, pale, like he had been carved from a candle. His breathing was ragged, the blanket lay across him as though a river winding through the hills of his body and pooled about his legs. Hannah pressed the onion poultice onto his chest where a deep-red mark showed the hours of treatment.

Egon lay his hand upon her father's head, an instant later he pulled it away, frowning. "He's burning to the touch." He turned to her mother. "Aunt Anna, which is the broken leg?"

Anna pointed to the left leg, tangled in the blanket. Egon threw the blanket over and put his hand onto the thick bandage. Lydia did not like the way it moved under his palm.

"It's warm." Egon said. "I need scissors."

Lydia grabbed a pair of scissors from her mother's sewing kit. "Here."

Egon slid the blades under the bandage, but thought better of it before cutting. "Aunt Anna, perhaps the girls shouldn't see this."

Hannah made to leave but Lydia did not budge. "I'm staying," she said.

"It's not going to look good," Egon warned.

"He's my father."

Egon turned to the bandage again. "As you say. Then open the window. Hannah, take a bowl and see if you can find any snow left under the trees."

"But the doctor said to keep him warm?" Anna's voice quavered as she spoke.

"I'd guess that was this afternoon."

"Yes."

"Well, that was then. But he's warm enough now, any hotter and it might hurt his mind. We have to cool his head to keep that from happening. Lydia, hold his leg for me. Aunt Anna, take his arm. He'll probably struggle."

Lydia and Anna took their assigned places.

"Take a deep breath," Egon instructed. "Try to hold it for as long as you can. The first minute will be the worst until the fresh air dissipates it."

Egon cut the bandage. Lydia felt her father jerk under her, she pressed down with her full weight. She could see her mother do the same. Another cut. Her father bellowed out something unintelligible but full of pain. Lydia felt the sting of tears in her eyes.

"Just one more," Egon said. He cut a final time and the bandage shifted. He winced as if he already knew what he would see.

Placing the scissors down, he carefully peeled off the bandage with his thumb and forefinger. What had once been a craggy chasm of flesh stitched together with black thread was now mountains of red and white and pale-yellow straining against its bindings. Lydia gasped and instantly regretted it as her stomach leapt to her throat causing a horrible croak, followed immediately by two more.

"If you're going to throw up, do it out the window," Egon said.

Lydia fought to regain herself, focusing on taking shallow breaths and holding her father's leg down as Egon took his knife, held it over the candle, and proceeded to clean the wound as best he could. Lydia noticed her mother looking away, glistening eyes to the ceiling.

"I have the snow," Hannah said. She let out something of a strangled cry as she inhaled the putrid air.

"Leave it on the floor and go," Egon instructed. "Aunt Anna, do you have any honey?"

Lydia's mother nodded, careful not to glance at her husband's leg. "In the cupboard, on the top shelf."

"Good. Hannah, bring it to me and then fetch the doctor, we'll need maggots. Lydia, make a cold compress for your father's brow."

The dawning hours were lost to Lydia as she soaked compresses in the icy water, her benumbed fingers no longer able to feel the cloth, laying the compresses upon her father's brow only for them to warm as quickly as she could make them. Egon applied honey to the wound and the doctor soon followed with maggots to consume the infection and the letting of blood. Hannah gathered snow, boiled water, whatever was asked, though she would go no further than the doorway to her father's room.

Egon wiped his arm across his brow, surveying the situation. "You should take some rest," Egon said to Lydia.

"I'm not tired," she said. It wasn't exactly a lie for she had no concept of how she felt anymore.

"You're exhausted. At least go out and take some air. Nothing's going to change in the next few minutes."

Lydia leaned against the wood slats of the house exterior, staring ahead at the greying light of the morning horizon, her apron flecked in reds and yellows and pinks. She barely felt the chill wind whipping her kapp about on the braid from which it still struggled to hang by a stubborn pin. She didn't even turn her head to look as the sound of a buggy approached.

Michael, pulled back on the reins. "Lydia, you look terrible."

"And where have you been?" she scolded.

Michael's cheeks took on a pink hue as he smiled, sheepishly. "Just out." He jumped down from the seat and pulled the reins over Old Dan's head.

"Until dawn?" her voice conveyed her irritation. He'd been out courting while she and her mother and sister worked through the night.

That tone caused Michael to turn and give her a harder examination. He dropped the reins and rushed over to her as though finally understanding. "Lydia, what has happened?"

"It's Da-" Her numb exhaustion finally gave way to sobs.

Michael caught her as her legs gave out and she slumped forward. "He hasn't...?"

"Not yet, but Michael, it looks like the claws of the devil climbing up his leg! Cousin Egon says the infection may have gotten into his blood, and if it has..." She buried her face in Michael's shoulder, his brown hair sticking to her dampened brow and eyelids.

Her elder brother held her tightly. "I will take care of us; you don't have to worry. We may be pressed, but God will never allow us to be crushed."

The memory of the market and Sam's warm grip as he helped her up. Was it really only yesterday? It felt like a month ago! She nodded into his shoulder. Finally, her body surrendered to the darkness, dark like the Indian's eyes that flashed before her mind before it vanished into the void.

♥ ♥

When Lydia awoke in her own bed, the evening sun was streaming in. It had to be at least five o' clock. Da! Lydia threw off her quilt and ran down the stair, almost running over Michael coming up.

"How is Da?" she cried.

"His fever's down. The doctor says if it breaks, he may pull through. Cousin Egon is tending to him."

"What of Hannah and mother?"

"Hannah took Rahrah, Essie, and Peter to stay with the Blesses. Mother is resting in their room."

The Blesses; at least her sisters and brother would be well cared for. That was Agatha's house. They had always wished for more children, built their house for a dozen, but only Agatha ever came. Though Agatha was only sixteen, the same age as Hannah, she was one of Lydia's dearest friends. She loved Lydia's youngest sisters and brother as though they were her very own kin.

Lydia looked over to the nursery where she saw her mother curled up in the small bed, hugging Peter's miniature blanket to herself. She could see her mother had been weeping.

Lydia turned away. "Tell me all the doctor said."

Michael took a deep breath. "He did say that if the fever doesn't break soon, he may have to take the leg to give Da the best chance to survive. Even then, with such a high break, the surgery would be risky. Ill as he is, it might kill him."

Lydia instantly imagined her strong, tall father, leg gone. She fought back tears. "Is that all?"

Michael nodded. "Seth Garten's come by."

"He has?" Lydia's heart skipped a beat.

"He's in the barn, feeding the cows."

"Oh!"

Lydia ran back to her room, pulling out her half-undone braids and rolling her hair up into a proper bun. She splashed cold water on her face, scouring it with a rough towel. She knew she must look a fright, but it was the best she could do. She took out a clean kapp and knotted it primly beneath her jawline. She hurried back down the stairs.

"Don't forget to take the milk pail," Michael called as she ran out the door. Lydia stopped short and ran back in, grabbing the bucket before rushing back out.

She could hear the cows complaining loudly. They hadn't been milked since yesterday; they were probably desperate! She did her best to compose herself and strode into the barn. She could hear the sound of milk spraying into a bucket.

"There's a girl," Seth cooed softly. "That feels better, doesn't it?"

Lydia followed the sound of his voice to Mildred's stall. She could not help but smile when she peeked around the corner of the stall to see Seth, his long legs bent like a grasshopper's as he sat on the low milking stool, milking the cow. She nodded, fighting back her nerves. She could do this.

She stepped forward, bucket between her hands in what she hoped was a most charming pose. "Seth! What brings you here?"

He looked up, his sparkling blue eyes and gentle smile sent her heart into palpitations, thumping so loudly in her ears she almost couldn't hear the cows any longer. She hoped he couldn't hear it.

"Good evening, Lydia." He snuffed. "You look terrible."

Lydia felt her face burning in shame.

"Well, your dress that is. Your face is as pretty as ever."

He might have struck her with a bolt of lightning. They were alone, so he could get away with saying such things, but the fact he had! She could feel the heat burning all the way to the back of her neck.

"How is your father?" he asked, his gentle eyes conveying genuine concern.

The question brought Lydia back to earth, at least, mostly. How could she be acting so silly with her father at death's door? "The doctor says he will have to take the leg if his fever doesn't break soon."

"Then we must pray that it breaks."

"When did you arrive?" Lydia asked.

"A few hours ago. Ald and I figured you might need help with the chores."

"Where is Ald?"

"Out in the fields plowing with that new ox of yours. It's a fine beast for the price of a few quilts. Brother Egon really did you right with it."

"It wasn't Cousin Egon who made the purchase."

Seth fixed her with a look of surprise. "I never figured you to have an eye for cattle."

Lydia flushed. "I don't." But how she wished she did at that moment! "Uncle Zeke rented his booth to a man who purchased him for me."

"That was good of him. Your Uncle Zeke has always been a fine judge of a man."

Lydia thought back to the Indian Quaker and his kindnesses. "Yes, I would say so."

"Well, how about you pull up a stool and help me milk these cows before they burst?"

Lydia laughed and pulled a stool over to begin milking Brownie. "I never pictured you milking a cow."

"Youngest brother, remember? I've been doing the milking practically since I was born. I only came in to feed them, but then I saw how full their bags were and I just couldn't leave them."

"I thank you that you didn't, I'm not certain when we would have found the time."

They milked in silence for a while, Seth moving on to Gertrude. "We're all praying for your father's recovery," he said, softly.

Suddenly, the tears were falling from Lydia's eyes, completely unbidden. "Thank you."

"God will hear us."

"But He doesn't always save everyone. Otherwise, Asher would still be with us." The words came to her lips without her even thinking them, as though they had been hiding under her tongue the whole time, waiting to escape.

Prayers had not saved her younger brother. He'd be fifteen now if the pox hadn't taken him. She hadn't even thought of him for months, but now, here his ghost hung in the air.

Seth's head hung low. "I know."

"I don't blame God; I know death is promised and the timing is not assured. I have accepted it may be His will to take my Da, but I am not ready for him to go, too."

"I don't think we can ever be ready. All we can do is pray and seek the comfort that death is not the end."

Lydia nodded.

A thought seemed to strike Seth. "But I think God intends him to pull through, else why would He have allowed Brother Egon to leave so quickly? And given him such fine weather for travel?"

Lydia thought a moment. "Yes, if my uncle's family hadn't been ill, he certainly would have stayed the night with us there. By morning it would have been too late! I hadn't even thought of it. I was too focused on thinking God was testing me, I hadn't even considered it was His providence!"

"It seems an odd way to provide, but He does know us better than we know ourselves and that sometimes drastic circumstances are the only way to move us."

"Like a loose pig," Lydia said, suddenly ten miles away.

"I suppose a loose pig would be such a thing," Seth said, his expression one of confusion.

Lydia blushed to her collarbone. She grabbed her bucket. "I had best see Da." She turned away so Seth wouldn't notice her face.

"Don't worry, I have things well in hand here."

"Yes, thank you." Lydia hurried out.

She leaned against the barn, pail dangling from both hands, allowing the cold wind to chase the color from her face. He must have thought her mind was addled talking about loose pigs like that! And then running off like a child! But there was nothing for it. She trudged back to the house, bucket sloshing loudly beside her.

The remainder of the evening was passed in much the same way as the night had been: applying cold compresses, cleaning and recleaning the wound, and gathering what little snow there was to be found. The doctor brought whiskey from his private store to pour in both the wound and in her father to numb his mind from the pain. At midnight, her mother awoke and joined them but proved of little help for, when she took his hand to comfort him, she dissolved into tears, straight back melting over the cradled hand, her forehead pressed against it on the bed. Lydia felt the sting of tears threatening to blind her eyes. She turned away and dipped the cloth back in the melting snow, willing the cold to numb her heart as well as her fingers.

It was late in the night. Anna Fischer had crawled beside her husband and now slept with her face buried in his neck. The doctor made to wake her.

"Leave her be," Egon said, roughly. "You know as well as I, this might be their last night."

Hours ticked by. Take the cloth off, douse it in the water, wring it out, hear the water splash. The lamp burned on. In its dim light Lydia could see Egon, passed out where he sat, his head resting on his arms beside her father's leg on the bed.

Hannah padded in softly on bare feet. "Would you like to go to bed?" she asked.

Lydia wiped her brow and looked into the face of her sister. Hannah's sky-blue eyes were circled in deep purples, her lips drawn, her skin pale.

"No, I'm fine." Lydia answered. "You sleep; you've been up since yesterday."

"If you're certain?"

Lydia nodded.

"Goodnight, Da." Hannah leaned over and kissed him on the brow. Then she paused, putting a hand to his head, feeling his cheeks. Lydia's heart stopped. Had he already passed? So quickly?

"Lydia, feel his brow," Hannah said.

Lydia dropped her cloth into the water and wiped her hand on her dress, placing it on her father's head. No, it was too numb, she couldn't feel a thing. She brought her forehead to his. She lifted it. Was it right? She wiped a chilled hand across her brow and leaned it against his again. She drew up with a smile. "It's broken!" A giggle escaped her lips. "His fever's broken!" She and Hannah embraced, laughing with relief.

Egon roused. "What is it?" he mumbled, gruffly.

"Da's fever is broken!" Hannah cried.

Egon placed his hand upon the sleeping man's brow. "Praise God." he sighed.

Chapter 5

His fever broken; Elias Fischer began the slow journey to recovery. After a fortnight, the doctor declared the infection had been wholly defeated and Lydia's father would be walking by Pentecost. As if God intended to further multiply their joys, a letter arrived announcing Aunt Sarah was with child, likely to be delivered in the summer. Even Anna's health was improving. It seemed the trial was over, they had survived.

Lydia and Hannah spent the warm days frolicking amongst the cherry blossoms and making delicate wreaths to decorate their father's room. The sisters liked to lie on the sun-soaked grass and allow the petals to fall on their cheeks like soft snowflakes.

One day, as they were passing through the little orchard to deliver lunch to Michael in the field, they passed by Seth and his older brother leading their monstrous draft horse, Dun Levi. Seth smiled and gave them a brief wave. Lydia colored to her ears.

Seth handed over Dun Levi's reins to his brother. He jogged over. "Good morning, Hannah, Lydia. How is your father?"

"He fares well," Lydia managed, trying to hide her rosy cheeks under the shade of the brim of her bonnet.

"We've missed him in church. The hymns just don't sound the same without his booming voice."

"He'll be glad to hear that," Hannah chirped, eagerly. "He misses singing with everyone. He says it's just not the same with only us."

Seth fixed his blue eyes on Lydia. "When do they think he'll be back?"

"The doctor says Pentecost, but Father is certain he'll be there for Easter."

"He's very stubborn about it," Hannah added.

"Glad to hear it. Well, best be getting Dun Levi back to the pasture. He's as stubborn as a mule without his mid-morning snack." He turned to walk away.

"Seth!" Lydia called, feeling her color rise further.

He turned with a smile. "Yes?"

Lydia's heart pounded as it had in the barn. "Thank you for your help. I'm sorry we haven't been able to have you and Ald over to dinner to show our proper appreciation."

"You don't need to worry about it. It was the least we could do for you." He fixed her with a significant look as though to make clear he meant her, specifically. "Have a blessed day." With a wave he was off to join his brother who immediately began speaking quickly in quiet tones with him.

"You like him, don't you?" Hannah asked after they'd passed.

"Who do you mean?" The question did nothing for her coloring.

"Seth!"

Lydia could feel the heat prickling about her face.

Hannah gaped. "You do! Agatha said she thought you did! And he likes you, too!"

Lydia held her hands to her cheeks to, if not cool them, at least hide them. "I don't know about that."

"He just said he did all that work for you."

"He didn't mean just me, he meant all of us."

Hannah walked backwards, smiling like a cat. "It sure seemed like he meant you."

"Even if he did, it's a far distance between liking someone and courting."

Hannah scrunched up her nose, eyes gleaming with mischief. She glanced over to where Seth and his brother had gone. "It doesn't look so far to me."

"Hannah! You...!" Lydia grabbed a handful of grass and flung it at her. Hannah shrieked, running off as Lydia chased her almost all the way to the field. They stood laughing as they panted for air.

Hannah's gaze became soft. "If you need it, you can take one of my quilts for your marriage bed. I know they aren't very good..."

"You've only been quilting a few years," Lydia said, consolingly.

But it was true, Hannah simply lacked the attention for quilting. It wasn't long before her stitches diverged from their line off into some odd direction as her daydreams took over and she was thousands of miles away in some Roman village, maidservant to a Centurion whose daughter had just died and was now bringing Jesus to heal her. A piece of fabric might hang haphazardly as Hannah offered the Son of God a cup of cool water to wet His parched tongue and He gave her a pat on the head. Or else she was giving Esther advice on how to ask her husband, King Nebuchadnezzar, to spare the Jews. Perhaps she was fanning Deborah rather than mother on a hot day, or was the good woman in Psalms selling her fine fabric in the marketplace when they went to Lancaster.

"Don't worry," Lydia said. "I'll have one made before the wedding."

"But we don't have any more cloth."

No, they didn't. Lydia knew this as well as her sister. All of grandmother's cloth had been used and Mamma had been far too ill to weave. Neither Lydia nor Hannah had much skill for it despite their grandmother's patient teaching. Perhaps Aunt Sarah might have some spare? She was quite talented.

"I'm certain God will provide," Lydia said.

When she returned home, Lydia joined her mother making the corn pudding. "Mother, do you suppose Aunt Sarah might have some spare cloth I could use for a quilt?"

Anna shook her head. "No, my treasure, she'll be needing all she has for the girls and the baby."

"Oh." Lydia hung her head; it had been selfish of her to ask. Of course there was none to spare with the new baby coming. She stirred the pot, adding another pinch of cornmeal to it.

"But perhaps I might have an idea. Rahrah, come watch the pot."

Deborah ran over excitedly with Esther following.

"Now Rahrah, you mind the pot, don't get distracted or you know what will happen," Anna warned.

Deborah stuck out her tongue and Esther slapped her hands over her mouth and giggled.

Their mother nodded. "That's right. And I'll be certain to give you the blackest bit."

"No!" Deborah cried.

"Then do as I say."

Deborah took the heavy wooden spoon in both hands and began stirring.

Lydia followed her mother up the stairs to the ladder which led to the attic.

"I wish I had better to give you," Anna said, pulling open the hatch, "But these will have to do."

Lydia followed her up into the room where Anna was rifling through an old chest.

Her mother pulled out a faded maroon dress, the shade made from the juice of inkberries. "This was the dress I wore when I married your father."

She handed the dress to Lydia. Lydia could feel the softness of the fabric, the same as that of her quilts, her grandmother's finest work. As she looked it over, she could see the elbows had worn through and the hem was badly frayed.

"You were probably too young to remember when I used to wear it to church. I couldn't bear to turn it to rags. And here," Anna pulled out another dress from the bottom, it was a soft, pale blue, with a yellow lace trim. "This was your grandmother's wedding dress from the old country."

Lydia took it in her hands, running the lace through her fingers. It was not stiff like that of the English, but delicately woven thread. "What dye is this? I've not seen anything like it."

"Cornflower. Mater said it was everywhere back home. I also have some of her old quilts." She pulled two quilts out, both torn and stained beyond mending. She pointed to a large rose spot on one. "This is where I spilled a glass of cherry juice I wasn't supposed to have taken to bed. I tried to wash it out but all it did was spread so I hid it in the woodshed and just pretended it was still on my bed. I shivered through three nights before Mater told Vater. Vater was so mad when he found out, but Mater only laughed and said she'd always known, she just wanted to give me the chance to admit to it, but then she saw I was as stubborn as she was so she had to tell before I froze to death."

She laughed, hugging the quilt tighter. "Her eyes had this way of sparkling whenever she laughed, even at the end when she was bedridden, they still sparkled. The stain always reminded me I was my mother's daughter, at least until Asher accidentally tore it in two riding it down the stairs. And here's your blanket I made for you when I was pregnant." This was a small blanket, a simple quilt of fabric squares, many of which were merely clinging to each other by threads. Anna looked sorrowfully at the pieces. "I know it will just be a rag quilt; I wish I could give you more."

"Oh Mother, it's more than enough!" Lydia said, embracing her mother and the fabric she held. "It will be a quilt made from a legacy of love. I could not ask for anything finer!"

Lydia set to work, tearing out threads, cutting off worn parts and frayed edges, designing the squares, and arranging her pieces. It would be a lot of work to turn them into a proper quilt. As the early spring days moved on, she invited her friends over for quilting frolics in the chilly evenings.

Michael often helped pour the tea and took the girls home once it became too dark. He also served as guide to the outhouse once night fell to keep them safe from wild animals (a duty that had seemed essentially important to the girls when they were smaller, but now was merely a habit). That Michael was always willing to help the girls was a given. He'd been accompanying them home since he could drive a cart. Often, one of the families would give him sweets and keep him over till the morning as a reward. Lydia found it funny that he still took such treats even as a young man.

On one sunny afternoon in the final days of March, Lydia sat in the rocker on the front porch and set herself to quilting. She still hadn't figured what she wanted to do with the yellow lace. She had considered getting rid of it, it was far too ostentatious for her, but she couldn't bear to part with something her grandmother had made as a young woman. Lydia hadn't even known she could tat!

She wished her grandmother would have taught her. Not that she wanted lace for herself, but the English were voracious when it came to it. She could make more money for the family, perhaps enough that they could sell their ox and buy a proper draft horse like the Garten's had. Of course, if she married Seth, Dun Levi and Willow would be her horses, too. But it was hard to believe Seth would want her when there were other girls from wealthier families who would die for a word from him.

It was not as though wealth were something aspired to amongst the Amish Brethren, but it was clear some families had more than others - whether that was a blessing was oft debated. Greater fortune led to greater temptation to the ways of the world. Money had led many a member of the Brethren away from the simple life Jakob Amman had taught would bring them closer to the Lord.

Her family had never possessed much wealth. Her maternal grandmother converted when she met Lydia's grandfather, a handsome German farmer who was never especially successful. They spent their very last pfennig to book passage to the new world and escape persecution in Germany where Anabaptists were not simply disliked, but openly detested. Lydia had heard the story of the three cages filled with the bones of Anabaptist leaders that hung from one of the German Catholic churches.

She hadn't known her father's parents so well. They were Swiss, enticed by rumors of fertile, black soil and endless expanses of flat land for farming in America. They set up their homestead in Reading, where Cousin Egon's parents still lived. They died when her father was ten of some malarial disease that also took his younger sister and brother.

She wondered what it would have been like to travel to this land, devoid of any inhabitants but for Indians. The courage it must have taken to set off from Germany and Switzerland knowing you could never come back, and what if the stories weren't true and it was only hostile environment and death that awaited? As she stitched a piece of cornflower blue into place, she imagined how her Grandmother Elsie must have felt lying in the berth of that leaky ship traveling across the great ocean. The terrible fear and yet the excitement! The trust in God that He would provide. Grandfather always said that every mile of the journey was traveled in prayer.

"What an ugly bunch of rags!" a sharp female voice brought her out of her thoughts.

She looked up from her sewing to see the sneering faces of Kirsa and Candace.

"Are you seriously trying to make a quilt out of those rags?" Kirsa said.

"The Fischers are so poor that's the only kind of blanket they can afford. They already dress in rags," Candace taunted, her dark curls bouncing with glee from under her bonnet.

"Do you really intend to put that piece of trash on your marriage bed?"

"She should put it in the rubbish heap to burn it."

"How embarrassing for you!" Kirsa said. "And for your husband."

Lydia's eyes burned with tears. These were precious pieces of her grandmother and mother, and yet she knew they were truly rags. Seth deserved a blanket made of new cloth, not a quilt of old rags!

"I'd be more embarrassed to be married to a woman who would make fun of someone's hard work," Ald said as he strode up, Seth behind him. Ald walked up to Lydia and examined her work. "A quilt like this I'd be proud to have on my bed, what about you, Seth?"

Seth nodded.

Kirsa and Candace paled. They crowded up to Seth like flies on something particularly sweet, as they always did when he was present.

"But Seth," Candace pleaded, "It's only rags. You can't tell me you'd really want to sleep on someone else's worn out things?"

"Rags make softer blankets," Seth said, simply.

Lydia's heart leapt. She felt the softness of the former wedding dress between her fingers. The once stiff new cloth, supple with time and wearing. Now it was the girls who turned red.

"You see, a man doesn't want something that looks fancy, he wants something that feels nice to sleep on. Now then, why don't you go off? I'm sure you've got more useful things to do at home," Ald said.

Kirsa appeared as though torn between wanting to cry and wanting to make a final retort. She grabbed Candace's arm and the two stormed off. Ald watched them leave with a smile of satisfaction.

"Thank you, Ald," Lydia said.

Ald just shook his head. "They're too old to be putting on airs like that. If they keep it up no man in town is going to want to marry them, doesn't matter how pretty they are. It's no good to have an avaricious wife."

"Yes, but I don't think it was avarice. I mean, they're right, these are only rags."

"It's not the quilt they envy," Ald grinned.

Lydia tilted her head as if to try to gain a better view of the situation, if not the quilt, what else could there be? Their families were certainly of better means than hers and they were at least as pretty as she, especially Kirsa with her honey-colored hair and fair features.

"Anyway, Seth wanted to ask you something. Seth?" Ald nudged his cousin forward.

Seth glanced about. Lydia noticed his cheeks were red, likely from the sun. He must've had his hat off in the field.

"Umm, yes." Seth rubbed the back of his neck with his hand. "I have a hymn singing gathering in my barn every other Sunday and I was wondering if you, and your sister, Hannah, might like to join us this weekend?"

Lydia brightened. "Yes, of course! Might we bring Gretel as well? I know she can't sing but she makes wonderful snacks." It was quite a thing to ask, but she simply couldn't imagine going without her dearest friend.

Ald seemed unsure, everyone knew full well what Gretel lacked in vocal quality she made up for in volume, but Seth answered, "Of course," Seth appeared even redder. "God made every voice to praise Him."

Lydia beamed. "I can't wait!"

Chapter 6

"How do I look?" Hannah asked, hurriedly tying her bonnet below her chin.

"Your apron's crooked. Here, let me fix it." Lydia tugged the end of the apron string so the bow came out; she pulled the strings so they were even and retied them.

"Tighter," Hannah said.

"It's vanity," Lydia mock-scolded, undoing the bow and tying it tighter to accentuate Hannah's slender waist.

"If I had your face, I wouldn't have to worry about my figure."

"I can't wait forever," Michael called from downstairs.

"Coming!" Lydia shouted. "Let's go." She pulled her sister out.

"Just a moment!" Hannah grabbed a pin from the table and stuck it in the back of the double-knotted bow Lydia had tied in her apron.

Michael drove them over to the Garten's barn in the hay cart, picking up Gretel and her dried apple bread along the way. They saw a number of other boys and girls walking and chatting around the barn.

"Look, there's Micah and Malachi Lapp, and Benedickt Nestle," Hannah said, sitting a bit straighter.

"And Elsie Haller! Wait. That's Evony she's talking to," Gretel said, eagerly. "Evony!" she called, waving.

Hannah and Lydia happily waved with her. The raven-haired beauty turned and gave her largest smile, waving back. *Of course Evony would be invited to such an event*, Lydia thought. *All the boys would work a week straight for her to smile on them as sweetly as she is smiling on her friends now.* Lydia could hardly contain a proud giggle for that thought.

Ald elbowed Seth. Seth started, looking over to where Ald was pointing. He grinned and they strode over to the cart.

"Good day, Lydia. Would you and yours like a hand down?" Seth asked.

"Of course."

Seth gripped Lydia's waist and helped her hop down. He let his hands remain a moment longer. Lydia looked up into his blue eyes and blushed, turning from his gaze before she resembled an apple. He let go and took up Hannah, letting her down as well, while Ald aided Gretel.

"What did you bring?" Ald asked Gretel. "It looks delicious."

Michael was speaking to Evony, "If you'd like, I can take you home with the girls."

"Of course, I'd appreciate a ride home this evening. Thank you." Evony said loudly enough for Lydia to hear clearly. Micah and Benedickt appeared absolutely crestfallen. Lydia stifled a laugh at their mournful expressions - they resembled dogs who had just been denied a piece of bacon.

The group sang and ate apple bread and spoke on every matter they could think of in the great red barn. Seth gave particular praise to Lydia for her courage, going to Lancaster alone and selling all by herself. "It's the mark of a great woman who can manage such a thing; not that it would be difficult for her with quilts as fine as those were."

"I did have help," she said, thinking of Sam smiling at her as he picked up her quilts from the ground and brought them to the booth.

"Yes, but you could have done it without."

"But I would not have found such a fine ox."

Seth laughed. "You're always so modest," he leaned in close, "It's one of the things I most admire about you."

Lydia blushed.

The following weeks were full of singings and frolics as spring began in earnest in their small village. Lydia's father was wholly recovered from his infection and was becoming restless, having to stay in bed so long. Lydia and Hannah took turns reading the Good Book to him and telling him the news of the town. Their mother was finally well; she hadn't coughed more than once at a time in a fortnight. It seemed to all the Fischer family the time of testing and trial had finally come to an end.

Lydia and Hannah were enjoying the warmth of the late April afternoon sun, Lydia with her quilt and Hannah with a litter of kittens, when Ald jogged up, hair slicked to his forehead with sweat, his bright red cheeks all the more so for his pale flesh.

"Is Michael home?" he panted, bent double, hands on the knees of his trousers.

"He's out back, chopping wood," Lydia answered as Hannah looked over from where she lay on her back on the sun-warmed wood, kitten held above her face, attempting to bat her nose. Lydia frowned, putting her quilting down in her lap, Ald was never one to exert himself if he didn't have to. "Why? What is it?"

"There's a man, who calls himself Stewart, in the main square," Ald managed between heavy breaths. "He's asking every able-bodied man to come hear him speak. He's carrying a musket with him."

Lydia stood in alarm, her quilt and needles falling to the porch, quite forgotten. "A musket? Whatever for?"

"I don't know; he said he'd tell us when everyone had gathered." With that, Ald ran off behind the house.

Lydia turned to Hannah; her sister's blue-roan eyes sparkled with excitement.

Lydia grinned mischievously. "Let's go see what's happening," she said, stepping over her fallen quilt pieces.

Hannah nodded and handed her tiny black and white kitten back to its mother. They hurried off to the square.

As they approached the square, they saw a broad-shouldered Scotch-Irish man in the barest of English garb (no more than his shirtsleeves, vest, and breeches!) holding a musket in his hand as Ald had said. He surveyed the gathering crowd of not just men, but women and curious children as well. He smiled, nodding in satisfaction. Lydia saw Seth standing nearer to the stranger. Ald jogged up to them with Egon close behind.

"You girls shouldn't be here," Egon said. "Not with a stranger about."

"We'll keep back, but please, let us stay," Hannah begged, hands clasped together.

Lydia followed her sister's lead, both giving the most pitiful, pleading looks they could manage.

"You know that won't work on me; I work with horses. You've never seen the way they look at you when they know you have a carrot."

The girls stuck out their lower lips and huddled together.

Egon turned away and slapped his thigh. "Aw, alright! You win. I'll stay with you, though. And we're staying back here - I won't have you girls within easy shooting distance of that musket."

The girls grinned, hugging their cousin.

"I'm going to go closer," Ald said, leaving them and joining the Garten boys near the front.

The bishop, a white haired man of eighty-six years, strolled up to the stranger, cane traveling before his right leg. He took off his hat in greeting, revealing the bald dome beneath. "I am Bishop Achim Breneman, and who might you be, stranger?"

The man with the musket did not bother to remove his light brown tam. "You may call me Stewart." His words were strongly accented in English,

Lydia was surprised he was even able to speak their language, most English didn't bother to learn. He must be a trader of some type.

The man, Stewart, spoke, "I have been sent by the Presbyterian brothers in Paxton to warn you of the imminent Indian threat. We have it on good authority that the Senecas are trying to convince the Miami to join them in an uprising."

There were whispers among the crowd.

"But that is not the worst of it," Stewart continued. "A number of tribes have called a war council near Fort Detroit!"

Fort Detroit? Lydia had never heard of Fort Detroit, nor, it seemed, had many of the others. The name sounded French. Perhaps it was one of the forts the English won in their war. If it were, then at least it was far away.

Brother Jacob stepped forward. "What you say, if true, is very concerning. But what has it to do with us? We are a peaceful people. We haven't been bothered by Indians in a decade."

Stewart scowled. "My father was a peaceful person and when they brought him home, he was in pieces and his scalp was mounted on some Indian's staff. Don't pretend you are immune! Not when Adam Garten and his family were killed when those savages followed him home from the field. His wife was pregnant, they found her unborn child in the family spring! Have you forgotten that? Or how you came to us to ask if we had seen Ruth Bless after she was kidnapped in the middle of the night?"

Lydia recognized that name. Ruth Bless was Agatha's aunt. There was a drawing of her in their sewing room. She remembered Ruth was not much older than she was now in that picture.

Ruth was thin of face and more plain than pretty, but she had something in her expression Lydia always found drew her eye, though what exactly that was, she could not exactly say. Something between sadness and spirit.

The Blesses always said she'd died young. To hear that she had been kidnapped by Indians; it would be unthinkable! No wonder they never spoke of it! She must ask Agatha about it as soon as she could.

"You remember how it was! A man might be found dead in a field he was plowing with an arrow through his chest. Or worse, to return home to find his wife and daughters ravaged and sons dead!"

Mothers covered their children's ears.

"Let them hear! Let them know the fate that awaits them if these savages are not eliminated! Let your daughter know she may be picking wild flowers one day when an Indian carries her off and forces her to birth dozens of half-breed children by just as many fathers. She will be passed around like a peace pipe! It doesn't matter if she is six or sixteen, they will treat her just the same. Let your son know he may wake up to a war cry as the Indian stands beside his bed and smashes in his head with their war club and the last sound he hears will be his wife or mother's helpless cries as they ravage her until she finally dies and then cut her to pieces like the Levite's concubine!"

The bishop stepped forward. "That is quite enough," he said as calmly as might be managed when such horrifying words had been spoken.

Stewart ignored the bishop. "It is not nearly enough! Let every man hear me! It is our duty to protect our land and our families. Do not be so fool to believe the red man can be driven out. Like the rat, he will return and often in even greater numbers! We cannot hold a plowshare or Bible in one hand and sword in the other forever! No. Like any vermin, the Indian must be exterminated!"

"But what of those who are civilized?" a man called from the back of the crowd.

Lydia pictured Sam in her mind. Surely, he should not be exterminated. He was a good man, not vermin. And Will Sock and his wife, were they not also called good by others? Were they not productive parts of their community? Perhaps those who had killed Adam Garten and his family and taken Ruth Bless should be brought to justice, of course they should, but all killed for the sins of a few? Was not God more merciful than that even to Sodom and Gomorrah?

"The red man is incapable of being civilized." Stewart answered. "He may be able to act the part, but his savage blood boils within, waiting for the moment to show his true barbaric nature. And then he shall rend and tear his neighbors to bits and hang their scalps, their ears, and their tongues upon his staff. That is the nature of the red man. To rape and murder and steal!"

"That is quite enough!" All eyes turned to Elias Fischer, who stood with his arm wrapped around his son's shoulder, cane firmly in his other hand. His face was ruddy and sweat-slicked from exertion. "Violence is not our way."

"It is not violence, it is survival! We must defend ourselves, as our government has made clear they will not."

"The governor acts with wisdom. Wisdom you seem to lack. Do you wish, by your presence, to bring down their mistrust upon us after we have had so many years of peace? Leave us, stranger. Do not return. You are not welcome here."

"You are a fool! They speak of nothing but expelling us from our lands by any means necessary. Peace is only a ploy to grow their numbers and amass more weapons. Do not believe in it! Mark me, there will soon come a day when you will see their treachery."

"You have said your peace. Now go." Lydia's father stared at the stranger. Despite his clear injury, even Lydia felt a shiver run down her spine.

"If any of you men wish to join us in our fight, come by the Presbyterian church of Paxton and Derry and ask to speak with Reverend Elder. He will be glad to bring you in as one of God's Rangers in the fight against the savage demons. I take my leave." The man, Stewart, bowed and strode off, followed by a number of boys including Malachi, the two younger Garten brothers, Seth and Nathan, and Ald.

"Lydia. Hannah. I shall speak to you when we are home," Elias said.

The girls bowed their heads. "Yes, Da," they said, walking off toward home with Egon following behind.

"You girls know better than to show yourselves to a stranger with a musket!" Elias Fischer sat at the maple table with his back to the fire in the darkening main room of their house which served as both living room and dining room, his two daughters facing him across the table.

"Yes, Da," Lydia said.

"You are an adult now, even though you are not yet baptized. You need to set a better example for your sisters!"

Hannah's shoulders dropped in relief as Lydia appeared to be the target of their father's rage.

"Yes, Da."

"And Hannah,"

Hannah turned, smiling through gritted teeth. "Yes, Da?"

"You are practically a woman yourself. You know better than this." He sighed heavily. "Do not tell your mother of any of what you saw, it would only worry her." He paused a moment, surveying his daughters' faces, sadly. "Do you have any questions about what happened today?"

"Who was that man and what business does he have here?" Lydia asked.

"Is there really going to be a war council?" Hannah's eyes sparkled with imagination. She was already picturing Indians in feathers and war paint sitting around big bonfires, Lydia could tell.

"I don't know if there is to be a war council. It is possible. There has been much speculation lately of the Indians and their movements. I know they are unhappy about the results of the war and some intend trouble, though, of what kind, I cannot guess. That man is from a group in Paxton who call themselves Rangers. They are mostly English. They are hoping to recruit people to help them rid the area of the Indians."

"Why?" Lydia asked.

"They believe that all the Indians should pay for the sins of a few. Unfortunately, a number of people agree with them. If they do something foolish, they may cause the tribes to retaliate."

"What will happen to the men who went with them? Will they be in trouble? They won't be shunned, will they?" Lydia's voice quavered thinking of Seth and Ald. Violence was strictly prohibited amongst the Brethren.

"They won't be in any trouble for merely listening. However, those who choose to follow in that man's path will find it a dark and terrible road. The ones who are unbaptized won't face censure from the community, though the murder of another man will certainly rend their souls. Those who have accepted our ways in the vows of baptism will be cast out."

Lydia breathed a sigh of relief, of her friends who had followed, only Nathan Garten and Malachi had been baptized. Her mind eased on that matter, she couldn't contain her curiosity any further. "Who was Adam Garten? Was he related to Seth?"

"He would have been Seth Garten's great uncle. They were among the first settlers of our town. Adam Garten built the spring house by the birch grove."

"Did Indians really kill him and his family?"

"Yes."

"Why?"

"I don't know, it happened before I was born. There may have been no reason."

Lydia was silent for a minute, staring at the flames as they danced behind her father, casting otherworldly shadows upon the walls. So many thoughts waged war in her mind. She had always feared the Indians until she met Sam, now she didn't know what to think. Surely, they couldn't all be savage murderers like that man said. "What do you think should be done about the Indians?" she asked.

"I don't know."

"Do you think they can be civilized?"

"I believe they can."

"Then why don't they?" Hannah asked. "Why not just live in houses and have farms like us? Then people wouldn't bother them."

"Some do. Many of them don't want to."

"Why not?" Hannah pouted. "Why would anyone want to live in bark huts in the woods?"

"I don't know, but many of them do."

"If they don't want to live with people maybe they should just leave."

"There are many who feel that way; that the Indians should move on if they don't want to join civilization, perhaps into the French territories."

"But isn't this their home?" Lydia asked.

Her father turned and stirred the fire with a poker. He did not answer.

That night, Lydia awoke to a gentle nudging in her bed.

"I had a nightmare," Hannah said, her long, silt-blond hair hanging all about her. "I dreamt I was hanging laundry out back and the Indians came in their war paint with their axes and they took me away. They were screaming so loud and they had great sharp teeth like *painters*." She covered her ears.

Lydia took her sister in her arms.

"Could I sleep with you tonight?" Hannah whimpered.

"Of course." Lydia pulled back the covers and Hannah snuggled in beside her. She stared at the ceiling as she felt the beat of Hannah's heart slow and her breath grow shallow and even. Thoughts ran through her head. Was this not the home of the Indians just as it was theirs? Couldn't they find a way to live in peace as William Penn had? "I wish I could ask Sam," she mumbled.

"Sam Meier?" Hannah asked, groggily, eyes still closed. "What would you ask him about?"

Lydia flushed; Hannah didn't know about the Indian man from Lancaster. She wanted to tell her about him, but then, it might scare her more to know their family in Lancaster was so close to an Indian man, even if he was the kindest of men. Perhaps, in a few days, Lydia would tell her, when her mind had settled. "Oh. I don't know. I'm sorry, I must have been talking in my sleep."

Chapter 7

"It's happened!" Seth announced, entering his barn as Lydia and the others sat singing the second hymn of the evening. "It's finally happened! Just as Stewart said."

"What's happened?" Evony asked.

Seth planted his hands on the table, surveying his friends. His expression was serious, but there was a glint of excitement in his eye. "Indians have attacked Fort Detroit."

Lydia and the others stood in shock.

Her hands flew to her mouth. "No!" she whispered.

"When?" Malachi demanded.

"How?" Ald asked.

"Have they taken it?" Benedickt said.

"May 9th. I don't know, it was under siege last they heard, but he said the Indians kept coming so they might have by now."

"Who told you this?" Lydia asked, already having an idea.

"A man named Connor."

Lydia felt nauseous. An English name. Probably one of those from the Paxton congregation. She didn't want it to be so. No, Seth wouldn't. Perhaps this Connor was someone just passing through. "A stranger?"

"Not to me. He's one of the Rangers. He gave me this." Seth pulled out a pistol from his large coat pocket.

Lydia gasped in shock. A pistol! How could he bring such an evil thing here? Everyone drew away from him as ants from pepper, all excepting Malachi who stepped forward to admire it.

"That's a nice piece," Malachi said, stroking the smooth wooden butt with a finger.

Seth held it up better for Malachi to see. "Yeah, look at the flintlock."

"Put that away, Seth!" Lydia's voice shook from fear. The only gun she'd ever seen was her grandfather's hunting musket.

She still remembered the only time she had seen her father take it from where it sat in the closet. She recalled the screams of their beloved old plow horse, his leg broken. The sound of the shot as she stood, resolutely facing the wall, knowing what was to come. That horrible thunder and then silence and the slight scent of smoke as it wafted in through the window. Guns were abominable. What they did was unnatural - life should not be so easily snuffed out!

"What would you want a pistol for?" Her voice was unnaturally high-pitched as she spoke.

He put the pistol back in his pocket. "It's only to protect the people I care for against the Indians. If one of them were to come for you or my mother or brothers... No one I love is going to come to any harm so long as I can prevent it."

Lydia's brown eyes locked with his. She spoke in a low, pleading voice. "Seth, it's not our way."

"It's not to attack people, only to protect us," Seth said, defensively. "The Israelites worked with sickle in one hand and sword in the other. This is my sword. The Indians aren't going to stop and we need to be ready to protect ourselves when they come. They lied to try to get into Fort Detroit, they will certainly do the same here if we give them the chance. Indians are cruel and savage - all of them."

"No they aren't. There are many good Indians."

"There is no such thing as a good Indian, they only pretend it to gain people's trust. The Indians attacking the fort were actually seen *eating* Englishmen! Who knows what they would do to women?" He turned to Lydia, taking her hand, he continued in a low voice, "I know it's not our way, but I want you to know you're safe here with me." He turned to address the others. "So, what hymn are we singing?"

Lydia sat down across from Gretel, fighting back tears. Her stomach felt as though it might give up its contents if she were to try and open her mouth. She could still see Seth's gun in her mind's eye, though it was wholly concealed by his coat. That he might use it, might kill a man to protect her!

And what if he was wrong? What if she wasn't in danger? Sam had grabbed her around the waist when she'd been attacked by that pig. What if he came upon someone helping her like that? Would he think that man was trying to hurt her and shoot him?

"Lydia, are you feeling sick?" Gretel asked upon swallowing a bite of tart. "You look pale."

"I don't feel much like singing," Lydia croaked and ran from the barn, tears flying from her eyes as she went.

♥ ♥

Hannah was furious at Lydia, refusing to speak to her for a week for embarrassing her that way. Gretel had tried to excuse Lydia's running off as just a sudden ill turn of health, but it seemed nobody especially believed it, yet none of them wanted to speak to her about it. She knew why. It was because no one wanted to admit Seth was wrong because then they might have to stand against him, and no one wanted to do that, not even privately.

The worst of it was Seth. She had felt so close with him before, she hadn't even realized how often he would come by until he suddenly stopped. Whenever they passed in the fields and she raised a hand in greeting he would simply turn his face away and carry on about his business as though she weren't even there.

She felt terrible! Worse so for knowing she was right. Were she wrong, she could apologize for having offended him, but what could she do when she was right? Perhaps she had misread him and he really wasn't as interested in her, anyway; she tried to console herself with such thoughts, but found herself despairing. He must have felt something and she had gone and ruined it! And even though she was right, it gave her little comfort when he turned away from her.

Of course, she couldn't talk to Hannah about it, she'd just say Lydia deserved it, that it was her own fault. And how could she tell her friends? She didn't want them to feel torn between her and Seth. Certainly, she couldn't talk to her parents or Michael! She wasn't even ready to admit she liked Seth, let alone reveal that to her family.

The news from the frontier did little to ease her mind as it trickled in. Fort Sandusky had fallen to the Indians. Then Fort St. Joseph and Fort Miami fell. Entire garrisons were killed. There was talk they were coming east. It only served to justify Seth's actions to himself and the other boys.

The last day of May came with no change from Seth. It being a warm day, most of the people gathered in the main square for conversation. Lydia was watching Deborah and Esther play with the other children along the lone road that ran through town.

There was a distant sound of thunder from the west. She glanced up at the sky expecting dark clouds upon the horizon. If they were coming fast, she might not have time to take Rahrah and Essie home before the clouds broke. But then, given how she was feeling, she might welcome a good soaking.

Her brow furrowed as she looked. There were no dark clouds in sight, only a few fat, cottony ones lazily drifting by. Yet the thunder grew closer.

Her head snapped up suddenly. Those weren't thunderclaps. "Rider!" she shouted.

The children stopped what they were doing and stared at her.

"Get out of the road!" She saw the horse coming now at full gallop, showing no sign he had seen the children. "Essie! Rahrah! Get out of the road!" Deborah realized what was happening and ran with the other children, leaving Essie staring at the fast-approaching man.

"Fort Pitt is under siege!" the rider shouted as he approached. "Fort Pitt is under siege!"

"Essie!" Lydia lunged forward, scooping up her sister just before the sharp hooves of the horse could mow her down.

"Woah!" the rider pulled up his horse hard. The dark creature reared, letting out a loud whinny of disapproval as it spun, walking on its hind legs, before dropping to all fours next to where the two girls rolled to a stop. "Are you hurt?"

"No. We're fine." Lydia glared at the man; Esther clasped to her body.

"I'm sorry, I didn't see her."

Realizing something had happened, though she had no idea what, Essie started bawling. Lydia shot the man a hard look before trying to calm her sister.

"What brings you to our town, stranger?" the bishop asked.

The rider took a skin of water from one of the elders, pouring the contents into his mouth and over his hair. His horse was so dark from sweat Lydia couldn't tell whether it were black or brown.

"As I said, Fort Pitt is under siege. I've been tasked with riding to Philadelphia to tell Colonel Bouquet. They're holding up for now, but if reinforcements don't come soon, they'll be lost for sure," he answered.

"What news of the territories?" Peter Garten asked.

"Lost. Pontiac's amassed at least a thousand men. The Indians are taking every town, village, and fort they can. Detroit is fully under siege. I barely outran them, but the people of the town I started from were not so lucky, I fear." He shook his head, solemnly. "They're coming east, it's only a matter of time until the tribes hear about Pontiac's victories and they want to join him. How far am I from Philadelphia?"

"Sixty miles," Brother Brandon Zook said.

"Too far for this horse. He's already gone all the way from Breezewood. May I borrow one?"

"Take mine," Seth said. "I'll saddle him now." Seth strode past Lydia, still holding her sister.

"Seth," she said, wanting to tell him it was good of him to lend his horse, but he just kept walking, not even acknowledging she'd spoken. It was too much! She could bear it no more! There was only one person she could go to who she could trust not to tell.

"Good day, Cousin. You look like something's troubling you. But then, you've looked that way a fortnight now," Cousin Egon said as she sat herself on the split-rail fence of their far pasture the following morning.

"You've noticed? Why have you not said anything?"

"You always tell me when you're ready. And if you don't, well it's none of my affair, then." He shrugged.

Lydia glanced about her to make certain no one was near. There were only fields and cows so far as the eye could see. "There's this boy,"

"The Garten boy, Seth," Egon said, dumping a bucket of water into the drinking trough.

Lydia colored. "How did you know?"

"He's pretty popular and it's clear he likes you, seemed right." He dumped the second bucket. "Come with me." He raised the buckets. Lydia followed behind.

As they filled their buckets from the well and walked back to the trough, Lydia spilled all her secrets to her cousin: what happened in the barn, how Seth was no longer speaking to her, how he had ignored her yesterday. "I'm sure I've ruined things with him and I don't know what to do!" she cried.

Egon snuffed, leaning against the fence post, the right corner of his mouth rose in a half-smile. "Now then, Miss Lydia, it's not so bad. Nothing broken beyond repair. It's only his pride that's been wounded and that's easily remedied." He patted the nose of Lydia's white ox that had come up to investigate if they might have some treat for him, as Lydia often did.

"But what if he hates me?"

"I don't think he could hate you. It sounds to me like he was hoping you'd have a different reaction than the one you did. He knows he did something he shouldn't have in taking that pistol and to have you be the one to tell him so... I suppose it embarrassed him. He wanted to show you he would protect you from danger, I think he might not realize you're not as afraid of the Indians as the other girls - I'm guessing on account of that Indian at the booth in Lancaster."

Lydia nodded.

"I thought so. You got to know one and found out they weren't quite the savages those Paxton Boys make them out to be; just regular people with a different way of living than us."

"But what can I do to make Seth talk to me again?"

Egon took a long strand of seeded grass, stripped it of its leaves, and stuck the stem in his mouth. He leaned back against the top bar of the fence, chewing thoughtfully. "I can't say I know a lot about romance, I've never been particularly interested in it, but I do know that often when a mare rebuffs a stallion, she needs to give him a little encouragement to tell him there are no hard feelings."

"How do I give him encouragement?"

"Do something nice for him. Doesn't have to be big. Just something to let him know you care for him. I think you'll find it won't take much to win him back." He smiled. "I know it may sound crazy to you, but most men fear being rejected by the girl they like, even popular boys. All he needs to know is that he's not in danger of it. I mean, I'm guessing he's not or it wouldn't be bothering you so much."

"No," she hesitated. Something was bothering her, but what, she wasn't sure of. A worm of uncertainty, but was it Seth or her own feelings for him that caused it? Or perhaps it was merely nerves? "At least, I don't think so."

"Good. Now that that's settled, let's take care of the far troughs before the heat of the day sets in." Egon squinted up at the sky from under the shade of his straw hat. "It's going to be a bad one."

As the cool bucket banged against Lydia's leg, she began to form an idea of what she might do.

♥ ♥

Egon had been correct in his prediction; by midafternoon Hannah was complaining as wisps of her thin hair stuck to her face. There was little to do except laze about listening as their mother read to the smaller children and embroidering.

As the heat of the day set in, Lydia went to the spring house and drew out a bucket of ice-cold water. Enjoying the breath of cool air in the spring, she fought to tear herself away from the chill and back into the thick, heavy air. By the time she arrived at the Garten's field, her dress was clinging to her skin uncomfortably.

She saw Seth hoeing the weeds from a row of onions in only his trousers, held in place by a single strap that ran diagonally from the left side over the right shoulder, and a straw hat. His lean frame was well-muscled from hard work in the fields and coated, in parts, with a fine layer of dust and sweat. It was scandalous to see him in such a state of undress, likely, he didn't think any girls would be by on such a sticky day.

The Gartens, having no daughters, almost ensured the only woman visiting the field would be his mother. Beside him was Ald, his sleeves rolled almost to his shoulder, revealing equally muscled arms. Though Lydia had seen most of the boys of Birch Run in various states of disrobe, for some reason, in this unexpected moment, she could not stop staring, admiring how handsome they were.

"Seth," Lydia said, holding the bucket before her in both hands.

Ald started and waved. Seth didn't look up, pretending to be focused on a particular patch of weeds.

"Seth, I've brought you some water." She put the water down next to him.

He stopped hoeing. Lydia could see his face reflected in the cool water, his eyes softened, the hardness about his features melted.

Ald elbowed him. "Lydia brought you some water. You should thank her," he jibed, a gleam in his eye.

Seth smacked him away with his hat. "You shut your potato trap!" He gazed at Lydia. "Thank you for the water. I hope you'll be at the singing on Sunday, after services?"

"Of course." Lydia nodded as she spoke.

"I'll see you there, then."

"So, you and Seth finally patched things up," Gretel teased.

"I knew they would," Agatha said in her soft voice, pulling a browning leaf from a lamb's ear stalk.

Gretel, Agatha, and Lydia knelt tending Lydia's garden. Today was their weekly garden frolic where they would go visit each of their garden patches and tend them together, then have supper and sleep over at one of their houses. This day was Agatha's turn. Lydia had waited eagerly for today, hoping she might see the portrait of Ruth Bless again and possibly ask Agatha what had happened to her.

"I wish I'd had your faith. I truly thought he'd never speak to me again," Lydia said.

Gretel dropped the handful of weeds she was pulling. "You can't be serious! After all he said about wanting to protect you? Lydia how can you not see he's in love with you? Everyone else can."

"Maybe it's true you can't see when someone is in love with you?" Agatha suggested.

"Are you saying you see it too?" Lydia was overwhelmed. It was hard enough for her to accept that Seth liked her, let alone that he might be in love with her.

Agatha smiled serenely. "Of course."

"The whole town knows. When Michael started whitewashing your house, I had to tell at least three different people you and Seth weren't getting married," Gretel said.

"But we aren't even courting! He's never even taken me home!"

"I know! But you know how people talk. And he'll be asking to take you home soon enough."

Lydia's face burned, turning her attention away from her garden patch to her brother's so her friends couldn't see how red her face was. Then something caught her eye.

Gretel leaned in. "When he does, you will say yes, won't you?"

"Gretel, is that celery?" Lydia asked, not fully believing her eyes.

"Is what celery- oh! Well, it's not rhubarb!"

"It's practically Michael's entire garden," Agatha said. "Almost enough for a-"

"Wedding." Lydia finished, grinning from ear to ear. "That's why he's been painting the house! Last year we couldn't have paid him to do it."

"Michael's getting married? To who?" Gretel asked.

"I don't know."

"You have no idea?"

"No, he's never brought anyone home. That sly fox! All this time he's been planning and none of us saw it coming!"

"Well, you did have other worries," Agatha said, helpfully.

"I wonder when he was planning to tell us?"

The remainder of the afternoon into the evening was spent speculating about the wedding, when it would be, and, most importantly, who the bride would be.

"Maybe it's someone from Lancaster or Reading and that's why you haven't met her yet?" Gretel posited as they were lying on the bed in Agatha's room.

"I don't know. Maybe Lancaster. He did come home late one night from courting. If she was in Reading, he wouldn't have been in until morning at least." Lydia turned over onto her back. "Ugh! I want to know who my new sister is going to be! I wish Evony were here, she always knows about who's courting with whom. It's too bad she hates gardening."

"Yes, but if she knew, wouldn't she tell you?" Agatha asked.

Lydia sat up straight. "Of course! Agatha! You're brilliant! The only reason she wouldn't tell us is if it were one of her friends and she was sworn to secrecy. I wonder who it is. Maybe Leah? Or Guy? Oh, wouldn't it be fun if it was Guy? She's so smart! She could have Essie and Peter reading in no time. And she always manages to make the most mundane tasks fun."

"Yeah, but it could be Dorcas," Gretel said.

Lydia stuck out her tongue. "Ugh, not Dorcas."

"She's not so bad," Agatha said.

"Well, she's very pretty, but she's so vain and she's always got to be the best. I don't think he could ever make her happy. No one less than a Garten could make her happy."

"Too bad the last Garten is in love with you," Gretel teased.

"Oh! You!" Lydia hit Gretel with a pillow.

Gretel shrieked and took the other pillow, hitting back. Agatha took a cushion from the rocking chair and joined the fray. A few minutes later they were all panting and red-faced, kapps askew, giggling between breaths.

"I'm going to freshen myself up, I'll be right back," Lydia said.

She walked down to the kitchen, taking some cool water from the porcelain bowl that sat on their counter and splashing it on her face. She took her moistened fingers and smoothed the flyaway hairs back, readjusting her kapp in the reflection from the glass window. Both the bowl and the window were some of her favorite features of the Bless house.

The bowl had come with the family from Switzerland and featured a pattern of small white flowers Mrs. Bless said were called Edelweiss. The window was one of only six glass windows in the town. It had been a gift from a Philadelphia glass blower to Agatha's grandfather after the elder Bless had helped him build his shop. The other five belonged to the Gartens.

Lydia always enjoyed looking through it at night for she could see both herself and the moon and stars. She tried to position herself so the stars joined the freckles on her face and thought of her grandmother up in heaven, her freckles now like the stars themselves. Was Ruth Bless up there with her?

Lydia climbed the stairs and was about to join the others when she saw the portrait of Ruth Bless through the open door to the sewing room which had formerly been Ruth's room. She stared at the young woman's face, plain and beautiful at the same moment. What had become of her?

"I wish I had gotten to meet her," Agatha said, startling Lydia. "Mother always tells such stories about her. They were the closest of friends. She was so happy when Mother married Father. Father never speaks of her. It pains him too much."

"Was she really taken by Indians?"

"That's what mother says. It happened long before I was born. They had the picture drawn to take around to Lancaster and Reading in the hopes someone might recognize her. But no one ever did."

"How did it happen?"

"I don't know exactly. Mother said she saw Aunt Ruth in the meadow with an Indian man. Aunt Ruth told her the man had gotten lost and was asking for directions to Lancaster. That night, Aunt Ruth went to bed and the next morning she was gone. The window was wide open. The Indian man must have been watching where she lived and taken her during the night. That's why Mother and Father make us lock the shutters every night, no matter how hot it is."

"I always thought it was to keep the bugs out."

"That as well," Agatha smiled. "I'll see you in a few minutes." She padded softly down to the kitchen.

Lydia took a final look at the picture. Poor Ruth, taken away from all she knew and loved by an Indian in the middle of the night. How terrified and sad she must have been. But it was odd. Something in those eyes told Lydia she would not have gone without a fight.

But then, fear did strange things to people, made them act in ways they never would otherwise. Just like Seth and his pistol. Wasn't he afraid, too? She'd been too hard on him. All he knew of Indians was the stories about his great-uncle's family. Of course, he would be afraid to lose those he cared for in the same way!

It was a long time before Lydia fell asleep between her softly snoring friends, and, even then, her dreams were filled with empty beds and open shutters clattering in the wind.

Chapter 8

The final Sunday of the month of May brought with it church service followed in the evening by hymn singing. Lydia had missed the better part of a month of singings with Seth and the others at the barn and was glad to, once more, rejoin their number. She sang with the joy of a chickadee heralding spring after a long winter.

Seth sat across from her and every so often he would catch her eye, causing her to involuntarily smile and blush and her heart to rise in song to join her voice in joyous harmony. All was as it should be and, for the moment, wars and battles and death were the furthest thing from Lydia's mind. All the shadows that surrounded her heart were cast away in the warming glow of God's love flowing through them as they sang.

As the singing ended and they began saying their goodbyes, Seth hung close to Lydia, as though waiting patiently for her to finish with her friends who seemed acutely aware of his presence.

"Hannah, would you like to stay at my house tonight?" Agatha asked, casting a glance over to where Seth and Lydia stood within hearing distance.

Lydia was paying little attention as she and Gretel planned to meet for lunch the following day. Seth, however, nodded appreciatively.

Hannah caught the meaning, smiling conspiratorially. "Of course! Lydia," she called, loudly, "I'm going with Agatha! I'll see you tomorrow!"

Lydia raised a hand in a vague wave.

Lydia embraced Evony goodbye and looked about her, seeing most of the crowd had diminished. The last few lingering young men and women chatted in small knots scattered about the house grounds.

"Lydia," Seth finally spoke.

"Yes, Seth?" Lydia looked up into his handsome visage, his blue eyes bright even in the dark.

He turned from her gaze quickly, hand to his chin. He took a deep breath, straightening himself up so that he stood at his full height. "Lydia, I was wondering if you might allow me to take you home?"

Lydia's heart dropped into her stomach and flew back up to her chest on the wings of a hundred butterflies. It was really happening! Seth was asking to take her home! Her mind was somehow simultaneously blank and racing.

Seth leaned in so his hat brushed the rim of her bonnet. "Well?"

"Yes!" she cried.

Seth smiled. "Good."

He took Lydia's hand and led her to the buggy, guiding her up the steps to sit beside him. Lydia's mind buzzed as he sat next to her and hit the reins. He glanced over at her and smiled again, she returned the look. It was the first time she had agreed to be courted and she found herself at a loss for words.

Her friends had all been courted before, Agatha and Nils had been courting for almost a year now, and Evony had given no less than a dozen men a chance to win her favor through courting. Even Gretel had allowed one boy to take her home, but that had only been that one time. Lydia had never really talked to them about it, figuring it would come perfectly naturally when it was her turn. Now she regretted it deeply.

Nothing about this was coming naturally at all! What would it be like? Seth had been over to the house many times over the years, but this would be different. She imagined them bundled in her bed together, talking through the night until the dawn when tradition ascribed he would return home. What would they talk about? Would she even be able to talk at all? She couldn't seem to now. But, then, Seth seemed perfectly happy to sit in silence. Her breathing quickened with the pace of her heart as they grew closer.

They stopped and Seth took Lydia's hand, leading her down from the buggy and into the house where she could hear her father's snores from their bedroom. Seth guided her toward the stairs, fixing her with a look that would normally melt her heart, but right now all it did was make her feel like she was going to throw up.

"No." Lydia said, stopping.

"No?" Seth was confused.

Her mind yelled at her feet to move forward, but they wouldn't even shake. No matter how hard she tried to will herself, she couldn't move. It was as though she had rooted to the spot. What was wrong with her? She mentally screamed at herself to move, but still nothing. There might as well have been a wall in front of her.

"No. I can't. I'm sorry." Lydia fought back tears of embarrassment. Here she was with Seth Garten! All they had to do was go up the stairs and lie down on opposite sides of the bed and talk. It was nothing! And yet she couldn't do it. She just couldn't make herself!

Seth cocked his head and smiled warmly. "It's your first bed date, isn't it?"

"Yes," Lydia answered, miserably, a stray tear falling.

He slid his finger under Lydia's chin, tilting it up to him. He wiped the tear with his thumb. "Hey, don't cry. I was nervous my first time, too. There's nothing wrong with it. We don't have to do it tonight. We're courting now, right?"

Lydia nodded.

"Then we'll have plenty of time. We'll probably be sharing a bed for the rest of our lives, we don't have to tonight. We can just talk down here if you like."

It felt as though a weight had lifted from Lydia's chest. "Thank you. I'd like that."

They talked awkwardly about the upcoming harvest for an hour while the smoldering fire slowly blackened and cooled.

Despite his kind words, Lydia could not help feeling as though she had failed, she could focus on nothing else. Perhaps if she asked him to come up with her now, no harm would be done. But she couldn't. It was as though there was a gulf between her and the words inviting him upstairs that she simply could not cross, no matter how much she wanted to.

As sweet as his words were, she knew he would never take her home again. Her first courtship was over before it had begun all because she couldn't do something as simple as invite him up to bed with her. They'd be separately bundled! It was just talking! She didn't deserve a man like Seth if she was too cowardly to do even this little thing! Seth, for his part, tried to make conversation, but it didn't seem any topic could gain her interest. Finally, they lapsed into silence.

Seth uncrossed him arms and, taking the poker, jabbed at the coals. There was no spark of life from them. He replaced the poker and turned to Lydia. "Thanks for having me over. It's been nice to finally spend some time alone with you."

Lydia hung her head. "Yes, thank you for bringing me home."

"Perhaps you might let me bring you home again next week, after the hymn singing at my barn?"

Lydia raised her large brown eyes to his smiling face. She couldn't believe it! He was asking her in earnest if he might take her home again! She hadn't ruined things at all, by some miracle! "Yes, I'd like that."

"Good, I'll see you then." He leaned in and gave her a kiss on the cheek. "I'll be looking forward to it."

Lydia lay in bed staring at the ceiling. Next week. Next week she'd be ready. She'd make sure of it. But even as she thought about it, she felt no less nervous than she had tonight.

She needed to talk to her friends. They could help. With their advice she'd feel more comfortable knowing how it had been for them. She'd call an emergency sleepover tomorrow.

♥ ♥

The following evening Evony, Gretel, and Agatha gathered under the excuse of a quilting frolic. Hannah had been asking Lydia all day about her night with Seth until Lydia finally shut her door and refused her sister entry.

The girls chatted for hours about this and that until finally Evony said, "So now, what's all this about? What happened last night that you had to call us all together?"

"Nothing," Lydia said.

"Nothing happened," Gretel giggled.

"No, really. Nothing. I froze. I couldn't invite him up. We ended up standing in the main room for an hour. It was so humiliating!" Lydia buried her face in her hands.

"Oh no! Lydia, that's terrible!" Gretel hugged her friend, joined by Evony and Agatha so they were a swaying mass of blankets and sympathy. Gretel drew back to look at her friend. "What did he do? Was he mad?"

"No, he was really sweet about it. He said we didn't have to. He even asked if he could take me home again next week. But I don't know if it'll be any different!"

"Wow. He must really be in love with you," Gretel said.

"I thought maybe you could help me. You've all been on bed dates before, what are they like?"

Evony rubbed Lydia's back comfortingly. "They're really nice, mostly. It's pleasant spending the night with someone beside you. Mostly you just talk for your first few dates, but sometimes you might kiss or hold hands."

"Unless it's Amos Caflisch," Gretel added bitterly. "Did I ever tell you what he did?"

"No." The girls shook their heads in unison.

"Well, we hadn't been lying there for five minutes before he starts trying to unbundle me! I kept trying to get him to stop, but he wouldn't. It was so bad I ended up having to sleep with my parents."

"Really?" Lydia was alarmed.

Evony rolled her eyes. "Unfortunately, there are some boys like that who think just because you're alone together suddenly all the doctrines become optional. But Seth's not like that. When we were courting, he never did more than hold my hand. If only he'd been a better man outside of the bed! But you remember what he was like back in those days."

"I'd forgotten you two courted." Lydia laughed. "He was pretty terrible. Remember how he used to call me Hideous Lydia?"

"Obviously he doesn't think you're hideous anymore!" Gretel said. "Remember the time he and Ald rigged that water basin up in the tree and then tricked us to walk under it? But he ended up getting Ald too!"

"That was so cold!" Lydia cried.

"And Ald chased him halfway to Oester's farm!" Gretel said. "I really thought he might make good on his threat to skin him alive if he caught him."

All the girls laughed uproariously at the memory of a soaking wet Ald chasing Seth, waving a large stick and shouting all manner of threat at his cousin.

"Agatha, what was it like when you started courting with Nils?" Lydia asked, catching her breath.

"Well, I was very nervous. He was too. Neither of us had ever courted before and we really didn't know what to do except that we were supposed to lie in bed. Mother told me not to let him muss my dress up, she said it must remain straight and wrinkle free all night and she would be checking in the morning. I was so afraid of wrinkling it, I lay as still as a log the whole night! Nils couldn't figure out why and he laughed when I told him. He told me what she meant. I was shocked! Though it would have been better if my mother had told me that than just not to muss my dress. I'd considered not even wearing it to keep it from getting wrinkled. Imagine what he would have thought then!"

The girls laughed.

"What's it like now?"

"Well, you know," Agatha blushed. "We've been courting for a year. Mostly we just talk, but sometimes," her face turned a deeper shade, "Sometimes we kiss and he holds me in my bundle. It's very nice."

"It really is. My love likes to hold me all night long," Evony said.

"And who is this mystery love of yours?" Gretel asked.

Evony smiled coyly, raising a brow. "It's a secret."

"Evony! You can't keep secrets from us!" Lydia said.

"Well, he's very sweet, and strong, and tall."

"All of them are!" Gretel said.

"You do have a type," Agatha added.

"Are you, at least, serious about this one?" Lydia asked.

"If he keeps holding me and kissing me the way he does! That's why you wait to get baptized, so you can have a little fun without worry," she answered.

Lydia felt a thrill up to her hair. How scandalous! Of course, Evony was only teasing, everyone knew lack of self-control on bed dates could land a girl in serious trouble, and Evony wasn't that foolish.

"What about you, Gretel? Have you a boy you fancy?"

"I do, but I'd never tell you," Gretel taunted.

"Oh pooh," Evony stuck out her bottom lip in a false pout. "Why not?"

"Because he'd be the first person you'd tell!"

"I am not that much of a gossip!" Evony placed a hand to her chest. "You've wounded me to the core."

"It's Moses," Agatha said.

"Agatha!" Gretel cried.

"Well, it is. And Jeremiah."

"How do you even know that?"

"And Malachi."

"I don't like Malachi anymore, not after he went with that English man. That's the good part about being single, I can like many men and drop them like a bad apple at the slightest sign of rot."

"And Malachi is rotten now?" Lydia asked.

Gretel realized she might have gone too far, afterall, Seth had also followed the man. "Not rotten, but he's boring to me now. I want a man who is brave without a gun, like your father, Lydia. Or maybe your cousin, Egon."

"Egon too!" Lydia laughed.

"Why not Egon? He's handsome and runs his own farm."

"And he's twenty years older than you!"

"It only means he knows how to take care of himself and won't need me to play mother to him as well as the children."

Lydia laughed. "Well, you'd better hurry, he's returning to Reading soon. Who knows when he'll be back again?"

Gretel spread her arms wide to the ceiling. "Good! He can take me with him." She fell backwards onto the bed and her friends.

"We'll miss you," Agatha said.

Gretel propped herself up on her elbows. "Not for long. We'll be back for all of your weddings. I wonder who will be first."

"Lydia!" Evony and Agatha answered together.

"If I can ever get past the first step," Lydia said, miserably.

"You will," Evony wrapped her arm around Lydia. "And, after that, it will be easy."

"But why is it so hard?" Lydia cradled her head in her hands. "It wasn't that I didn't want to, I couldn't! I truly couldn't! It was like there was some invisible barrier blocking me."

"Perhaps it's just not right," Agatha whispered, tugging at a loose thread on the blanket.

"Agatha! How could you say that? It's Seth Garten, of course it's right!" Evony said.

"We're trying to encourage her," Gretel glared at Agatha, "Not make it worse."

"What does God say?" Agatha asked.

"I don't know, I haven't asked Him," Lydia said.

"He's one of the best young men in town, and she's one of the best women, surely God would want them to marry! I can't think of a better match," Gretel said.

"I'm just meaning, maybe it would be good to talk to the Lord about it. I'm sure He'd approve." Agatha was backing down, but it didn't lessen the effect of her words.

"Maybe she's right," Lydia said. "What if I'm not supposed to marry Seth? Maybe I need to bring this before the Lord."

"Fine," Evony appeared irritated. She knelt on the bed with her hands clasped together, eyes cast to the ceiling. "Oh Holy Father, who should our dearest sister, Lydia, marry?"

"Seth...Seth Garten..." a voice that was clearly Gretel hissed from behind.

"See, there you are. Confirmation."

They all laughed, but for Agatha.

"Evony, that was the most irreverent thing I have seen since Seth was kicked in the stomach by Schwartz three years ago," Lydia said. "Don't worry, Agatha, I'll pray about it. Thanks for the reminder. Maybe it was my forgetting that caused the problem. He wanted to remain the center of it and I was forgetting Him entirely."

"Yes, that is probably why," Agatha agreed, but it was clear to all she didn't mean a word of it.

The girls returned to their chatter until they slowly succumbed to sleep. It was somewhere around three in the morning when Lydia awoke. The room was dark but for a few orange embers in the wood burning stove. Had she heard something? The night was silent, now.

She moved to extricate herself from her friends and found one absent. Evony was gone! The breeze from the window flitted through her loose hair. *Oh no! Oh Lord, please don't let her have been taken by Indians!* she prayed mentally as she walked toward the window. No, there was a lantern shining brightly from the outhouse. Poor Michael, having to take her in the middle of the night like this. She smirked.

Lydia turned her attention to the sky where the moon fought to shine through the dark clouds. She could smell rain on the breeze. Tomorrow morning it would come.

Perhaps now might be a good time to do as Agatha suggested. "Dear Lord," she began. But then she stopped. What was she supposed to say next? She normally didn't have trouble praying, but for some reason, tonight the words weren't coming.

She sighed, looking back to the glow of the lantern hanging on the side of the outhouse. Had her first thought really been that Indians had taken her friend with not even the slightest reason to believe such a thing? "Dear Lord," she started again. "Help me in my fear. Give me courage and understanding that I might not blindly believe the worst in those I do not know. Do not let divisive words create a wall of suspicion between me and people who are different from me. Don't let my heart be influenced that I forget to love them as you love them. And help my friends to see through their fear to the people beyond it. Let me be willing to see," the image of Seth holding the pistol came to her mind, "and help him to see, too. Oh Lord, show me the way to show them. Give me your peace. Amen."

Though she had prayed earnestly for the Lord's peace, it seemed the thing most elusive to her in the following days. The closer Saturday came, the more nervous she became until she found herself hoping for some kind of illness that she might have an excuse to put it off for another week.

She was despondently poking at the potatoes on her supper plate when her mother came in. "Brother Jacob has brought us a letter from Lancaster," Anna said, slitting the letter open with a knife.

"What does it say, Ma?" Hannah stood and danced about her mother, trying to get a better view of the letter. Anna held the letter aloft so Hannah couldn't see it. "Is it about the baby?"

"Yes, Ma, what does it say?" Lydia asked, and the younger children echoed.

"Hannah, let your mother alone so she can read it," Elias said.

Hannah crossed her arms and fell back into her seat. It was hard for Lydia to believe she was sixteen when she acted this way.

Anna began reading, "It says: My dearest Anna and Elias, it gratifies me to hear that Elias's leg is on the mend and that he will be able to walk normally by Pentecost. It seems, to me, great evidence of our Lord's hand in his recovery that he would be walking again on such an important date. I do hope you, Elias, and the children will be able to visit after the baby arrives. I must confess, I find myself struggling with this pregnancy. The child is carrying quite larger and higher than I am used to, and I find I'm needing more help than my husband can give. Would it be possible for you to send one of your daughters to help me during this difficult time? May God bless you and your household. All my love, Sarah."

"I'll go!" Her mother had scarcely finished before Lydia volunteered.

"Are you certain?" Anna asked with trepidation. "We can send Hannah."

Lydia guessed they already had heard about she and Seth, likely from Hannah who never could keep a secret when it came to her sister, and didn't want to interrupt the courtship if it could be avoided. Especially since it was so new.

"Yes. It will be a good education for me and will give me time to finish my quilt," even as she spoke, Lydia felt as though waves of relief were carrying her anxieties away.

Her mother looked pensive. "If this is what you want?"

"It is." Lydia said decisively, spearing a piece of potato.

Anna folded up the letter and put it away, rejoining the family at the table.

Lydia felt a kick at her ankle from next to her.

"But what about... Seth." Hannah dropped her voice to a whisper on the last word.

"I'll write him. I'm sure he'll understand." In truth, she didn't care if he did or didn't. She was going. As she ate, she silently thanked God for His providence. Agatha was right, as she always was, something was wrong. What, Lydia wasn't sure of, but some time away would give her a chance to figure it out.

Chapter 9

A balmy breeze blew through the loose strands of Lydia's hair as she rode beside her cousin in his buggy. Every mile marker bringing her further and further from troubling thoughts of Seth until she was only thinking of her time with her little cousins, a comforting peace settling upon her soul. Egon's silence was a further balm, though he had chuckled initially when he found out she would be accompanying him as far as Lancaster, as if he'd somehow expected it.

The penultimate May morning was as pleasant as she could wish for travelling. Deer and rabbits grazed in abundance as their buggy trundled along. It was so different from when she last took the trip to Lancaster, when her heart was filled with fear for her father, for her family, if she couldn't sell her quilts. Now she had her new quilt, almost half finished, packed and sitting behind her, the early rays of the sun warming her freckled cheeks and shoulders as the forest gradually gave way to houses.

"We're here," Egon said, pulling his horse to a stop in front of the marketplace.

Lydia regarded him quizzically. "I thought we were going directly to Aunt Sarah's house?"

Egon smiled in that enigmatic way of his. "Well, I thought you might like to come by here first."

Lydia looked out into the square toward her uncle's booth. There was the Indian man, Sam, working next to her uncle. He glanced up, then again, a smile spread across his face, the same smile she remembered from that day months ago. It was like that first scent of rain on the wind after an oppressively hot week! She smiled back, giving a slight wave. Sam nudged her uncle and pointed toward the buggy.

"Lydia!" her uncle's voice boomed from across the square as he strode toward the buggy, arms spread wide.

"Uncle Zeke!" Lydia hopped down and was almost immediately caught in her uncle's embrace.

Her uncle pulled back. "Here! Let me have a look at you. I swear, you get prettier every time I see you."

"You always say that, Uncle Zeke."

"And it's always just as true. But don't tell your Aunt Sarah I said so, she wouldn't want me to encourage vanity in you. I know Sheerah and Phoebe will make enough of a fuss about you."

"I can't wait to see them!"

"If you all are ready, I'll be heading off," Egon said, tipping his hat.

"Nonsense, you must stay with us for supper to thank you for all your help with my brother's family. Sarah's expecting you," Uncle Zeke said.

"As much as I'd love to, I'd best be getting on if I'm to make Reading by evening. Give my thanks to your renter, Sam, for me. That ox is working quite well."

"I will, but I thought it was you who'd bought it."

"No, I had no part in it, it was all him."

"Of course he never mentioned it, but then, he's not that type." Uncle Zeke shrugged.

"Tell you what, why don't you invite him to supper in my place? That way nothing will go to waste. Seems a fitting thanks if you ask me."

A frown tugged at the corner of her uncle's mouth, the furrow between his brows deepening. "Hmmm, I'm not sure if Sarah would be keen to that."

"Oh please, Uncle Zeke! He helped me so much! Aunt Sarah won't mind, even if he's not family," Lydia cried.

Uncle Zeke thought for a moment, then nodded his head. "I suppose. If it's that important to you."

"It is," Lydia confirmed.

"Alright then, I'll invite him." Uncle Zeke smiled indulgently at his niece.

"Thank you, Uncle Zeke!"

The smile of indulgence disappeared at Egon, despite Egon's own grin. "Safe travels, Egon."

"And a good day to you. Enjoy your supper, Lydia," Egon's green eyes glinted under his sly smile.

As Egon drove off, Uncle Zeke spoke in words so low Lydia scarcely heard them, "That cousin of yours certainly knows how to stir the pot."

"I'm sorry, Uncle?"

"Oh, it was nothing, love. Let's be off to see your aunt."

"But what about Sam? I was hoping to say hello."

"There'll be time for that at supper, assuming he's free and would want to come. Your aunt is waiting for you."

A few hours later saw Lydia baking with her cousins. Sheerah, an eight year old with hair the same shade of dusky blonde as Hannah, was helping her to form small hand pies which they were filling with strawberries the girls had picked earlier while Phoebe, golden-haired and six years of age, carefully rolled pieces of the pie dough into balls for the older girls to flatten.

"Sister Junia says Mamma is going to have a boy. But I think we're going to have another sister," Sheerah said.

"Another sister?" Lydia replied, humoring them.

Both the girls nodded. Clearly this had been discussed before and the conclusion was unquestionable.

Lydia smiled at the pair. "Well then, what do you think we should name her?"

"Puah!" Phoebe cried.

"Puah!" Lydia exclaimed. "And who is Puah?"

"I... ummm..."

"Come on Phoebe, you know it," Sheerah encouraged her. "From yesterday."

Phoebe put a fist to her forehead, leaving a blotch of flour on her brow.

"We read about baby Moses..." Sheerah provided.

"She saved the babies in Egypt!" Phoebe cried.

"Very good, Phoebe," Lydia said.

Phoebe beamed.

"I think we should name her Priscilla, because it's pretty," Sheerah said.

"But what if it's a boy?"

Sheerah shook her head. "It won't be a boy."

"Perhaps not, but if you ever were to have a brother, what would you want his name to be?"

The girls looked at each other, then spoke in unison, "Egon!"

Lydia laughed. "I'm sure he'd be flattered to hear that."

"He's our favorite," Sheerah said. Phoebe nodded in agreement.

"I think he's everyone's favorite," Lydia said, crimping the dough around the edges of the miniature pie. She took her knife and sliced a cross on the top of the lump of the middle, exposing the strawberry filling. "At least, among the children." She looked at the knife and suddenly had an idea. She smiled to herself as she began cutting a piece of dough into the shape of a pig.

Sheerah stood to gain a better vantage point. "What are you doing, Lydia?"

"I'm making a special pie for my friend who is coming to dinner."

"What's your friend's name?"

"Sam. He works with your Da." Lydia finished cutting the top piece.

"You mean the Indian man? You're friends with him?" Sheerah was incredulous. "Momma always says we shouldn't talk to him."

"That's probably because he's a stranger to you. But he's very nice." Lydia hoped this was the reason, though the sad sickness in her stomach testified to the likely truth.

"Why are you making a dog for him?" Phoebe asked.

"It's supposed to be a pig." Lydia held the piece of dough up. "Though, I guess it does look kind of like a dog."

"I'll make it a curly tail! Then he'll know it's a pig!" Sheerah volunteered.

"Why are you making him a pig?" Phoebe persisted.

"He helped save me from a runaway pig." Lydia proceeded to tell the story of her meeting with Sam as they finished the little piggy pie.

"I want to make him a pig, too!" Sheerah concluded at the end of the story.

"Me too!" Phoebe echoed.

"Of course!" Lydia was a bit saddened to think her pig wouldn't be special, but it was just as well, wasn't it? It was only out of gratitude, but such displays could be seen for more than what they were by her uncle. She didn't want to be sent home, not when she had only just arrived.

The girls insisted on cutting out their own pigs. Sheerah's looked very much like a circle with legs and Phoebe's was not much more than oddly shaped flattened dough with a long, loose curl of dough set in the middle, but both were proud of their creations and declared them the most beautiful pig-pies in the world.

They waited impatiently for Uncle Zeke to arrive home with Sam. But when he did, it was without companion.

"Where is Sam?" Lydia asked.

Uncle Zeke hung up his coat. "I'm sorry, we were busy this afternoon. I forgot to invite him."

Aunt Sarah appeared, hands on her hips. "Well then, Hezekiah Fischer, you had best march right back to the market and invite him."

Uncle Zeke pulled her aside and said in a whisper Lydia only just caught, "But you told me you never wanted him under our roof. Remember the last time I asked him over for supper?"

"After all he's done for our family, for our Lydia, no one deserves a seat at our table more than he!"

"What has he done?"

"One of the quilts was ruined by a loose pig. He bought it at full price."

"Full price?" Uncle Zeke almost said the words at full volume in his surprise. "But he hardly has anything, himself, between his rent and food."

"I overheard Lydia tell the girls. He gave her his lunch and procured the ox for her. Had you told me this, I... I would have long ago allowed him a seat at our table."

"He never said a word about it! I would never have even known she was here if Brother Yoder hadn't asked about her."

"Well, we know now. Go and fetch him." Aunt Sarah pushed his coat back into his arms. "And lower his rent." Uncle Zeke hurried out the door he'd only just come through.

But something bothered Lydia, even beyond her aunt's desire not to have Sam in their house. Had her aunt and uncle set the rent of their stall higher than it should have been for the same reason her father had asked an unfair price on butter from that Indian man? To discourage him from renting? Had not

Jesus spoken against what was not all that different from usury?

Asking such a question was liable to upset her aunt and, more than anything, Lydia wished to avoid that. She set the table with a troubled heart, trying to console herself that the wrong was now being righted.

Sam arrived with her uncle half an hour later. He mostly spoke to her uncle and aunt; it would have been inappropriate to be overly familiar with him so early in his visit, or for he to be so with her. No matter how well they had gotten on before, he was still technically an outsider, a stranger, and therefore obliged to speak principally to the man of the house. He'd know this as well as she, but as Lydia lay out the plates she gave him a shy smile.

"Thank you, Miss Fischer," he said as he received his.

Sam spoke little during the meal. He did have a laugh at the pig pies, particularly when Lydia apologized that the strawberry juice made it look as though they were bleeding from their eyes and mouths in rather gruesome fashion. He said it was no trouble, he'd just eat that part first and proceeded to take an oversized bite from the one Lydia had made.

"See," he said, holding up the decapitated pie, "no more trouble. Of course, now he's headless... That's not much of an improvement, is it?" He gave an exaggerated frown. "Guess I'll just have to take care of that as well."

Phoebe and Sheerah tittered as he quickly devoured the rest of the pig. Lydia covered her lips with the side of her hand that he would not see her laughing, though, it was clear from the way his dark eyes shone he'd caught it.

Though he had spoken little during the meal, it was determined he was good enough company to invite back the next week and the next, until he became a fixture at Sunday dinner; his initial reticence giving way to the same comfortable conversation Lydia knew from their first lunch together.

The third Sunday in June came in as fine as could be wished. Fireflies danced outside the windows, enchanting Phoebe and Sheerah, inspiring them to eat their suppers faster that they might have the chance to go out and catch them before it became too dark.

Sam regaled the adults with hunting tales, and, while the children tried to listen, the temptation was too great.

"May we please be excused?" Sheerah asked, placing her sister's plate on top of her own and fixing her father with the most hopeful, large blue eyes she could manage.

"Of course, but stay close to the house," Uncle Zeke answered.

"Yes, Da," Sheerah said.

They were off and out the door before Uncle Zeke could even finish the words, "And keep an eye on your sister!" He sighed, leaning back in his chair. "Best let them be young while they can," Uncle Zeke said. "Go on with your tale, Sam."

"So, as I was saying, I was up in the high ridges out by Chamber's Fort after otter. This was maybe five years ago. I'd set my snares on a pair of snowy otter slides and was just making to leave for camp for the night, as the dark was falling fast, when my moccasin caught on a patch of ice and I slid down like an otter into the river."

Lydia gasped.

Sam chuckled. "Yeah, that's about what I did, as well. That kind of cold... you can't even properly feel it. It's like falling onto stone, except it swallows you. I tried to pull myself out, but I couldn't get a grip on the packed snow. I'll tell you, all I could think was to claw at the shore even though the only thing it was doing was tiring me out. Then a still, small voice said to me, *"Peace. Be still."*

Lydia leaned in, listening intently as Sam continued.

"That was the last thing I wanted to do. But I remembered the story of Elijah and the still, small voice and I knew I had to trust it. So, with every fiber of my being protesting against it, I stopped fighting the current. I lay back in that horrible, black water and let it take me. Those might have been the longest minutes of my life, as all I could think about was how cold I was in this liquid tomb when, suddenly, I hit a large branch that had fallen across the river. I was able to use that to pull myself up and out. I'll tell you, it was a cold walk back, but something inside of me burned like a fire, keeping me from freezing. I just kept talking to God, asking Him to just get me back to camp, that was all I needed."

"Then what happened?" Lydia asked.

"Well, I'm here now, so you know the short of it. But that wasn't the only time God saved my life out on the trail."

Lydia continued to listen as Sam spun his tales late into the evening. After Aunt Sarah put the children to bed, Lydia took up her quilting, listening as she stitched a pattern of flying snowy geese from her grandmother's snowy white apron - a relic of the old country she had never worn in the Americas for fear of being seen as too ostentatious.

The shadows of Sam's arms gesturing in emphasis of his story grew as the kitchen fire shrank to coals. Uncle Zeke's snores could be heard from the rocking chair where he slept, Bible still in his lap.

"So there Wa'ya and I were, two skinny turkeys tied to his flank and a whole pack of beaver and otter pelts, heading up to camp when I heard the first howls. Then more answered from the other side. I could hear the sound of rustling all around us. If the air hadn't been so still that night, Wa'ya or I would have smelt them; but, as it was, we didn't have the faintest clue they were there until they had us surrounded. They were so close I could hear their panting. It was like fish in a dark pond, you couldn't really see them, but you could see their shadows rippling through the trees. There had to be at least twenty of them! Wa'ya reared. I had to yank him down before he could bolt," Sam made a motion like he was pulling a lead-line down with all his strength, "cause if he did that, well, we'd both have been lost."

Lydia's fingers stopped moving as she listened.

"I knew we weren't getting out of this without sacrificing something, so I cut the turkeys, even though they were the first real food I'd caught in days, and I leapt on Wa'ya's back, fired a shot through the trees in front of us, and heard a yelp. I didn't even need to give Wa'ya a kick, he just needed permission. He tore right through the path my arrow took."

"Did the turkeys stop the wolves?" The edge of the chair bit into Lydia's legs as she leaned further in.

"If it stopped one or two, I wouldn't know; but the rest of them didn't even hesitate, they just came right after us. It'd been a long winter and, I suppose, we were too large a meal to pass up. I wasn't sure what to do. I couldn't go back to camp - a tent and a few hot coals wouldn't mean nothing to them now that they'd set their sights on us. We'd need to find shelter fast and we were too far south of Chamber's Fort to make it. So, I just said, *"God, if it be your will, show me the way."* And, right then, I felt a gust of wind so hard it nearly knocked me off my horse. Keep in mind it'd been as still an evening as you could imagine up to that point. So, I figured this was God trying to show me where to go. I followed that gust of wind, and then another, and another, shepherding me about the woods like a blind sheep. And then, as suddenly as the wind had come, it was gone and the forest opened up into an overgrown clearing where a set of burned out cabins stood. We got in to the first one that was still sound just in time. I slammed that door just as a wolf lunged at it and held the door as it crashed against it with a loud yelp. I could hear them scratching at the door and walls, trying to find a weak spot, but to no avail. Wa'ya and I hid in those cabins the rest of the night, and, the next morning, that's where I moved camp to."

Lydia was in awe. "You think God used the wind to take you there?"

"I don't have any other explanation for it."

"It's amazing how you say you talk to God like He is someone there with you."

"He is. The trail would be pretty lonely if I didn't have God to talk to. It'd only be me and Wa'ya."

"You make it sound like He is a friend."

Sam raised his brows. "He is. I mean, I don't talk to Him all the time; most of the time I just work in silence, but I always appreciate when He shows me some moment of beauty or some bit of providence. It's one of the reasons I like my work so much; it gives me all the time I could want to reflect on God and just be with Him in His creation. Speaking of creations, that's quite a quilt you're working on."

"It's only a rag quilt. None of the fabric matches."

"There's nothing wrong with that." Sam took up a corner of the quilt and examined it. "It reminds me a bit of one of those calico cats, you know, the ones that have spots filled with tabby stripes. Like rag quilt cats." He smiled.

Lydia returned his smile. "I like the thought of that: Rag Quilt Cats."

Sam seemed lost for words for a moment as their eyes held the gaze. Then, he shook his head slightly, coming to himself. "Here, the night's getting cold." He took the mostly finished part of the quilt and wrapped it around Lydia.

Lydia gripped the soft blanket closer to herself, feeling not only the warmth of the quilt, but of her heart at his kindness. It was such a little gesture, yet it seemed to hold a magic to it. She brushed her cheek against the cornflower blue of the border, enjoying its softness. She gazed appreciatively at Sam. "Thank you. I didn't even notice the chill until now."

Sam just smiled, the warmth in his eyes matched that in Lydia's chest. They sat in silence a few minutes, Lydia stitching, Sam silently watching. Finally, a thought crossed Lydia's mind.

She looked up to Sam. "I find it so interesting to hear you speak of God so. I often heard Quakers weren't Christians."

"Not all are, but most believe in God. I'll tell you, I've seen far too much not to believe in God. After all He's done for me and those around me, I'd be a fool to deny Him. It'd be like denying the sky or the ground or the air."

"Are you a Christian?"

Sam stuck out his lower lip and furrowed his brow as he thought for a minute. "I suppose I probably am. I really don't think of it a lot. I like Jesus. I often find myself thinking of him. How he was both God and man, part of both but never fully either. How he didn't have to come down and save man, how he didn't have to take on being man, how he could have just given up on us at any time. As a man, I would have. But that part of him that was God just wouldn't give up on us. He said, I will forever be a stranger existing in two worlds at once to help these people."

He paused a moment. "And I think what it would take to take on such a mantle. To willingly never fully be part of either world anymore. To give up heaven and put on flesh and join with humanity, but, at the same time, to know all he knew from heaven. How would you be able to live in a world where you had knowledge of everything? Where you knew how it was going to end? Who would betray you, who would deny you, and, somehow, let it happen - and still treat them with love knowing all that? I admire that. I don't think I could choose that, were I given the choice. To never fully have a home." Sam stared out the window to where the stars peeked out between the clouds.

Lydia frowned slightly. "I'd never thought of Christ that way. But, I suppose you are right, even when He was resurrected He still had His body, with the holes in His hands and feet and gash in His side. He didn't go back to the way things were before. He kept a part of His time on earth."

"Like a scar," Sam said, distantly.

"In a way, I guess. But perhaps that's how He wanted it."

"Perhaps," Sam pursed his lips, thoughtfully. A comfortable silence, once more, fell upon the pair. Lydia with her stitching and Sam with his stargazing.

"Will you be returning to the mountains by Chamber's Fort when you leave in November?" Lydia asked, laying the square in her lap.

"I reckon so. Beaver's been getting scarce; I might have to head further inland."

"Why do you do it? Why risk life and limb in the mountains? Why not start a farm here in Lancaster? You're still young enough to tend it yourself. You can't be yet thirty."

He chuckled. "You're right about that, I'm twenty-six as of May 1st." Sam turned, fixing Lydia with his black eyes. "Honestly? Never could get much from farming. I enjoy trapping. There's something about the snow and the silence and the freedom that lets my inner light burn brighter than it ever could on a farm. I never feel closer to God than when I'm trudging through some snow covered deer path setting and checking my snares. Might sound strange to you, but if I never slept on a bed with a soft pillow, that'd be fine by me. All I need is my God, my tent, and my horse." He smiled with a slight laugh. "And my quilt."

Lydia felt the color rise to her cheeks which she dearly hoped was concealed by the dim, orange glow of the dying fire.

He put his hands on his knees and pushed himself up. "Well, Miss Lydia, I'm afraid I've kept you up well past bed time."

Lydia stood quickly, causing her square to fall to the floor. "No, you didn't keep me up. It was my pleasure." She extended her hand, for what favor, she wasn't certain she knew, but the idea he might give a kiss to it made her heart flutter. "I hope we can talk again soon."

Sam was momentarily taken aback, as if he had never heard such words before. He smiled his wide, warm smile. "I'm glad. I'm glad you enjoyed it." He swept down and picked up her fallen square, placing it in her hand. "I hope so, too." He left, shutting the door behind, leaving Lydia with caterpillars twisting in strange knots in her stomach.

Chapter 10

"Tha savages have taken Fort Venango and Fort Le Boeuf! Tha entire garrison was brutally murdered at Fort Venango! Two more men were murdered at Fort Le Boeuf! Seventeen souls in all! All lost this weekend! And they are coming this way." One of the Paxton Boys, a name that belied his age of nearly forty years, announced from atop a crate near the post office, opened missive hanging from one hand. Presumptively the letter described the details of the attack. The black of the beard poking through his chin and jagged Scottish features gave him a ragged aspect that his dress of leather breeches, loose work shirt, and undone cravat only affirmed. On his back he carried a musket.

Lydia feigned disinterest as she walked past the gathering crowd and entered the post office to fetch the mail for her uncle. She listened carefully as she stood in line.

"Next," the clerk called. "Yes, Miss?"

She was pulled from her distractions to her task at hand. "Letters for Hezekiah Fischer and family."

The clerk handed her two envelopes.

"There are rumors the Indyuns have spies in our villages reporting on our arms and weaknesses. Indyuns like that Conestoga Will Sock!"

Lydia's head snapped to look at the Paxton man at the mention of the name Will Sock. Was he truly accusing the old man of being a spy?

"I take it you are Lydia Fischer?" the clerk said, forcing Lydia's attention back to the desk.

"Yes." She desperately wanted to leave so she could hear more of what the man was saying.

"Seems you've had a few letters." He handed her three letters.

She recognized her mother's handwriting on the first. The second did not even ask for recognition, for it had the names of Agatha, Gretel, and Evony scrawled on the front of the envelope, embellished by curls and pictures of flowers. The third she did not know, the writing on the front was neat, the letters all uniform in size and shape. Could it be from Egon? But then, he was never much of a writer. She turned it over to see the seal, its features warped by the heat, but the fact there was a stamp on the seal left little doubt who the letter was from, she only knew of two families who had their own stamp and would be writing her, and she held a letter from the other already.

"Thank you, sir. Good day to you." She took the letters and walked over to the counter, tearing the seal. She scanned the paper, eyes falling upon the signature of Seth Garten. It was all understanding and sweetness and left Lydia with a slight sick feeling in her stomach. Perhaps she should have been clearer in her letter to Seth of her feelings, or lack of the correct ones.

She opened the letter from her friends. It seemed they were more keen in their evaluation of her leaving as being what it was, fear of courting with Seth. They told her of how Seth missed her, reminded her that sometimes love took time to develop, and assured her that it was a good sign for a strong marriage that they weren't merely burning for each other, as the apostle, Paul, would put it. How would they know?! None of them were married!

Lydia threw their letters in the rubbish bin. But, just as quickly, she fished them back out. What if they were right and her absence would breed fondness to dispel her fears and indifference? Had she not been blushing and day-dreaming of Seth only a month ago? She must have some feelings for him! He'd done nothing to change them but to give her exactly what she had hoped for.

"We must expel the savages from our midst!" the voice of the Scotsman rang through the air.

Lydia gathered the letters and made for the door, stepping outside into a rather larger crowd than had been there only minutes ago.

"What if they won't go?" a man shouted from the audience.

The Scotsman gave a crooked half a smile. "Oh, they'll go, one way or the other."

Lydia's eyes grew wide. Others in the crowd were taken aback as well.

"You can't mean to murder them?" an older man with white streaks running through his squared beard asked.

"They have murdered ours! Why shouldna we revenge ourselves?"

"But these Indians are guilty of no such thing!"

"Does it matter? They took seventeen of ours, we'll take seventeen of theirs. An eye for an eye, just as in the Bible."

Lydia's brow furrowed, it was true such a verse was in the Bible, but regarding negligent violence harming a pregnant woman's baby, not revenge. How strange to hear it used so far from its meaning.

"No. We cannot condone such actions," the elder Amish man said. "We shall not participate in the spilling of innocent blood."

"There's no such thing as an innocent Indian. Mark me, if you don't take this chance now, they willnae give you tha chance later."

"Now or later, we shall not fight."

"You may allow yourselves to be lambs for the slaughter, but I ask, if we do what we must to defend ourselves and, by consequence, you, will you, at least, not get in our way?"

Lydia felt ill. Did that horrible Paxton man mean to ask if her kinsman would let innocents to be hurt, possibly even murdered? The older man only allowed his chin to fall, then turned and walked away, followed by the other Amish men of the village. Lydia watched, troubled. That wasn't an answer.

One of the young men turned and saw her. "Lydia!" He jogged over, sandy-grey hair whipping from under the sides of his hat in a style that was influenced greatly by his Dutch mother.

"Good afternoon, Wendell. How is Birgitta?"

"Well. She was hoping to see you. She wanted to know if you were going to stay after church for the singing this week."

"Tell her I am looking forward to it," Lydia paused, weighing whether to ask about what she had just witnessed, what the meaning of it was. No, she didn't know Wendell especially well, nor did she really know what she would say if the answer was what she feared.

Taking her silence as signal she was finished speaking, Wendell continued, "Good. She and Heidi will be happy to hear it. They are quite fond of you."

"And I of them."

"I'll convey your answer. Would you like me to walk you home?"

"No, thank you. I intend to stop by the market on my way. My aunt asked me to deliver lunch to my uncle since I was out."

"Your uncle rents his booth to that red man, isn't that right?"

"Yes. Sam."

"Aren't you scared of him?" Wendell asked, a quaver in his voice.

"No. Why should I be?"

"Well... you know..." Wendell was touching the tips of his two forefingers together in a nervous gesture.

Lydia's eyes flashed with an internal fire. Oh yes, she did know, but she was through condoning it, pretending politeness so as not to offend. Perhaps she might not be able to reason with a Paxton man, but she was not going to allow a boy such a Wendell to have his words go unchecked. Sam was one of the best men she knew and she'd not have it suggested otherwise. "No, I don't know. I don't see why I should be afraid of a good, Christian man."

Wendell stared wide-eyed, his jaw slack. "He's a Christian?"

"Yes, he is."

"Are you sure? I mean, how do you know?"

"I've spoken to him about it."

Wendell paled; he looked as though he might fall if a stiff wind blew at him. "You- You've *spoken* to him?"

"Why not? He is my uncle's tenant; he sups with us every Sunday. And I assure you, his faith is as strong as anyone I've ever met. Stronger even."

"I didn't know they could be Christians for real," Wendell's shock melted into wonder.

"Of course they can. They are people the same as we are."

"Yes, now that you say it, I suppose it would be the same way Lebi experiences faith. Simple and beautiful," Wendell said.

Lydia mouth moved as she fought through her shocked rage for the words. Levi, often called Lebi as his tongue never could easily form the "v" sound, was called simple from birth and though never truly ignored, he was treated with that dismissive sweetness one might use with a small child. "Levi's faith is not simple, it is the same as ours. You think he doesn't understand but he has learned more psalms by heart than most of us have bothered to read thrice. And so is Sam's. I wish I had half the passion to know God that they do. I wish I could understand Christ as they do! They know what it is to be a stranger among people."

Lydia felt a large hand on her shoulder and turned to see the black-stubbled chin of the Scotsman. "Is this man botherin' you, lassie?"

The stench of stale cider on his breath turned her stomach. Her heart pounded in her chest. This man, this horrible man, was *touching* her. His hand rubbed the crest of her shoulder in a way that might have been meant to be comforting, yet nothing in the motion gave such soothing to Lydia. She stiffened as another large, rough hand landed upon her other shoulder.

"Would you like if I got rid of 'im for you?"

Her eyes darted about to see if there were any men nearby to help her, finally they rested on Wendell's blue eyes, but they only reflected back her own terror.

"No. He's not bothering me," she said, fighting to keep her voice from trembling. "He's a friend."

"Dinnae sound that way from where I was." Both hands were gently rubbing her shoulders. "Seems I might be a better friend to a woman such as yourself."

"It was merely a disagreement. Nothing more." Her eyes still stared into Wendell's. Her mouth formed the word help, yet he only stood, as paralyzed as she. Lydia felt the thick ropes of muscle in the Scotsman's hands. She would never consider herself weak, years of farm labor had given her strength unknown to the English lady, but this man? She could feel in those hands the power to lift her as easily as a bale of hay.

"Well, if'n it be nothin' more, why dinnae you come with me and we can have a chat. I'd like ta listen ta that pretty voice of yours some more."

"You bother her!" A rough female voice croaked.

Lydia glanced past the large hand covered in black hair on her shoulder to see an elderly Indian woman. The Scot uttered a vile epitaph and slammed one of those large hands down on the old woman. She crumpled to the ground.

"No!" Lydia fell to the ground next to the woman, trying to revive her. She looked up at the man, defiantly. "How could you? She's an old woman!"

"The same as I'd hit a biting cur. It's an Indyun *soith*, not a woman. Let her alone, she'll be fine. I didnae crack her skull that hard. Indyuns dinnae feel pain like us."

Lydia didn't acknowledge his words, tending, instead, to the bleeding wound on the old woman's scalp.

"Wait... Dinnae tell me you actually care about these animals?" The words dripped with disgust.

Wendell saw his moment. "She does! She was just telling me that they could be Christians!"

"God didn't make the red man, it was the devil who marked them his creation with the color of their skin! They lack the mental capacity for faith. Their prayers are no more than a parrot's repetition of what will get it a cracker! It is a deception to get yeh to drop yer guard, let them in!" The Scot let his eyes fall to the hem of Lydia's skirt, her carelessness in her concern revealing not only her ankles, but her calves as well.

"That's what I said!" Wendell cried, trying to grab the man's attention. "But she won't give up on it. She even eats Sunday supper with them."

The woman began to revive in Lydia's arms.

"How are you?" Lydia asked, gently. The woman said some words Lydia couldn't understand, placing her hand on the wound where Lydia's handkerchief stuck. "Yes, you were hit."

"Wait..." the Scotsman's lewd smile twisted to disgust. "You really are an Indyun lover! Yer jest a red man's whore aren't you? Pretending to be pure." He spat on them.

Lydia winced at the foul-smelling liquid on her face, but only wiped her sleeve over it.

"Come on, boy! Best stay away from this wench's corner lest she tempt you to Hell. Let's have a cider and craic. I'll buy."

Wendell looked imploringly at Lydia for what he should do; go with the brute or stay and help her, possibly further incurring the English wrath?

She mouthed, "Go."

He nodded, or perhaps it was that his entire body shook, but he went just the same, leaving Lydia with the woman.

"Come on," she said, pulling the woman's arm over her shoulder and hoisting her up.

The woman smiled at her, the flesh of her face crinkling, showing teeth almost worn to the gum, she uttered more words Lydia could comprehend no part of.

"I'm sorry," Lydia said. "I don't understand. Let's take you to someone who can help."

Lydia half-walked, half-carried the old woman toward the square. She could hear the commotion around her, she must be quite the sight, but she didn't care. She just kept walking, willing herself forward. The woman seemed to grow heavier on her shoulders. Her steps became harder, staggered, yet still she continued. She couldn't ever remember a mile feeling so far.

From a distance, she could see Sam and her uncle struggling to see what was going on. Then Sam pointed and shouted something that looked like "Lydia!" His eyes flashed with horror as he jumped over the booth ledge and ran toward them. Lydia felt a wave of relief rush through her knowing they were finally safe. Her body, which had not issued a single complaint the entirety of the walk, now felt the full weight of the woman and the exhaustion from carrying her so far. Her knees buckled underneath her; she couldn't have stood again even had she wanted to.

"Lydia!" Sam cried. She felt his hands on her shoulders, removing the weight. She leaned into his chest, lifting her head enough to see Sam take the woman. He seemed to recognize her.

"Tkwëhtä:'ë:' Ë:ní'ta:'! What happened?" Sam said.

"He... He struck her..." Lydia managed.

"Who stuck you?" Sam asked the woman.

She answered something in her own language, indicating to her head, then to Lydia, then she stuck out her tongue. "White devil."

Sam turned to the young woman leaning against his chest, securing her to him with his arm. "Lydia, are you alright? She said the man was trying to... to take liberties."

"He tried. She stopped him."

Sam's arm tightened around her, her body relaxed, her head resting against the softness of his linen shirt. They were finally safe.

"Lydia!" Uncle Zeke panted as he knelt down beside them. "Are you hurt?"

"I'm fine."

"What happened?"

She heard Sam whispering the explanation to her uncle. She was half-aware of the growing shade around her and noticed the dark moving about on the ground.

"The Paxton Boys? Are you certain?" she heard Uncle Zeke say.

"Yes." Sam nodded.

The shadows seemed to encroach closer.

"Get back!" Uncle Zeke ordered. "Give them some room to breathe!"

The sun suddenly broke through. It was then Lydia realized the shade was from a cloud of human make, not mist. And she was in the arms of a man.

She pushed away. "I'm fine. I can stand now."

"Are you certain?" her uncle asked. "I can carry you home if you like."

"No." Lydia fought her exhausted body to her feet. "I can walk."

Sam handed her his waterskin. She took a drink and felt a good deal better.

"Good, I'll take Tkwëhtä:'ë:' Ë:ní'ta:' home," Sam said. "Zeke, will you be alright if we close early today?"

"Of course. I'll take Lydia home."

"But Uncle, can't I go with the old woman? I want to make certain she arrives home safe."

"Sarah wouldn't be too pleased if I didn't take you home, she'll worry when she hears what's happened. I imagine there's already someone who's told her."

"I'll be perfectly safe. Sam will be with me."

"I won't let any harm come to her so long as I live," Sam swore.

"That's the part I'm afraid of," Uncle Zeke mumbled.

Sam took a deep breath and released it. "I know."

Lydia planted her foot in the dirt. "I'm going with you. You may need help. Perhaps they will be less likely to trouble you if I'm along."

"That's not how it..." Sam shut his eyes and shook his head. "There'll be no convincing her otherwise, will there, Zeke?"

"No. Not when someone's hurt. Was it just the one man, Lydia?"

"Yes. He took Wendell off in the direction of the pub."

Sam sighed. "Well, he probably won't be out until nightfall at the earliest. Fine, you can come. But it's a long way, are you sure you're up to it?"

"Yes."

"Alright, you'll ride with Tkwëhtä:'ë:', I'll walk alongside. I'll have her back by moonrise, Zeke."

"See that you do. I don't need Sarah worrying more about her than she will."

The old woman dozed between Lydia's arms as Wa'ya plodded along the road with Sam leading him. She watched Sam from above. His walk was easy, calm. His shoulders followed the fluid motion of his body. They were not as squared or broad as Seth's, nor did he have that same straight way of carrying himself.

The two could not have been more different in form. Seth was tall and lean, his frame well-muscled; Sam, while he had a few inches on Lydia, could hardly be called tall and was of a more regular build, neither stout nor spare. And, though she knew he possessed strength, she'd never felt the rope of muscle when he'd held her.

She liked the way he walked, a hunter's gait, like he was aware of everything around him and ready to change course at a moment's notice, his eyes ever on the path except to occasionally glance up at the women. Not like Seth, who seemed to expect the path to be straight and clear, eyes always up from the earth. No, there was something about the way Sam moved that held her transfixed, the motion of his shoulders, of his back, the set of his hat that told her he was watching the ground, the warmth in his eyes when he looked at them. It set the caterpillars to crawling in her stomach.

He glanced up again, catching her eyes. Lydia felt her cheeks redden.

"What does her name mean?" she asked, trying to regain herself.

"Red Moon. It's Seneca."

"She's Seneca?" Good, the caterpillars had ceased their crawling in her stomach. It was strange he should make her feel so nervous when she harbored no fear of him.

The corner of Sam's mouth pulled down as he weighed his answer. "Well, yes and no. Her grandparents were Seneca, but she'd tell you she's Conestoga."

"Like Will Sock?"

"Yeah."

"I thought the Conestoga were their own tribe?"

"They are, in a way. They formed from members of a few different tribes generations ago. They used to be a lot bigger, but the area's been hunted out and every year there's less and less land to hunt on, let alone to farm. They can't make a living out here anymore so they've mostly headed west to the Ohio territory. But some, like Red Moon, don't want to leave. Her son, Kwa'yö:', has a farm and they do well enough to get by."

"Kwa'yö:'?"

"Rabbit. He'll insist you stay for supper; his wife's quite the cook."

Lydia felt her weariness returning, she massaged her brow with her thumb and forefinger. "Must we?"

"No, it'll be your choice, of course. But I know he'll want to thank you for helping his mother. If not for you, she would still be lying on the ground."

"If not for me, she'd have gone home safe, under her own power," Lydia spat, bitterly.

Sam smiled that cursed charming smile of his. "Seems to me we've had this discussion before."

"And it was my fault then, as well. If only I'd been able to keep my temper. Birgitta and Heidi will never speak to me once Wendell tells them what happened."

"Now why would they do that?"

"Because I told him off."

"About what?"

"He said your faith was simple, like Levi's. And, I don't know. I just got so mad. I don't know what came over me."

Lydia felt Wa'ya jerk to a stop, she looked down to see Sam had ceased walking. She couldn't see his face beneath the wide, black brim of his hat.

"What do you think made you mad about him saying that?"

"That he was insulting you. That he was being cruel about Levi. I don't know! Lots of things. I wish I had your faith! And he just insulted it."

Sam huffed. He turned his face up to her, smile bright as the sun itself. "Don't be letting anyone hear that, they'll call you an Indian lover."

"They're probably already saying that." Lydia pouted unconsciously.

Sam's smile fell. "Does it bother you that they might?"

Lydia thought a moment. "No, except that they mean it to be cruel. I don't think caring about people should be an insult. I always thought everyone felt that way."

Sam huffed again and shook his head. "You know, Miss Fischer, you really are something else."

Lydia was taken aback. "You think me odd?"

"Not odd, just... I haven't met many people like you and I wished I'd had. We'll be arriving soon, best wake Red Moon."

Within a quarter of an hour, they'd crested a hillock overlooking a small spray of cabins where Indian men and women went about their daily tasks while a set of children played with the dogs. It was unlike anything Lydia had ever seen before and yet, strangely familiar.

Stands of crops grew near the houses, some of the women walked through them, pulling up weeds and plucking bugs from the stalks. One she recognized as a broom and basket seller from the market – she'd never even realized the woman was an Indian! She'd always took her as one of those dark Germans from the Mennonites as she both dressed like and associated with them. Older women sat in a semi-circle, weaving baskets, talking and laughing. They reminded Lydia of the grandmothers in her village, sitting and sewing in the same way when the day was fine.

The men, the few that there were out in the middle of the day, were gathered about one man. That man wore a queersome mix of clothing: English calico shirt tied at the waist so the tails just covered a colorful breechcloth, leaving only his leather leggings visible and these hung from just above the knee, exposing his thigh. His clothes were decorated by bands of beadwork belted across his body. He wore his hair strangely shaved at the crown and sides so only a tuft of long hair tied with brightly colored feathers was left. From his ears dangled colorful stones set in shining metals, stretching the band of flesh that hung loose from his ears further down, swinging as they moved. Most of the others were dressed the same as the Mennonites Lydia saw in town were, which struck her as both strange and comforting.

"Why is that man dressed differently than the others?" Lydia asked Sam.

"He's from the Seneca; he's been trying to convince the Conestoga to join with them. He tells them they are too weak and small to fend off the English. But good old Shebaes has told him they have no interest in such things."

Lydia suddenly felt a thrill of fear at the sight of the man. She recalled what the horrible man, Stewart, had said they would do to a woman like her. She glanced over to Sam, stalwart as ever. He wouldn't let any harm come to her. But then, he was only one man and unarmed.

"Perhaps it would be best if I stayed behind?" she said.

Sam's back tensed, then relaxed. He placed a clenched fist on Wa'ya's shoulder. "Are you scared?" he asked, quietly.

Lydia closed her eyes. She didn't want to risk him seeing the tears of shame stinging them. She'd wounded him. The man who'd been nothing but kind to her and she'd hurt him. Where had all her courage, all her fine words, gone? She nodded; her throat too thick to form the words.

The fist released, hand laying on Wa'ya's soft fur. "You can stay here if you like. I won't force you to come with me. But, if you can trust me, there's someone I'd like you to meet."

Lydia swallowed, taking a deep, wet breath. "Yes."

She heard a soft chuckle from Red Moon, though she could not guess why.

Sam whistled and gave a coo-ee sounding call. The men and women turned. Sam raised a hand in greeting. The men responded with similar sounds and smiles. One of them, a man the age of Lydia's father whose features might have been hewn in stone and polished to their finest, took off sprinting toward them as fast as a deer. He caught up to them and he and Sam exchanged quick greetings before Red Moon interrupted.

She and the man spoke rapidly and then he and Sam helped her down. The man carefully led Red Moon to where the other men were and they gathered about her. She appeared quite pleased and began telling her tale of how she'd gotten the wound on her head while one of the other elder women attempted to treat it.

"That man is Kwa'yo, or Rabbit, if you prefer, Red Moon's youngest son." Sam said. "When his brothers went to Ohio, he stayed behind to watch after his mother."

"What does he prefer?"

"His name."

"Then I'll do my best," Lydia said as Kwa'yo sprinted back up to their little party and motioned for them.

"Come with me," Kwa'yo said. "You must have dinner with us. My family will want to thank you for bringing our mother home." They followed him toward one of the far cabins.

"He speaks Amish?" Lydia whispered, stunned. Very few of the English could even speak their language, but for those who lived nearby.

Kwa'yo called out in his native tongue and the voice of a woman answered from within. A delicate hand pulled aside the deer skin covering the door and a thin woman appeared in the doorway clad in a blue dress. Her skin was as brown as the shell of a dried walnut, her loose-hanging hair was not straight and black as jet like the other women of the village, instead holding soft curls of mouse-brown streaked with grey. But, most arresting to Lydia, was her face. It was not particularly beautiful, the features harsh about the jaw, yet neither was it plain. There was something in the eyes she knew, a strength. Something in the set of the lips that was so familiar to her.

"Welcome," the woman said with a warm smile.

And then Lydia knew. She knew that smile. She'd known it for years. She'd only just seen it not more than a month ago though she'd never seen this woman smile before in her life - only the same stony expression had ever played on her still lips. But now the frozen woman smiled, lines raised on her cheeks creating creases beside her eyes, her blue eyes, glittering in the sun.

Lydia could barely speak for her shock. "You! You're Ruth Bless!"

Chapter 11

"You said you know my brother? How is Abel?" Ruth asked as she set the table after Red Moon had been treated and put to bed to rest.

The cabin was cruder than the houses Lydia was accustomed to, it seemed a queer mix of Indian and Amish with a bear skin on the floor serving as a rug, yet the furniture was English, if old. Two teenage children, a boy and a girl, watched Lydia curiously.

Lydia had tried to speak to them but they either did not understand or did not want to appear as though they did.

"Have a seat." Ruth indicated toward a chair next to Sam. "Children, supper."

The boy and girl seemed to understand those words for they came to the table and chattered quietly to each other.

"He is well," Lydia answered, still too astonished to do anything but as she was told.

"I imagine he and Jo must have a dozen children by now," Ruth said.

"Only one, my dear friend, Agatha."

"Just the one? Such a pity. Jo wanted so many. What is my niece like?"

"She is like a lamb, quiet and sweet."

"How old is she?"

"Sixteen."

"Sixteen? The same as my Ga'nígöhdáshä'! I wish they could have grown up together, they'd have been like twins," Ruth said, wistfully.

Twins in all but feature, Lydia couldn't help but think. Agatha was tiny with long, wavy, blond hair whereas Ruth's daughter was tall and had the fine features, complexion, and jet-black hair of her father, yet somehow, on the girl they were even more handsome. She would have been a match only for Evony in that.

But her brother was similar to his mother. He shared her brown waves, tied low at the base of his neck in a ponytail. His skin held her same brunette complexion but of a shade slightly duskier. The addition of his father's high cheekbones under large, brown eyes only served to complete the portrait. Were he older, she was certain Hannah would fall in love on sight of him, though, beautiful as he was, she might anyway, despite her preference for the older boys.

"How old is your son? Fourteen?" Lydia asked.

The boy mumbled something.

Ruth scolded him. "Timothy! She's a guest. Don't be rude. And you can answer her for yourself."

"Fifteen, last month," Timothy answered, sullenly.

"Oh, I'm sorry," Lydia said, slightly flustered.

"No, I apologize for my children," Kwa'yo said. "They have never been very friendly to strangers. But they do improve on acquaintance, I promise you. When you come again, they'll probably have a hundred questions."

Based on the disdainful looks she was receiving from them, Lydia found that hard to believe. Fifteen and sixteen were hardly easy ages to get on with if they didn't take to a person, and that could depend on the day. She didn't like to think she'd been that way, but she likely had, if her parents were to be believed.

"My niece," Ruth said, moving the conversation back. "Is she courting now?"

Lydia inwardly sighed with relief. "Yes, she's been courting Nils for a long while now."

"Nils? What's his family name? How old is he?"

"Troxler. He's eighteen."

"A Troxler. They're a good family. Is he Benjamin's son?"

Lydia nodded.

"That is good, Benjamin would raise a child well. I was close with him." Ruth laughed at the memory as she sat down. She laughed so much like Agatha. "We almost courted. What did you say your last name is?"

"Fischer." Lydia watched as Ruth began spooning out stewed sweet potatoes.

Ruth's brow furrowed. "Fischer... I recall an Elias Fischer. He moved in from Reading the year I left. Is he your relation?"

"He is my father, yes."

"Who was your mother?"

"Anna Strunk."

"Oh yes, I remember the Strunks. They were from Germany. I suppose now you say it, you do look much like her. Prettier, though, than both your parents. I don't know where those eyes of yours came from."

A spoon clattered to the floor. Sam apologized and picked it up.

"Da says they are from my grandfather Fischer."

"I wish I knew, but I never met the man." Ruth Bless spooned a stew of venison, corn, and potatoes into her bowl.

Lydia could contain it no longer. "Forgive me for asking, but how did you come to be here? Mrs. Bless said she'd seen you speaking to a strange Indian in the clearing and you told her you were picking flowers and he was lost and you were giving him directions. And then, that night, you were gone."

"I was lost, until I found my true North," Kwa'yo said, giving Ruth a kiss.

Ruth smiled, sadly. "I know it was wrong. I should have told her the full truth, but I was afraid what she and Abel might do if they knew. It was not wholly a lie, I did meet Kwa'yo, when I was picking flowers."

"Three months before, I was chasing the biggest buck I had ever seen," Kwa'yo said. "And I came upon this beautiful girl among the flowers."

"He couldn't speak our language and I couldn't speak any of his."

"I tried to ask her if she had seen the buck go by. But she did not speak French, Dutch, or English."

"It was before there were so many English in our area."

"You speak French and English?" Lydia asked.

"Yes, some, and Dutch. I learned from traders," Kwa'yo answered.

"Perhaps not all the best words," Ruth laughed.

"No," Kwa'yo agreed. "It was probably good she did not understand me."

"So how did you ask her?" Lydia pushed.

"He tried to act it out!" Ruth couldn't contain her laughter.

Kwa'yo put his hands to his head with the fingers spread like antlers, moaned like a deer, and then pointed in a direction. This caused everyone but Lydia to laugh. It was all too strange!

"I laughed. He was so handsome, though I think he is even moreso, now. So, you can imagine this handsome Indian comes running out of the woods and starts making deer sounds and pointing."

"And when I saw her laugh, I forgot about the buck," Kwa'yo said, taking Ruth's hand. "She gave me a flower, made me a crown, and suddenly, I felt like I was a king."

Lydia noticed the children rolling their eyes to each other, but still her heart bounced slightly at such a freely given pronouncement of affection. She hoped her husband would be as open about his love for her.

Ruth picked up the story. "We met every day I could get away in that clearing. We taught each other to speak the other's language."

"How did you know to meet if you couldn't speak to each other?" Lydia asked.

Kwa'yo answered, "I just came back the next day and hoped the beautiful girl would return."

"I prayed God would let me see him again. I would have waited there all day in the hopes he would return, but he was already there."

"We were in love and love doesn't need words. But I still wanted to be able to ask her to be my wife in her language."

"He tried to be sly about asking me the words, but I knew. It wasn't a week later my sister caught us. I should have told her, but she would've tried to talk me out of it. I knew if it was found out I was engaged to an Indian I would be shunned."

"Shunned!" Lydia cried. "Why?"

"I was baptized and Kwa'yo wasn't. He didn't want to be Amish and, if I am to be honest, I didn't want him to be. I admired his freedom, freedom I didn't feel. He made me see that as fine as it was, my life was a cage. He was a beautiful free thing and I couldn't bear to bring him into the same cage I was living in. I wanted him to be free and I wanted to be free with him. I wanted to be one with God's creation, not force it to submit to my will, the way I would be forced to submit to my husband's will. So, I decided to run off to be with him. That night, I left a note for Abel and Jo and by midnight, I was free."

"A note? But everyone believes you were kidnapped!"

Ruth shook her head. "That stubborn illiterate brother of mine!"

Lydia looked confused.

"Oh no, he's not really illiterate, he just chooses what he wants to understand and what he doesn't. Like my children." She gave the two a pointed look. "He probably threw my note away and said I'd been kidnapped because he couldn't take the shame of his sister running off with an Indian."

Lydia couldn't believe what she was hearing! It had all been a lie! Ruth Bless was alive and well and Agatha's father had known it! He had deceived everyone and all for his pride. Poor Agatha had been afraid without cause! The Indians were her family; she had an uncle and cousins among them.

"Do you ever miss us?" Lydia asked.

"Yes. I miss Jo and my brother. I miss walking through town and church meetings. Some days I'd give almost anything to walk down the main road to church on Sunday. It pains me that my niece has grown up without me - that Jo spent so many years in hurt and I wasn't there. I wish I could have watched my friends marry and have children. The hardest thing I have ever had to do was leave my home knowing I could never come back."

"I don't think I could ever do such a thing," Lydia said. "I'd miss my family too much."

"Yes, I would have said the same. The only thing harder than the idea of life without my family was life without Kwa'yo. I simply couldn't imagine it. I would have wasted away. We made our own home and filled it with love and children. I wish you could meet them but they've all gone off on their own ways now, except for Timothy and Ga'nígöhdáshä'."

"But if that was a lie then what about Adam Garten? Were he and his family really murdered by Indians?"

The children dropped their silver.

Ruth frowned. "It was a long time ago, a tribe that no longer lives here. But, yes. When Adam Garten first arrived, he staked his land by the spring. The Indians were unhappy for they used that spring and their chief held conference with him. He promised to share the spring with the Indians. That winter, while they were in their winter campgrounds, Adam Garten built the spring house. You know how it has that heavy black iron door on it?"

Lydia nodded.

"That was to keep the Indians out, so they couldn't chop or burn it down. Then he put a huge padlock on it; it was still there when I lived in Birch Run, because of the drought."

"I've not seen it."

"They must feel it's finally safe. The Gartens never could bear to share more than they could comfortably spare." There was a sour note in Ruth's voice. "When the Indians returned and found they had been betrayed they sought to speak with Adam, but he fired upon them with his musket, wounding three of them. He meant to kill them."

Lydia couldn't help but picture Seth with his pistol; the pistol he meant to use for the same purpose.

"So, the next night they came and took their revenge on him and his family. I will not say they were right-"

"I will," Kwa'yo said.

"But I will say they were led to the violence through the greed and violence of Adam Garten."

Lydia pushed her plate forward.

"Are you not hungry?" Ruth asked.

"No. I'm just not feeling so well."

"She's had a long day," Sam said. "I'd best take her home."

"Oh, I'm sorry to hear that." Ruth stood and took Lydia's plate. "I do hope you'll come by again when you are feeling better."

"Of course," Lydia croaked, fighting to keep her meal down.

Out of the cabin, Lydia gulped the fresh air.

"Food didn't agree with you?" Sam asked.

Lydia shook her head.

Sam leaned over to look into Lydia's eyes from under her bonnet. "Ah, I see. Wait here."

He left for a few moments while Lydia waited, rooted to where she stood. He returned with Wa'ya. The horse nosed at Lydia, causing her to smile in spite of herself.

"I thought that might help," he said. "Why don't you hop on and we'll go home?"

"No. I shouldn't ride him. You should ride him. I rode the whole way here. It is only four miles; I can easily walk."

"Listen here, I can't ride while you walk. If anyone should pass us, they'd... they'd think the wrong things."

"Well then, we'll both walk."

Sam began looking her head over.

She twisted away. "What are you doing?"

"I'm trying to find where you tucked those mule ears of yours! I've never met a woman so stubborn in all my life! Is this because of what they said in there?"

"No. Yes. It's not fair for you to have to walk the whole way simply because I insisted on coming!"

"And I let you. I could have refused. Despite what you might think, you didn't force me."

"But Uncle Zeke-"

"His words don't mean a hill of beans to me if I don't want to do what he asks. I pay him, not the other way around! If he doesn't want my money, I can go on to Philadelphia. I'd rather not, it's further than I'd like. But I don't answer to your uncle, I only answer to myself, and I'm free to refuse you or accept you if I'm inclined. I let you come because I might need the help and, truth be told, for the company. And I thought it might be good for you to meet Ruth. Might help you understand a few things a little better. And, from the look of it, you do now."

Lydia burst into tears. "It was all lies! All of it! And they knew! And still, they kept lying to all of us! I don't know what to do. Do I expose them to the community? But then they might be shunned! But wouldn't it be just as wrong to let them keep lying?"

Sam stared at the ground. "I wish I had the answers for you."

"It just seems like no one is who I thought they were! My whole world is coming undone! I thought we were a people set apart. But we're just as full of lies and violence and usury and prejudice and cruelty as the world!" Wa'ya nuzzled into Lydia. She wrapped her arms around his large head and cried into his forelock. "Thank you, Wa'ya. At least you are what you appear to be."

"They're humans, the same as you and I."

She looked at Sam, tearfully. "But we were supposed to be better!"

Sam heaved a deep breath. "Come on, we've got a long way to go before dark."

They walked in silence for some time, Wa'ya between them, Lydia contemplating all she had learned. Her heart ached for Agatha who had never known her aunt, for Ruth Bless, who could never go home, for those Indians betrayed by the Gartensw, for the family of Adam Garten who had died for his sins, for all the terrible lies and half-truths the Paxton Boys told to make the people fear the Indians.

But she was glad to know, even if it were terrible, even if it rent her heart, she was no longer so blind. "Thank you for taking me."

Sam just smiled in his quiet way.

The mood considerably lightened, Lydia found herself chattering about all things and yet nothing in particular as Sam listened, occasionally making the odd comment, but mostly just hmming and yessing with a smile of slight amusement on his face as she went on.

As they approached town, they heard the sound of hoof beats pounding toward them. Sam froze, listening. Suddenly, he pulled Wa'ya off to the side of the road and turned the horse so he was concealed behind it from anyone coming.

"What is it, Sam?" Lydia asked.

"Just keep still. Take hold of Wa'ya's bridle so it looks like you're leading him."

"Why?"

"Just trust me."

Lydia took the bridle in her hand as the hoof-beats drew closer. She squinted through the dim light of dusk, trying to make out the figure. "It's Uncle Zeke!" she cried.

Sam let out an audible sigh of relief.

"But what purpose does he have coming out this way?"

Her mind immediately turned to Aunt Sarah. Had the baby decided to come early? Or worse, was there something wrong? Her panicked thoughts flowed like water through the run, turning seconds to eternity. Was this the last chance she might have to see her aunt alive? What about the children? She could stay on; she could care for them until Uncle Zeke found a suitable wife. Her mother could manage without her for a while.

Uncle Zeke pulled up his horse roughly, causing it to whinny with displeasure.

"What is it Uncle Zeke?" Lydia asked.

"Get on," Uncle Zeke ordered. "Don't ask questions, there's not time for it."

Lydia mounted quickly, fearing the worst for Aunt Sarah and the baby.

"Sam, I suggest you go home by a different way. Perhaps take a week off from the booth. I'll only charge you half-rent for the month," her uncle said.

Sam tipped his hat. "Understood." He mounted Wa'ya and was off through the meadow.

Uncle Zeke gave his horse a kick and they started off, not at a gallop as Lydia would have expected such a meeting to portend, but at a fast walk.

"Is it Aunt Sarah? Is she alright?" Lydia asked.

"Sarah's fine. Lydia, I want you to stay away from the market for a while. Don't come by the booth. Do you understand me?"

"But why?" Lydia protested.

"Do you have any idea the trouble you've caused that man with your stubbornness? Not that he would ever tell you. I should have never allowed you to go. But I was afraid if something happened with that woman on the road, Sam might need help and I let that override my better judgement. Right now, we have to clean up this mess. If they see you with me, we might convince them you weren't with him."

"Him? Do you mean Sam? Why would we need to trick them?

"I know you don't understand, but that little display earlier caused a lot of talk about town. People are saying he took you."

"But that's not true!"

"It is true. And you need to realize that."

"But I insisted we go, and nothing scandalous occurred."

"That you went off alone with an Indian is scandal enough! What happened after is a matter of gossip."

"But Sam would never do such a thing!"

"I know that and you know that, and I let my trust in him blind me to what he is."

"Just because he's an Indian doesn't mean he would ever-"

"It's not about that!" Uncle Zeke interrupted. "It's not about whether we know he would or not. They've already decided he did. Some of the men from Paxton are out looking for him. If they found you with him now, they'd kill him. We're going to ride through town and, if anyone asks, you'll say he took you straight to your Aunt Sarah's where you spent the rest of the day until she asked you to fetch some white oak bark. She already knows and will vouch for you. The people here know he's associated with our family through business, and they'll soon come to see all that happened was an act of foolish kindness on your part to an old woman. But that's only if we don't give them anything to talk about. If you can't stay away, I'll have to send you home. Do you understand?"

"Yes, Uncle." Lydia hung her head as they rode home. She hadn't realized the trouble she'd caused; she'd never even considered it a possibility! But she couldn't simply have ignored the old woman and she didn't regret meeting Ruth Bless. Had she not gone, she never would have known the truth. And wasn't the truth what mattered? Not all this hate and prejudice.

The days passed by and Lydia did as her uncle told her, avoiding the market and helping her aunt. Whenever anyone asked about what had happened, she only repeated her uncle's story and repented in tears each night over her lies, pleading that God keep any further inquiries away that she would not have to lie to them as well.

That Sunday, Sam came by for supper, a large bruise around his eye and cuts on his lip a few days healed. When she asked, he only said Wa'ya had accidentally knocked him with that big hard head of his. He did not stay late as he had before, leaving as soon as the meal was eaten, sparing no glances for her. And Lydia wept again seeing what her stubbornness had wrought. She prayed to God for answers. Should she stay away from Sam? But even as she asked it, she knew that was not the answer.

Chapter 12

She threw herself into her community. There was not a quilting bee nor a hymn singing she was not at. The effects of her outburst to Wendell had been tempered by her Good Samaritan act of kindness to the Indian woman. Having no reason to disbelieve her story regarding the Indian man who worked with her uncle, the questions soon ceased and her reputation was restored. An injustice her fair face brought her which was not extended to Sam.

The men from Paxton found their time occupied with their farms and businesses, though they still passed through on occasion looking to stir up outrage with the newest reports of violence from the Indians. The heroic escape of McDougall and his troops brought cheers, but the news a few days later of Captain Campbell's brutal slaying by the tomahawk of the Chief of the Chippewa sent a chill down Lydia's spine as the sieges of Fort Detroit and Fort Pitt dragged on beyond human endurance.

The other youths wondered aloud how long the forts could hold out. Fort Detroit was well aided by the French who had designated it the last stand before the Indians could make incursions into Canada, but Fort Pitt was isolated, cut off from its closest help from Ligonier and Niagara, forts which had already fallen.

"If Fort Pitt falls, the Iroquois Nation will join with Pontiac," one of the boys at the hymn singing whispered to the boy next to him as they were all taking their seats.

Lydia leaned in closer as the other boy asked, "Do you really think so?"

"Of course. They've been wanting the mouth of the Ohio back since they lost it."

"But that means the Seneca and the Susquehanna!"

"And the Delaware will probably follow suit."

"Do you really think the Delawares, too?"

"Why wouldn't they? They'll raze all the settlements to the ground. We'll have to go to Philadelphia and pray there will be enough boats to take us back to Switzerland before the city falls."

"You think they could take Philadelphia?"

The boy nodded. "If they all got together, Philadelphia would be no match for them. They don't fight fair on a field and Philadelphia isn't built for a siege. It has no walls. They could send their braves in in the night and slaughter like the devil and there'd be no way to hold them back."

Lydia couldn't help but feel rising anxiety in her chest as she heard this. She needed to talk to Sam, to dispel the power of these rumors on her own mind.

♥ ♥

After a fortnight had passed and the sultry mid-July heat settled on the sleepy Pennsylvania town, Lydia's aunt, now so heavy with child she struggled to walk about the house, came to her with a parcel wrapped in burlap. "Your uncle forgot his lunch, could you please take it to him?"

Lydia knew better than to object to Aunt Sarah in her current condition, even if Uncle Zeke told her to stay away. She took the parcel and walked the short distance to the market square. There was Sam, standing at the booth. Involuntarily, she took a deep breath. It felt as though all the weight she'd been carrying over the past two weeks lifted.

He was busy with a customer; he didn't even notice her. She watched him for a minute. There was such a peace that settled over her as he worked, she wished she didn't have to trouble him. With that thought, sadness stole over her.

She was a trouble for him. She'd given him that black eye as surely as if she'd struck him herself. Would he even want to speak to her? Of course not. She had best find her uncle and give him his lunch and leave. But she didn't see Uncle Zeke anywhere.

Sam glanced up and saw her. He smiled, raising his hand in greeting. How did one smile have power to cause her emotions to war within her? She suddenly very much wanted run as far away from him as possible and yet towards him as fast as her legs could carry her. She felt the weight of the burlap parcel in her hand. Lydia swallowed, managed a smile, and walked toward him.

"Uncle Zeke forgot his lunch. Aunt Sarah asked me to bring it for him," she said, laying the parcel on the wooden counter beside a red fox pelt.

"I'm sorry, you've just missed him. He's gone off to the pub for lunch."

"Oh. Sorry to bother you." Lydia turned to go.

"No, wait. Why don't you stay and have lunch with me?"

Lydia scanned the area for anyone watching. "Are you certain it would be alright? I wouldn't want to cause you further trouble on my account."

"I know what I'm asking, and I'd like it if you'd stay."

Lydia nodded. "I'd love to."

She met Sam in the grassy area behind the booth where they had first broken bread. Sam dug out a potato from the hot coals with a large stick. Splitting it into quarters, he ladled a thick gravy of meat, carrots, and mushrooms and put one half on a plate he handed to Lydia. For himself, he put the potato in the wooden bowl she recognized from all those months before.

"Here, I have the lunch for my uncle." Lydia opened the burlap sack to reveal a cheese and pulled-chicken sandwich, she tore it in half and gave Sam the portion she judged the larger. She took a forkful of soup and chewed the meat thoughtfully. "Turtle?"

"Tried to take my finger off by the stream this morning." Sam held up a bandaged digit.

Lydia tried to hide her laugh behind her fork. The two fell into conversation moving from the weather to the shop, until, eventually, turning to Lydia.

"Hannah, my sister, is probably my closest friend, but she lives in her own world most of the time. When I come home, Rahrah and Essie - I'm sorry, Deborah and Esther - will probably have a thousand stories to tell of their adventures that will be pure nonsense and only really consist of going to the woods and waving sticks, but according to them they'll have frightened off the entire Philistine army with the help of their leader, Gideon. Or maybe they'll have stood too close to the fire playing that they are Shadrach, Meshach, and Abednego. It's hard to say. Once, they found a cave and Hannah swore it was the lion's den Daniel had been thrown in one day and Jeremiah's pit the next!" She laughed.

"She has quite an imagination."

"Yes, but she is sixteen, now, and I worry she won't make much of a wife if she can't become more sensible. Half the time when she cooks her mind wanders and she burns the supper."

Sam chuckled. "I'm sure some man will be happy to trade the entertainment of her stories for burned meals."

"Perhaps, but I don't know if I've met any such man. When I left, she wasn't speaking to me, again."

"Why is that?"

"Because I was leaving Seth Garten just as he made clear his aim to court me."

"Oh." Sam stirred the fire with his digging stick. "And she thinks you'll lose his attention?"

"No. She thinks I am being cruel in leaving him right now, even though she knows our aunt needs the help. She said I am toying with him and I should just accept him."

"Do you want to accept him?"

Lydia looked down at the bit of potato still left "No. Oh, but I am so confused! I thought I did but I don't think so anymore. And it's not as though he's changed! Well, I suppose he has changed. Maybe that's why. But I liked him so well up until he asked me to ride home with him and... I'm sorry, I didn't mean to say all of that. It's just... perhaps I just find you easy to talk to."

"It's nice someone does. Don't worry, I won't tell." He put a finger to his lips and smiled. His eyes twinkled with mirth. "So, you have three sisters?"

Lydia breathed a sigh of relief at the change of subject. "Yes, and three brothers." Lydia glanced down at her food. Just as with her troubles with Seth, the words had tumbled out without an ounce of thought or bidding. "I'm sorry, two brothers."

"It doesn't make him any less your brother. When did he pass?"

"A few years ago. He got sick, we all did, but he never got better."

"What was his name?"

"Asher, on account of his ash-colored hair when he was born."

"And your other brothers?"

"Michael, he's two years older than me. Don't tell Uncle Zeke and Aunt Sarah, because they'd only make a fuss, but I believe he's planning to marry soon. And then there's Peter; he's between Deborah and Esther."

"All Biblical names."

"Yes, it's a Fischer family tradition to give us an example to live our lives by, except for Cousin Egon's family, they wanted to choose names from our home country to remember where we came from. Do you have any sisters or brothers?"

"Don't know. How is your aunt coming along?"

Lydia felt her cheeks burn. Of course he wouldn't know if he'd been taken so young! That he so quickly changed the subject only showed how little he cared to speak about it. And here she was chattering ceaselessly about her own family and their names and connections - how hard it must be not to have any knowledge of those! Like a feather floating on the wind. "The baby should be here any day now."

"That's a fine thing. I'll be praying for her and the baby. Well, you'd best be going, I need to get back to work."

"Of course." She stood. "I know she'll appreciate the prayers. Will you be coming on Sunday?"

Sam raised his great, dark eyes to Lydia. "Would you want me to?" The sincerity in his voice pained her heart.

"Of course! And you must stay longer than last time. I was sad not to be able to speak with you."

"It does me good to hear you say that."

"It's true. I value our conversations more than any! I only wish I could come to see you as often as I'd like, but Uncle Zeke warns me against it with those Paxton men about. And all I want to do is talk to you about what they're saying! Everyone is so afraid and I don't know whether I should be afraid or not."

"Lydia... Miss Fischer, your uncle will be back shortly, and he wouldn't condone me talking to you about such things, but," he glanced about him, "if you are able to come by Friday when Zeke usually meets with the other men at the pub, maybe we might be able to discuss it more."

"I'll try my best, but aren't you worried someone will see?"

He smiled. "I suppose you make me want to be reckless, Miss Fischer."

Lydia's heart flew up to her throat, then sank like a stone to her stomach. It felt like all those caterpillars had formed into one giant chrysalis and a monstrous butterfly had burst out inside her.

"Now you'd best go before you're missed," he said.

"Yes," Lydia said, not quite certain how to make her feet work. "Yes, of course." There, now they were moving again and she was jogging back to her aunt's house. She had to. Whatever feeling this was inside compelled her. Walking wouldn't do at all.

A few moments ago, she hadn't even been able to walk - what caused that? *You make me want to be reckless, Miss Fischer.* Oh! It felt like a cold wave washed through her, taking her very blood with it. She leaned against the corner of a house placing a hand on her brow. There was no fever; it felt cool to the touch. How did only a handful of words affect her so? She continued leaning, letting the sweet sensation of the words pass over her with every recollection.

"Lydia! Lydia! There you are!" Sheerah cried. "You're pale. You're not sick, are you?"

"No, just the heat of the day overcame me a moment. What is it, little sparrow?"

"It's Momma! She told me to find you. She said my sister is coming."

Lydia's eyes flew open wide. "Go fetch Sister Hagan, then come straight back home."

"What about Father?"

"In such matters, men are only in the way." Lydia raced off to her relative's house.

Tearing open the door, she found her aunt sitting on the floor with her back against the wall, her reddened brow coated in perspiration, causing strands of her hair to stick. Phoebe was crouched next to her, patting her hand and trying to snuggle against her. Sarah was trying to console the child but every score of seconds her body shuddered and her jaw clenched. The baby was coming fast! Sister Hagan might not even arrive before it did.

Lydia took a deep breath. She'd seen this four times with her own mother. Essie had been fast, too. "Phoebe, could you find me some rags and put a kettle on. Your mother needs hot water."

"Is she hurt?"

"No, she'll be well soon, I only need to help her to bed. Now, please find the rags for me." Lydia knelt beside her aunt, wrapping an arm around the woman. She hadn't realized until this moment how small and thin Aunt Sarah actually was.

In her mind, Aunt Sarah was always taller than her and strong enough to carry Lydia on her shoulders, but she wasn't much bigger than Hannah, was she? And, only twelve years older. In ten years would she, herself, be having her third child? Lydia wondered as she helped Aunt Sarah to the bed.

Being a wife and mother still seemed to be some distant future, but Sarah had been Lydia's age when she married Uncle Zeke, and then Sheerah had come within the year. In less than a year she might be where her aunt was, lying in bed in terrible pain as her womb was opened by her first baby. The idea filled her with an anxiety she'd never felt when picturing life with her first child.

She tried to calm her nerves by picturing the familiar scene she'd imagined hundreds of times. Her lying in bed nursing the pink little babe as her husband, Seth, looked on them. Of course, it would be Seth, who else could it be? But the idea of him gazing down on her and her child set her skin to crawling. It was wrong. It was so wrong. She removed him from the scene. The crawling stopped.

Her aunt's sudden grip on her wrist broke her from her thoughts. It felt as though the bones in her arm were caught in a vice!

"Breathe, Aunt Sarah! Breathe! Sister Hagan will be here soon." Lydia spoke as calmly as she could to the red-faced, sweat-soaked woman. The belly had dropped, it was almost shaking for the spasms. Sister Hagan would not arrive in time even if she flew. Clearing her mind, Lydia focused on her breathing as she positioned herself to receive the baby.

In an hour's passing, Lydia stood beside her uncle and the children watching as Aunt Sarah nursed a dark-haired boy swaddled in a large piece of Lydia's quilt Phoebe had, in her rush, mistaken for a pile of rags.

"What should we call him?" Uncle Zeke asked. "Ezekiel? Or perhaps the shepherd, Amos, would be more fitting? Or Joseph, that he might work diligently and follow God humbly."

"I was thinking we might name him Daniel," Sarah said, quietly, as she gazed on the sucking babe at her breast.

"That's a mighty big name to live up to." Uncle Zeke thought for a minute, placing a hand on the child's head to stroke his dark hair. "But I think you're right. Daniel Fischer it is."

The next few days were alive with things to do. Letters were written and sent to friends and relatives announcing the birth, people from all over Lancaster came with pies and flowers and words of congratulations, each having to see the new baby for themselves. Sleep was a seldom gained luxury reserved only for Phoebe and Sheerah while the adults cared for Daniel who seemed to suffer from an aversion to sleep matched only by his love of his own voice. Lydia hadn't even realized what day it was until Uncle Zeke yawned and stretched and said he wouldn't be going to the pub today; he was in no shape to be out and about.

"Uncle Zeke, might I go into town today? I told a friend I would meet them for lunch."

"Of course! All you've done is work since Danny came. You've more than earned a break from it. Though if you would, bring back some cheese and flour, we're just about at the end."

So, it was less about consideration for her than for the groceries, but Lydia didn't mind, it made for a good excuse.

She strolled along the streets glancing in the shop windows. Every day it seemed there were more and more English wares in them, even in the Brethren's shops.

"Good morning, Lydia," a pair of young men said in unison as they passed.

"Good morning, Tobias. Good morning, David." She returned the greeting with little notice of how they stared at her as she walked by. Her mood was buoyant as she slipped through the stalls to the back area where she could already smell a rabbit stew. She paused to close her eyes and savor the aroma; the carrots, the onions - it was heavenly!

Sam appeared from the other side of the booth. "Have a seat, I'll be there in a moment."

He took a pack of furs from Wa'ya's saddle and carried them around to the booth. Lydia sat, watching the soup boil. She leaned back and let the sun shine on her face.

Wa'ya whinnied. She turned to the fine young stallion. "Yes, hello to you, too, Wa'ya." She stood and walked over to him, picking a few blackberries from a bush as she went. She stroked his long white blaze. "I'm sorry I don't have any alfalfa for you, but perhaps you'll take these berries?" She hadn't even opened her hand before he was nuzzling it to try to get at the contents. "Oh, you greedy thing! Here!" She opened her hand and instantly felt his lips and tongue where the berries had been. She kissed him at the center of his forehead.

"You'll spoil him, you treat him like that," Sam said. "Then he'll be your horse and none of mine. He'll follow you around like a duckling. A one thousand pound duckling."

"We could use another horse at home."

"He'll eat your fences. You've been warned."

"Hmmm... maybe not then." Lydia gave Wa'ya a final pat on the nose and took a seat on one of the logs by the fire. "You made rabbit stew again?"

"I remembered you seemed to like it when we had it last." Sam removed his broad-brimmed hat and set it next to the log, revealing his hair as black as midnight, cropped short, shorter than Lydia was used to seeing on a man. Probably a preventative measure for fleas and lice, given he worked closely with dead animals.

"I did. It's my favorite."

Sam ladled the soup into a bowl, handing it to Lydia, then produced a second and began filling that.

"You got a new bowl!" she cried.

"Well, seeing as I knew you'd be stopping by, I figured it was best to be prepared this time so you wouldn't feel like you were putting me out." He sat down next to her on the log. "Now, I heard it was you who delivered your cousin all alone? You must've been scared."

"I was, though thankfully I've helped with my sibling's births so I mostly knew what to do. He made it easy on me. I don't know what I would have done had he come backward like Rahrah."

"Have you ever given thought to being a midwife?"

Lydia gazed into her soup, considering. "Maybe. When I'm older and I've had a few of my own."

They fell into talking about Daniel and the birth and before she knew it, the hour had passed. "Oh no! It's well after noon now and we've not gotten to talk about any of what's happening!" Lydia pouted.

"It'll hold till next week. It was nice not having to think on those things for an hour but to just have a talk with someone who doesn't – oh, well, that's none of your concern." He stood up and took her bowl.

"Who doesn't what?" Lydia asked, handing the bowl over.

"It's of no matter." He shuffled off to where his horse stood and put the bowls in his pack.

Lydia stood. "Who doesn't what?"

"I'm not telling you!" He plucked his hat from the ground and set it back on his head, shading his eyes so she couldn't tell if he were annoyed or amused.

"I won't move until you do."

"Then stand there like a statue all day for all I'm going to say."

"Don't test me, Sam, you know I will."

"How does a woman get to be so stubborn? Fine! Who doesn't look at me and only see an Indian. Are you happy now?"

"No. How could I be happy about that? What about Uncle Zeke?"

"What about your Uncle Zeke?" The way he said the words gave Lydia to know her dear uncle was, sadly, not the exception she'd hoped.

She lowered her head. "I'm sorry. I didn't mean to offend."

"Don't feel sorry, you can't help you're stubborn as a mule." His nose crinkled with a smile.

A smile that did little to raise Lydia's spirits.

"Yes, I can. It's not a godly trait. It has caused no end of trouble for me and now for you, as well. I'd do anything to be rid of it!" Tears threatened to fall from Lydia's eyes.

Sam stepped to her. "You'd better not. You hear me?" He leaned over to meet her brown eyes with his warm, black ones. "I love that about you, how stubborn you are. You are the most impossible woman I've ever met and if you dare change that even a bit, well, I'll never make rabbit stew for you again."

"Never?"

"Nope. Not one hare or cottontail ever again." A grin spread across his face revealing his teeth all the way back to the molars.

Lydia giggled, wiping her dress cuffs across her eyes to dry the lingering tears. "That's a cruel threat."

"I mean it. Now get on, they'll be missing you." He waved off toward the square. "I'll see you next Friday."

Chapter 13

The following week, Daniel had finally calmed down enough that Lydia and Aunt Sarah were able to take him out of the house. He was quite enchanted by the sights and sounds of town, seeming to find it far more soothing to sleep among crowds of people than in his own cradle.

"He looks so happy with you!" Birgitta squealed as Daniel grabbed her finger.

"I assure you, when we are inside, he is never this way."

"No wonder you've been out so much lately," David, a tall, dark-haired man of Lydia's age loped up beside them. He stared at the baby tucked against Lydia's breast. "You look quite natural with an infant."

"Thank you, David. I have enough younger siblings that I'm well practiced."

"A good thing for a woman to be. Might I touch him?"

"Of course." To Lydia's mind it appeared David was quite a poor hand at touching a baby for he tried to pet it down its body like a cat, his fingers brushing against her apron bib. "No, David, try just stroking his head. He enjoys that."

David clumsily did as she said, still catching her apron too much. Daniel started to grunt his displeasure.

"That's probably enough for now," Lydia said, pulling away from the young man.

"Where are you girls off to today?" David asked.

"We are going to a sewing frolic at Naomi's house. It's such a lovely day we thought we might use her porch," Lydia answered. Birgitta lifted a pair of baskets, each filled with sewing supplies and fabric.

"Ah, then don't let me hold you back. Perhaps I'll see you at services Sunday? Will you be able to stay for the hymn singing, Lydia?"

"I don't know. I shall have to ask my aunt, but if she doesn't require my help, I imagine so."

"I hope you will. Toby and I miss hearing your lovely voice."

Lydia reddened at David's praise.

"Good day to you both." He tipped his hat and strode away.

Birgitta started giggling. "Well, it seems you have gotten David's attention."

Lydia joined in her giggles. "I suppose so."

"Would he be someone you'd like to court with?"

"I don't know. He seems nice enough, and he's handsome. But I think I'd want to know him better first."

"But that's the point of courting!"

"Birgitta, he's practically a stranger to me! And not especially good with children. Did you see how he tried to pet Daniel?"

"Like he was a spring lamb!" Birgitta laughed. "What about my brother, Wendell? He thinks the world of you. Then we could be sisters!"

"Even after I scolded him?"

"He holds no ill will towards you for that. It was in the name of love of others, after all. He understands, as younger people, our tempers sometimes can flare, but mellow once married."

Mellow. Change. Naturally, she wished it, too. It would not do for a wife of the Brethren to be as stubborn and hot-tempered as she. No man would wish to be married to a scold.

But Sam said he loved that about her. The thought brought a sorrow to her heart. Her mind responded with proper sense: *But then, he could afford to, he would not have to live with it his entire life.* "Of course." She thought for a moment. "No. I don't think I could leave my family."

"It's not so far," Birgitta protested.

"Yes, but it's far enough."

"I understand, but I'll still be praying you change your mind."

The following Friday, Lydia made her excuses and went to the market. There was Sam, holding up a long, dark fur for a man and woman to see. A deep warmth like a hearth on a cold winter's day filled her heart at the sight of him. She glanced about for any Paxton Boys and, seeing none, made her way over to the booth. "Good day, Sam."

"Good day, Miss Fischer. I'll be with you in a moment."

"Thank you."

Rather than go to the fire pit behind the booth, she gazed upon Sam's wares. She hadn't taken the time to appreciate them before, but there were quite a number of fine things among the pelts. Of course, there were the normal gloves and stoles, but there were many luxury items, far too fine for Amish women. These were for the French and English. Lydia stroked a red fox fur lady's hat trimmed in white with a large blood-red gem in the center.

"I think you'd look better in the stole," a male voice said.

"She doesn't need anything to look better," David answered.

Lydia turned to find herself almost pressed against the booth by Tobias and David. Instinctively, she leaned back slightly, smiling. "Good day, David. Good day, Tobias. What brings you to market today?"

"Oh, we just saw you walking and decided to say hello." David said, slipping on one of the gloves. He clenched his fist twice and examined it. "Hmmm... Not bad, for Indian wares."

"Are you interested in those gloves?" Sam asked, stiffly.

David pulled the glove off and dropped it back on the wooden counter. Sam quietly turned the glove back to right and moved to another customer, but Lydia could see him glancing back at them.

"So, did you speak with your aunt?" David asked.

"Yes," Lydia answered.

"Will you be coming to the hymn singing on Sunday, then?"

"I should be able to."

"Good, it's about time we had you back," Tobias said.

"We'll see you Sunday," David said.

Lydia waved and turned back to Sam to see him intently watching the boys leave.

"I'm sorry they were rude to you," she said.

Sam shook his head. "It's no matter. Are they friends of yours?"

"I know them from church and singing. It does matter, though, you should be treated better. You've done nothing to deserve such rudeness."

"Except being born," Sam muttered.

"Don't say something like that! I'm glad you were born and I'm glad you're here! Sam-" the words stopped in her throat.

The emotions welled in her chest but she wasn't sure what they were supposed to take form as to speak them. She didn't know what this was but that it was powerful and heady. She cared for him; she admired him. But it was something beyond those things, else she'd know it as the same thing she felt for Cousin Egon. What was it? He tilted his head to the side, as if inviting her to continue.

She'd best try with what she knew. "You're important to me and it tears at my heart to see people treat you so poorly."

Sam took off his hat and put it to his chest, tilting his head to the sky, he mouthed a few words with quite a passion. He turned to her. "Tarnation, Lydia! You're going to do me in talking like that," he said.

"I'm sorry. I should have waited until we were in private."

"That's not quite my meaning, but I suppose it is better you said it here." Sam ran his fingers through his black hair, replacing his hat on his head. "Are you ready for lunch?

As the pair ate in their usual places, Sam said, "So tell me, what's been worrying you?"

Lydia poked at her food with her spoon. "Lots of things, really."

"Let's start with the first."

Lydia thought a moment. "Are the Seneca planning to join with Pontiac? A few of the boys at the hymn singing were saying that if they joined, the Iroquois Confederacy would follow."

"As far as the whole of the Iroquois Confederacy, it's not too likely. Some Seneca chiefs have been talking about it, I wish I could allay your fears and say they weren't, but there are a number who have been looking to create a confederacy to rebuff the English."

"Just the English? Why not the French, too? Is this part of the war?"

"No, the war is over, and that's what really led to the problems. I won't say the tribes particularly like the French, but the French aren't really interested in colonies here. They care more about trade and they see us as tools in that. Same as the Dutch. Most of the land they take from us is for forts and trading posts. They don't treat us especially well, but they give us gifts and treat our people with a certain respect. What do you know about Pontiac?"

"They say he's a savage, bloodthirsty Chippewa chief who hates all white men and won't stop until he's scalped a thousand of them."

Sam laughed. "Well, first off, he's Ottawa. And you know he grew up with white men at Fort Detroit? Some of his closest friends are white, and French."

Lydia's brow wrinkled in confusion. "I don't understand."

"Of course not. You see, Fort Detroit, and the other French forts for that matter, aren't like here where Indians and whites live separately and don't really mix except to trade. In French settlements, Indians and French people lived together, and children of both played and were able to be friends. When the war came, the Indians had to pick a side. Most chose to side with the French because they saw how the British often chased tribes from their land rather than respecting their right to be there. Most English see us Indians as less than dogs. To be honest, there wasn't any other choice they could have made to try to protect our land and way of life."

"So, what happened to make Pontiac do this?"

"Well, when the British took over Fort Detroit, they made it clear they had no intention of treating the Indians with any kind of respect, whether it be for their person or their land. You can imagine that didn't exactly instill confidence in Pontiac that they would be treated fairly in the future and, with a number of other tribes wanting war, he felt if there was a time, it was now, when the British were weak and the French might come to their side. It was a gamble."

"But the French haven't come to their aid?"

"No, they haven't. But, like I said, it was a gamble. They didn't feel they had a choice. They could either fight now or wait to lose their land and fight then when the English were stronger."

"But shouldn't there be some other option?"

Sam shook his head. "It seems there should be. In a just world there would be. But this isn't a just world."

Lydia put aside her empty bowl, resting her chin between her fists. "I don't think it's right, but I suppose I understand why Pontiac has done this. Still, it frightens me."

"It frightens me, too. There's no good outcome. If they succeed, it'll mean more wars. But if they fail..." He need not finish; the British were not known for their forgiveness.

"Why can't we just live together as you say they did at Fort Detroit? Why do the British hate the Indians so much?"

Sam put down his emptied bowl and sighed. "They don't hate us. We're only in their way."

They sat in silence a few minutes as Lydia thought. It was so horrible that men might murder other men simply to take their land, not even out of hatred or malice, simply greed. "It's not just the war that frightens me. The Paxton Boys keep talking about killing Indians. They even said Will Sock was a spy... And they hurt you."

Sam exhaled a deep breath and nodded. "Yes, they did. Two of them caught me out by the pub. They got tired of me when I wouldn't fight back. I wish I could tell you all will be well and they are only talk. I hope they are." He stirred the fire. "It takes a lot to go from drunks throwing a few punches to murder. But there's enough of them they could cause trouble. So long as the war stays on the other side of the state, I imagine they won't go any further with it. I'm sorry, I'm not doing much to calm your fears, am I?"

"You are. Truly. I feel better knowing what is happening and why. Everyone has been saying it is because Indians are bloodthirsty savages who want to kill us for being civilized, that they hate us because we are Christians and they are heathens. It calms me to know the reasons, even if I don't know if I agree with them."

"Well, I'm glad to know I did that much for you." The sound of rustling about the booth roused them both from their talk. "That must be Zeke. You'd best get going before he sees you."

Lydia stood and made to jog off into the stand of trees.
"And Miss Fischer?"
"Yes?" Lydia turned.
"Thanks for what you said earlier. Nice to know someone is glad I was born."
Lydia beamed. "Of course I am!"
Sam removed his hat and ran his fingers through the raven-black hair before replacing it. His expression recalled to Lydia when she would pour a pitcher of warm water on Hannah's hair during their bath. "Miss Fischer, you'll do me in with that smile."
"What is that to mean?"
"Nothing. Now git. Oh, and be careful of those boys."
"I will!" she waved and ran off, wondering what he meant that she would do him in with her smile. Given that he mentioned the Paxton Boys after, he probably meant she should watch how she responded to him to avoid appearing too friendly and attracting their attentions.

That Sunday, Lydia sang with a joy she had not felt for a long time. She still had her fears, but they'd lessened from looming shadows to a more concrete reality, a reality she could pray for. She could pray for understanding between the English and the Indians. She could pray for an increase in generosity, fairness, and love for his fellow man in the heart of the English and for the softening of Pontiac's heart and a willingness to seek compromise. She could pray for peace between the two nations. And she prayed most for the Paxton Boys, that their hearts would be turned from fear, hatred, and violence to charity, instead. As she sang, she held these prayers in her heart, lifting them up to the Lord.

"You sounded beautiful tonight," Tobias said as they slowly shuffled out of the house which today served as church, forming into smaller knots.

"Beautiful? She sang sweeter than a bluebird," David argued.

"Thank you both. Oh, Birgitta, will you be walking home?" Lydia turned to her friend who was speaking with a young man.

"No, John is taking me home. But Wendell's just left, you can catch him if you want him to walk with you."

"No, thank you. I still want to speak with Heidi about our next sewing bee."

Lydia and Heidi discussed the bee for some time as the crowd of youths dwindled to only five. "I'll see you next Thursday, then," Lydia said, waving as Heidi went off into the darkness with her younger sister.

David sidled up to Lydia. "Lydia, Tobias brought his father's buggy, why don't you let us take you home?"

"No, thank you. The night is so warm and it's such a short way, I'd much rather walk."

"Go on," David hissed to Tobias, waving him off. Tobias glared at him but did as he was directed. David turned once more to Lydia. "Why don't you let me walk you home, then? I'd hate for you to come to any trouble on such a dark night."

"I'll be alright, you don't need to trouble yourself. It's not even a quarter of a mile. I like to use the time to talk to God."

"To talk to God?"

"It's something a dear friend taught me, to speak to God as though He is beside you, like a friend."

"Isn't that irreverent?" David asked, though he did not appear especially concerned.

"I wondered that, myself, but I have felt I've grown closer with Him through it."

David smiled, taking Lydia's hand in his. "Well, perhaps we might use the time to grow closer as well, rather than risk irreverence."

Lydia's eyes widened, suddenly realizing what he was saying. He wasn't asking to walk her home out of kindness, he meant to court her! "I'm sorry, David. I'm flattered, but I'm not interested in courting with you."

David's aspect changed, darkened. "Are you already courting with another?" he demanded.

A shock of alarm ran through Lydia. "No," she said, backing away from him. But he still held her hand firmly in his.

"Then what objection do you have to courting with me? Do you think I'm not good enough for you? Not good enough for your bed?"

"It isn't that!" Lydia pulled at her trapped hand. "I'm just not interested in courting with anyone right now!"

"A girl like you should show proper gratitude when a man asks to court her. Perhaps what you first need is a man to teach you some humility." He bent Lydia's arm painfully, her knees buckled beneath her.

"Let her go." A large shadow of a man appeared from the blackness of the night. His skin was dark, almost as dark as his eyes under his wide-brimmed black hat. His fingers twitched on his large hands, as though ready to grab the skinning knife at his hip.

David's eyes rounded in terror. He dropped Lydia's hand.

"Leave." the man ordered.

Lydia had never seen a man run so fast, leaving her alone.

She breathed a sigh of relief. "Sam."

Sam knelt down, taking Lydia by the hand. "He didn't hurt you, did he?"

"Just my hand, some. I was more frightened than anything. I've never seen a man turn so quickly."

Sam helped Lydia to her feet, taking a moment to examine her hand. "It looks alright. Would you like me to walk you home?"

"Yes. But perhaps we might walk for a bit before. I don't want to be alone right now and it's such a lovely night."

"Of course."

She and Sam walked a fair way in silence before Lydia asked, "How did you know I needed help?"

"To be perfectly honest, I almost didn't come. I'd heard some rumors around town about those boys and how they treated girls they were supposedly courting. I told you to watch out for them, figured that would be enough. But, while I was working in my tent, God kept bothering me to go check on you. I told Him you could take care of yourself, but He wouldn't let up. Finally, I couldn't take it any longer. I told Him once I finished the glove I was stitching I'd go, but He wouldn't even let me do that. So, I left it half sewn on my cot and went to find you."

Lydia laughed as she pictured Sam trying to sew while God insisted he go until he finally dropped his work in exasperation.

"I swear it's true, you can check my tent if you don't believe me."

"I believe you," she said with a smile. "I've just never thought of God as insistent."

"Trust me, the more you get to know Him, the more you'll understand."

"I hope someday I'll know Him as well as you. Thank you for helping me."

"Don't thank me, thank God. If it were up to me, I'd still be sewing that glove in my tent."

"And I'd be..." Lydia shuddered. "I thank you both, God for sending you, and you for listening."

♥ ♥

They walked that way for some hours, talking happily about this and that as they passed through the back streets of the town until they heard spritely music emanating from the English dance hall. Lydia rushed over and gazed through the warmly glowing windows, watching the English couples dancing.

"I've never really watched dancing, it looks like they are having such fun," she said, wistfully, as Sam joined her.

Sam smiled, extending a hand. "Would you care to dance, Miss Fischer?" he joked.

Lydia laughed. "But I've never danced before! We aren't allowed to dance."

"Nor have I. Quakers see it as frivolity. But if you won't tell, I won't." He held a finger to his lips. "Now then, Lydia, would you care to dance?" The look in his eyes had turned from mirthful to earnest. Lydia felt a thrill through her heart when he spoke her Christian name.

"I'd love to."

She placed her hand in his. It was large and rough and warm. She wrapped her thin fingers around its edge, feeling his thumb cover them. They spun around in the street in a poor imitation of the dancers in the window, laughing as they tripped and miss-stepped, knocking knees and stepping on toes. She couldn't remember when she'd had such fun! She felt so secure with her hand in his as he clumsily led them about.

Then Lydia glanced up into Sam's black eyes. Suddenly, the world dropped away and it seemed as though they were tied through an invisible force. Those dark eyes held her gaze. They were no longer dancing. The smile that played at his lips vanished for something else, and she felt herself irresistibly drawn to them. Her breathing quickened as her face flushed. She looked down just as Sam glanced away. She could feel his fingers brush hers as they separated.

"I suppose I'd best get you home," Sam said, still avoiding looking at her.

Her face burning, Lydia managed to speak. "Yes... and thank you, for the dance."

They walked home in silence, Lydia's heart racing. She cast glances at Sam, but every time she looked, he was staring straight ahead. What had that been back there? Had he felt it as well? Perhaps that was why he was acting so strangely now.

It had felt so powerful, even now she still felt it - a tie she could not explain, a moment of pure clarity when Sam had been the only thing in her world. And what troubled her most was how she would do almost anything to have that moment back. What were these feelings? Did she like Sam as she had Seth? No, she had never felt this much for Seth in her life! This was something far deeper, something she'd never known before. Was this love? Did love happen like this? Did it feel so strange and unsettling? None of her friends had ever spoken of having such a feeling.

She glanced over to Sam again; he was still facing forward like a soldier - eyes drifting neither to the right nor the left. Clearly, something was troubling him. Had he felt it to? Or had she done something to offend him? She wanted to take his hand, to ask him. But she didn't, remaining silent in her troubled contemplation as they finished the walk and bid their goodbyes, Sam still refusing to meet her eyes, yet he allowed a smile that suddenly turned Lydia's stomach upside-down and left her unsteady on her feet, her face flushing once more.

She leaned against the door, turning the knob and almost falling inside in her state of complete disarray. Thankfully, no little ones stirred as she made her way to her room and lay on her bed, replaying the evening in her mind: the dance, his smile, that moment. She closed her eyes as she let the sensation wash over her once more. If only she could live in that moment! That moment when the world fell away and Sam was all there was. Just Sam.

Chapter 14

Lydia counted the days until Friday when she might speak with Sam again. She tried to lose herself in her work, reminding herself that the time would pass faster if she did, but it was of little use. More than once Sheerah or Phoebe found her in the middle of a task, staring ahead and forgetting what was at hand.

She played a thousand different conversations in her mind with Sam. What if she told him of her feelings? What would he say? What if he felt the same way? What if he didn't? What if she didn't tell him and just attempted to pretend all was as it had been, would he notice her distracted mien? What if he confessed first?

That would surely be the easiest route, then all she must do was say she felt the same. But nothing of Sam's character allowed her to believe he would speak first on the matter. Or, perhaps, he already had and she'd been too blind to notice. At night, when she was alone and could remember all he had said and how it made her feel, she wondered had he not been telling her for weeks?

She wanted to be confident in her belief that her feelings were returned, yet the idea she was misreading him and he would reject her left her terrified. She would speak to him about it, of course, when next they were alone. Even if he didn't return her affections, at least she knew he would be kind about it.

In all her imaginings she could not picture him being unkind. Perhaps teasing, but never unkind. But how she dearly wished he would return them! She had never known a man who listened to her, respected her, liked the things that were her (like her willfulness). He did not wish for her to change, he wanted her to remain who she was and, more than even that, he enjoyed who she was! And she enjoyed who he was.

He was a quiet man, a hard worker, humble, but not above teasing her if the mood suited him. He had a dignity about him, even when disparaged to his face. It was not a proud arrogance, like other men, but a strength in knowing who he was and his abilities. He was thoughtful and kind to all. He gave respect to everyone, even those who treated him poorly. And he knew God.

Beyond merely knowing God, he pursued God, listened to God, allowed God to move him. He had a faith Lydia could only admire. It inspired her, informed her that faith could be more than praying to the skies, but that God was actually interested in her welfare. Not just interested, but concerned for it! Had not God told Sam to find her when she was in danger, even before she knew she was? How could she want for anything more in a man than what Sam was?

Thursday arrived and, with it, Lydia's eagerness that it be tomorrow became almost all-consuming. She couldn't concentrate on her chores at all.

"Lydia! Watch the pot!" Aunt Sarah cried.

Lydia started, realizing the pot of stew was boiling over, splashing out and sizzling on the stones below. She stirred it quickly, ignoring as drops of boiling liquid singed her hand. "Sorry, Aunt Sarah."

"Really, I don't know what's gotten into you this week. Are you feeling ill?"

"No," Lydia replied. "Just a little out of sorts." She wasn't ready to tell her aunt of her feelings for Sam, at least not until she knew how he felt as well.

They liked Sam, but were she to tell them, she could not imagine them encouraging her in the relationship. He was a trapper and a Quaker - neither qualities that they would be keen to allow their niece to bind herself to. That is, if they could see past his skin - that lovely, deep shade of copper that caused so many to despise him on sight. Even if he were to convert and become a farmer, they still might not accept him.

She desperately wanted to believe that in coming to know him these past months they might have abandoned such prejudices, but had they truly? If she must face their opposition, she would want to be certain it was for something real, not for the silly, fevered imaginings of a young woman.

Uncle Zeke stomped in, hanging his coat, his expression stony, in his hand an unfolded letter dangled.

"What's happened, Zeke?" Aunt Sarah asked, bouncing her baby nervously.

"You've had a letter from home." Uncle Zeke handed the letter to Lydia.

"Oh no! Is it Da?"

"Your father's fine, love," Uncle Zeke sat down heavily next to Aunt Sarah. "Best let you read it, rather than hear it from me." He whispered something to Aunt Sarah whose face suddenly became drawn.

Lydia straightened the letter and read:

L, It must be from Hannah, only she began her letters to Lydia that way.

I asked Ma and Da to let you hear it from me, that it might upset you less. L, Michael's announced his engagement. I knew it! Lydia thought triumphantly.

He is marrying Evony. The letter floated down to the floor. Evony! When had this started? It must have been for months given the celery and the whitewashing. And neither of them thought to mention it!

She scrabbled for the letter, plucking it from the floor and reading on. *I am certain you are as surprised as I was. She is to be baptized this Sunday. They have announced their wedding will be in a fortnight.*

A fortnight! No. That couldn't be right. Weddings were autumn and winter affairs, not summer. Why have a wedding so early, unless... No. Michael would never! Neither would Evony! Lydia was one of her closest friends. She would know! They weren't that kind! Sure, Evony might make the occasional joke, but those were merely jokes. They were good Christians! There had to be another reason.

She read on. *L, Evony's been gaining weight for the past two months, I only just noticed it a week ago, she's been using her apron to hide it, but I think she might be with child.*

Lydia's world stopped.

With child, she read again. Michael's child. For how long? Had this been the reason for Evony sneaking out of the room? No, that was only a few months ago. To be showing enough that Hannah might suggest a baby, she'd have to be at least six months along and it was now July.

She remembered Michael coming home early from courting the night when father had taken that near fatal turn. Had Michael been violating their code of chastity even as his father was lying in bed, near death? With her best friend, no less! How often had she unintentionally facilitated this? How often had Evony used their friendship? Used her?

No wonder they must have a summer wedding immediately! They must do it before the reason behind it became clear; not that the rest of the town wouldn't know when the child came only a few months later! They wouldn't say anything, of course. Evony had not yet been baptized and, though Michael was, he was marrying the woman so they would forgive it - but they would know. They would know her brother had, with full intention, violated their codes, that he should be shunned, that if he had refused to marry her, or she him, he would be.

Lydia was furious! She was furious with Michael for being so irresponsible, furious with Evony for betraying their friendship, and most of all furious with herself for ever bringing Evony into their lives! She could almost feel the shame wrap around her like a cold, sopping, wool blanket. She wanted to crumple up the letter and throw it in the fire, but she forced herself to read on.

Ma and Da ask that you would come home immediately to help with the preparations for the wedding. And, for myself, I need you home. I have no one to talk to and I need someone! It's been hard enough without you, but now, I cannot bear it!

Da will be by tomorrow morning. Please don't be too angry with them, they are doing the right thing and we know he did intend to marry her. We must remember, we are called to forgive.

At the moment, forgiveness was the last thing Lydia could think of giving. How could they have done such a thing! The letter shook so much she could no longer read it as her hot tears smeared the ink.

"A child is always a blessing," her uncle said, his voice rough. "No matter how it comes to be."

She swallowed back her words of fury. "I need to pack," she said. Marching up the stairs to her room, she let the door slam behind her.

It was hours before her tears finally cooled the rage. She removed the things she had stuffed in her bag and folded them properly. It was true what Hannah had written, Michael had been planning to marry Evony for quite a long time, he'd planted celery and painted the house months ago, probably before he knew she was pregnant. Wasn't the point of courting intent to marry? It wasn't as if they were strangers; they'd known each other most of their lives. While these arguments did little to ameliorate Lydia to Evony's pregnancy, it did, at least, allow her to reconcile herself to their marriage.

But now what of Sam? She could hardly bear to think of it! She was leaving. There'd be the wedding, then she'd have to help with the baby. It was not as though she could easily visit Lancaster - at ten miles it was too far to simply walk, and he certainly couldn't visit her! A stranger *and* an Indian looking for a young woman? Quaker garb or not, the people of Birch Run would never allow it!

Perhaps this child was God's way of telling her she and Sam were not in His divine plan, she thought, staring out the window. Even telling herself this, she didn't want to say goodbye. It felt wrong, somehow. It was too soon! But tomorrow, the sun would rise and her father would come to collect her and that would be it. Not even enough time for a farewell.

No! She would have that, at least. There was little she could control at this moment, but she would have that one thing!

At supper, she made her proposal. "Aunt Sarah, I was thinking I might go to the market tomorrow morning to buy a wedding gift."

"Of course. Your father will stop there first, anyway, to see his brother. He can take you from there with a good deal less trouble. Zeke, would you take Lydia's things with you when you go off in the morning?"

Uncle Zeke looked up from his grouse and potatoes. "I will."

"I'm relieved you are willing to accept them," Aunt Sarah said.

"He is still my brother; I don't wish to be a stranger to him." She could still not speak of Evony - perhaps time would reconcile her to her future sister, but she was not ready for that quite yet.

"What are you thinking to purchase?"

"Perhaps a skein of yarn, or a pan for their kitchen when they build their house."

"Those would both be thoughtful gifts, I'm certain they'll be happy with them."

The following morning, her uncle took her things with him to market while Lydia made the breakfast and said her goodbyes to the girls who were sad to see her leave but were only too thrilled to know they would soon be going to a wedding. They were too young to understand this wasn't a truly happy occasion and Lydia had not the heart to ruin it for them.

Lydia set off in the dew-soaked grey of early morning. She didn't know what she would say to Sam. He'd know she was leaving - her things would make that clear enough - but what would he think? Would he be sad?

She stopped at a stall and bought a few spools of linen thread. Evony was far better at sewing than knitting and Michael always needed something or other mended. Then she bought a broom from the Conestoga woman who smiled at her in recognition. Lydia managed to smile back through her misery.

"Lydia!" her father's voice boomed from the road where he stood next to the buggy with Uncle Zeke.

As much as she was glad to see him standing, it was the last sight she wanted to see. He was too early! They'd have no time to speak.

He pitched Lydia's bag behind the seat. "Come on, time to be off."

She glanced over to the booth. Where was Sam? Had he left to avoid saying goodbye? Her heart was crushed. She wouldn't see him afterall.

She turned to her father and there, there was Sam, inspecting the horse. Lydia smiled and jogged over as Sam patted the beast on the shoulder.

"He's a fine animal, Brother Fischer." He turned to Lydia. "Heading home, Miss Fischer? It's been a pleasure having you here. Will you be wanting a hand up into the buggy?" He smiled at her indicating to the other side of the buggy.

She fought to contain her eagerness. "Yes, please. Goodbye, Uncle Zeke, I'll see you soon." She hugged her uncle, then walked over to where Sam stood. "I'm sorry, I have to go," she whispered.

"I know." He was so close she could feel his breath on her ear.

Her heart raced. She wanted to feel his arms wrapped around her. To rise on her toes and press her lips to his.

"I'll be here until the first week of November," he said. "Then I'm off to the western mountains for the winter."

"May I write to you?"

"I'd like if you did," he leaned in close as he made a platform with his interlaced fingers, whispering in her ear, "Lydia."

She felt her mind grow foggy, she stepped into his hands and placed her hands on his shoulders as he boosted her up, dearly wishing he'd let those fingers slip that she could *accidentally* fall into his arms, but he didn't and, moments later, she was waving to them as the buggy pulled away.

November was so far off, she consoled herself. She would find a reason to visit before then and see those dark eyes and hear his rough voice again. As the buggy jostled, she felt something in her pocket. Taking it out, she beheld a piece of white fabric stained mostly cherry red spotted with blueberry purple, a note pinned to it. *For your quilt* it read in quickly scrawled letters.

It took Lydia a moment to realize what she was holding. It was a piece of Sam's shirt from the day they'd met! She'd been so upset at the time she hadn't even realized his shirt had been stained as well as her quilt. When had he slipped it in there? She held the little piece of fabric to her chest.

"What have you got there, Lydia?" her father asked.

"Just a piece of fabric for my quilt from a dear friend," she said.

"That was nice of her," Elias Fischer said, not especially paying attention. "Best put it back in your pocket or it might blow away."

She did as he suggested, occasionally running the fabric through her fingers as they drove on.

They arrived home two hours later to a house in clear state of wedding preparations. Hannah and her sisters were the first out of the house.

"Lydia!" Hannah leapt into her sister's arms, spinning both around. The other children crowded around them. "I missed you so much! How is the baby?"

"Daniel is well. He has very healthy lungs."

Hannah laughed, then said, conspiratorially, "Seth wanted to be here, but I told him you'd be too tired from traveling. I hope you don't mind."

"You did exactly right. Has he been by often?"

"Often enough that people are asking if he's courting me! But I always set them straight. Not that I would mind... He's been worried about you. There are more Indians in Lancaster and he's heard rumors of spies for Pontiac there."

"Well, that's all they are. Rumors. And neither of you should be listening to them."

"You should have written him more," Hannah chided.

"I wrote him as often as he wrote me."

"But you know he doesn't like to write! A woman has to encourage a man to keep him interested."

"From what you say it sounds as though my lack of encouragement has not hurt his interest," Lydia said, trying to hide her irritation. Was Seth Garten all Hannah could talk about?

"That's because he really loves you. You should treat him better."

"I will try. Now then, Rahrah, Essie, let's see Ma and Peter and have some lunch." She smiled for the children that they wouldn't know her heart was aching to be ten miles from there eating stew with a man with dark eyes shaded by his broad-brimmed black hat.

"Lydia!" Evony emerged from the house.

"Come on Essie, Rahrah, let's let them talk," Hannah said, shepherding the two girls into the house.

Though still lovely as ever, Evony had certainly gained weight; Lydia could not miss the unmistakable bulge of her belly, the bulge of her and Michael's baby. She burned with anger.

Evony did not miss Lydia's expression. "I'm sorry. I know I should have told you! I *wanted* to tell you!"

"But you didn't," Lydia said, coolly.

Evony's eyes dropped to the ground. "No, I didn't. At first it was so new, I wasn't certain we would stay together and I didn't want it to make things bad between you and I if it didn't. And all that hiding made it easier to hide more things. And then, when I knew I was... I was in trouble... I was so ashamed! I couldn't bear to say anything! I prayed so hard God would make it not so, but with every month it became more and more obvious. Agatha's not even allowed to speak with me anymore, neither is Gretel, but she still does, only a few words here and there in passing. I've never felt more alone!"

Lydia watched as dark spots appeared on the dirt.

"You've always been my best friend. Please don't leave me now as well! I know I deserve it, I lied to you so, so many times, but please forgive me!" Evony begged.

Lydia took a deep breath, clearing her mind of all but the weeping woman in front of her. *Oh Lord, help me to find the mercy you showed so many women,* she prayed. She watched her friend, the very girl she had learned to read with, had played with, who had taught her to crochet. "You shouldn't upset yourself so; it's bad for the baby."

Evony turned her tear-stained face up to meet her friend's warm, brown eyes. "Do you forgive me, then?"

Lydia took Evony's hands in hers. "I do. I'm still angry, but that will fade in time. It wouldn't do for sisters to hold hatred toward each other."

"I understand. I couldn't ask for more than that, but for one thing?"

"What is that?"

"Will you stand with me at the wedding? My own sisters have refused, and you've always been my closest friend."

Lydia considered for a moment. It was a difficult decision. She didn't want to appear to openly support what had led to this situation, but Evony was her best friend, soon to be her sister. She hadn't lied out of malice. "I'll need to think about it."

Seth came by in the evening, but Lydia asked Hannah to give him her regrets and send him home. "What do you want me to say?" Hannah hissed to her sister who was sewing on the bed in her room with her back to the door.

"The truth; that I'm too tired to see him today."

"Well, when can I tell him you'll see him? I'm not sending him home without an answer."

Lydia pondered the question. "Tell him I can see him in two days."

"Two days!"

"Yes. I should be well recovered by then. We can talk after they put up the wedding house."

Hannah eyed her sister slyly. "Will he be staying over?"

How could Hannah even think such a thing at this time! "For now, I think it'd be best if we just talked. It's been two months since I last saw him. Let us get reacquainted."

"You could get better reacquainted if he stayed over," Hannah muttered.

"Isn't he waiting while you argue with me?"

Hannah's hands shot up to cover her mouth. "Oh!" She rushed from Lydia's room where her sister sat sewing a square centered around a strangely colored piece of shirt fabric cut to form two hearts, one cherry red and the other, blueberry purple.

♥ ♥

The day of the wedding house raising came quickly. Seth, Ald, and the other men of the town arrived early in the morning with Cousin Egon joining them a few hours later. By evening, the temporary house loomed large against the sunset. It was more a walled pavilion than a true house, easily able to fit the two to three hundred guests they expected under its grand awnings. Anna Fischer and her daughters served the men supper in the very house they had just built.

"Might I have more water?" Seth asked as Lydia passed him, seated with his back against the wall.

"Of course." Lydia filled his cup. "Thank you for helping with the wedding house, it was very kind of you."

"We're courting, it's only natural I would help. Why don't you have a seat and we can talk for a bit?"

"I suppose. Hannah, would you mind?"

A slyly grinning Hannah quickly took Lydia's pitcher.

She and Seth spoke of her journey and the crops for some time as the crowd of men thinned. When it was only them and a few elders talking loudly on the other side of the room

Seth said, "I heard Evony asked you to stand with her at the wedding."

"Yes, but I haven't yet decided if I will," Lydia said, avoiding Seth's eyes as she looked across at the few remaining people.

"If you are worried I will think less of your morals if you do, you don't need to. I know you are of good virtue."

"Thank you. But I still worry what the others will think."

"It doesn't matter what they think, I'm the one who's pledged himself to you. Jealous people will spread rumors no matter what you do, but I know your friends and the elders will understand you're doing it for your family and there's nothing more important than that."

"No, there isn't."

Seth shifted closer to her; Lydia saw the flash of a wooden pistol butt from under his vest. She stiffened.

Seth noticed her change of aspect. "It's only for protection."

"It's for killing men."

"It's for killing Indians."

Lydia was stunned. "Indians are men. They have the same souls we do."

"No they aren't." Lydia hadn't noticed Ald come over until he spoke. "They're just animals. It's no different than killing a rabid dog. They don't have souls any more than a dog or one of those apes you read about in Kings. People get confused because they can talk, but it's no different than parrots. They just repeat something they've heard; they don't really understand human language."

Lydia's mouth struggled to form words. She looked to Seth, but he offered no rebuke. "You can't really believe that? Surely, Ald, you can't believe that?"

Ald shrugged. "It's what grandfather says. Remember, they murdered his brother and their family. Tore apart his wife and baby like ravenous boars. No human being with a soul could do that to a baby."

"You know as well as I human beings are quite capable of any violence. Is that not why we left Europe? Is that not why the cages hang from the cathedral of Munster? It is horrible that men might do such a thing but that does not make them inhuman! They are just as much men with souls as we are!"

Seth laid a hand on Lydia's arm. "Lydia, you are such a kind, compassionate soul, it's what I love about you. I wish I had your certainty, but I have never looked into the black eyes of an Indian and seen a soul."

Lydia pulled her arm away, Sam's beautiful black eyes shone in her mind. "I have."

Seth glanced over to Ald, who gave a nod. "Then I believe you. You have met more Indians than me, I'm certain, being in Lancaster so long."

"Do you really?"

"Of course. And to show you I'm in earnest," he pulled out the flintlock and tipped it over, dumping the powder and shot cartridge on the floor of the wedding house. "You'll not see me carry it any longer, if it means that much to you."

Lydia was almost in tears. She felt the salvation of Seth's soul from the enemy. He would not kill! He had seen! Finally seen! "Oh Seth! It does! It truly does!"

Seth grinned. "I'm glad. I couldn't bear having a piece of metal come between us. Now then, I know you won't be having me stay, but might we take a walk? I've missed speaking with you and I don't really want this evening to end just yet."

Lydia nodded. "I'd like that very much."

Seth became a regular visitor to the house and, true to his word, Lydia did not see the horrible gun at his hip again.

They took walks about the town and Lydia found herself thinking how natural it felt to be beside him, strolling through the square. This was all she could wish for, all any Amish woman could ever want, a simple life with Seth.

Her mind wandered to the future. It was right, she and Seth. Strolling through town, greeting their friends, taking Sunday supper with her family and dinners with his until they had enough children to fill their own table. It was what her life should be; the life she had always dreamed of. Then why did it all feel so wrong?

Seth was handsome and kind, he'd never shied from hard work. He'd be a wonderful father and a good provider with a large, established family they could lean on if need be. And he loved her. She saw it in his eyes every time he looked at her.

Many women would consider themselves lucky to find a gentle man who was fond of them, a man who would take care of them and the babies and never raise a hand to them in anger. To be loved by such a man, truly loved, was more than could be asked. It felt like an extravagance to hope for! She was so blessed, and yet she could not feel it, and she chastised herself for her inability to feel anything but mildly ill at the thought of their future together.

A few days before Evony's baptism, on the final day of July, Lydia still had not made her decision as to whether to stand with her friend at the wedding. She'd wanted to have an answer for Evony by the baptism, she'd promised herself she would, but she was still not certain. It was easy to say she forgave her friend, but she still found herself burning against her. She hated her anger, hated her failure to forgive as purely as she was told forgiveness should be.

"Ask the person whose opinion matters to you most," her mother finally advised after days of listening to her daughter agonize over the decision. Though her mother had almost certainly meant Seth, the thought of him never even crossed Lydia's mind. She took to her quill and penned a letter to Sam asking what he thought she should do, secreting the envelope away to the post office so Hannah would not ask who Sam might be.

When she arrived in town, there was a great commotion. She could hear the whining drone of Scottish pipes and the pounding of drums. Down the road leading into town, she could see men in green scotch bonnets with orange puffs at their tops, tall black pointed hats the like of which she'd never seen and orange uniforms faced in green followed, their knees visible beneath the hem of their kilts.

These soldiers were flanked by British regulars - she knew them from drawings in books. At their head, riding atop a decorated brown war horse, was a young, brunette Swiss man with a large nose, wearing a fine red coat, saber glinting from his side.

She found Gretel and Agatha amongst the throng of people. "What is it, Gretel?" she shouted.

"The regulars! Colonel Bouquet and his men are passing through!"

"They're going to save Fort Pitt," Agatha said.

"They're so handsome!" Gretel said.

"Hey, what about me?" Ald interjected from behind.

"You're fine enough, I suppose." Gretel waved her hand dismissively at him.

"Only fine enough!" he shouted, but Gretel ignored him. It seemed she was hardly the only one under the spell of the soldiers as the women waved and cheered.

Bouquet raised his saber to stop the soldiers near the point Lydia stood. The bishop appeared from the crowd. Colonel Bouquet bowed his head to his elder. "Pardon me, kind sir, would it be possible for my men and our horses to find refreshment here? We've been marching a long way in this heat and they are thirsty."

"Of course. Whatever you have need of," the bishop answered.

Lydia felt a pull at her arm. "Come on," Gretel said. "Let's grab some pails and fetch these handsome men water!"

The men drank gratefully as the women fussed about them. A few of the children brought the young Scotsmen flowers and nice rocks as good luck charms.

"Essie! Don't touch that man's pipes!" Lydia scolded as Esther placed both hands on the giant bag of the instrument and pushed down, flattening it with a great, discordant wail. Hannah giggled, pulling Essie away from the instrument.

The freckled, blond soldier laughed, removing his bonnet to reveal his sweat-slick hair, dermal effusion stood out red along his brow. He probably wasn't much older than Hannah. "Never ye worry, she cannae hurt it none."

It took Lydia a moment to understand his words. Her English was fair, but his brogue was so thick it sounded more like rumbling stones than words.

He gave Essie a pat on the head. "Purty lil' poppet, nay so much as 'er sister. Might ah 'ave some water, fair beauty? It'll be a long way we 'ave to go and water from one as purty as yeh will keep meh 'eart strong even if meh legs wish ta fail."

Lydia blushed at such a bold pronouncement but handed him the pail.

He dipped his hands in the water, forming a bowl, and drank from it. Hannah laughed.

The young man smiled brightly at her. "What's so funny?

"You are like the men of Gideon who cupped the water in their hands!" Hannah exclaimed.

"God make our battle so easy! Too bad meh name's not Gideon, it's Andrew."

"Hannah," she said. "And the pretty one is my sister, Lydia."

"Yer both beauties. Wish ah had time to get to know yeh. But ah'll keep yer faces in meh mind. Give meh a reason to fight."

Lydia would rather not be his reason to fight, but she did not say so. Hannah blushed, giving her pale face the shade of cherry blossoms.

The man stood. Taking up his pipes, he blew into them. A slow, droning whine began to grow. "Would yeh like me teh play yeh somethin'?"

"Yes!" Hannah cried; Lydia nodded in agreement.

Andrew stomped his foot as he began to play an unfamiliar tune which was both beautiful and sad, all at once. When he finished, a crowd had gathered. A few of the Scotsmen wiped away tears from their eyes. "Ah hope that's not the last time ah play that song," he said, sadly.

"It won't be!" Hannah cried. "You will come back and play it again for me."

"Of course. Now that yeh've said it, yeh've charmed me." He smiled. "I'll come back and play it for yeh, jest for yeh. Give meh somethin'."

"What?" Hannah asked.

"A ribbon or a handkerchief, teh give me luck. And when I pass by again, ah'll return it to yeh."

Hannah quickly searched her person but found nothing.

"Hannah, don't," Lydia whispered in their normal tongue. "He's a stranger."

"But it will give him happiness. Is that not a virtue? He's going off to fight the Indians. It will give him luck."

"It will be a tie to him. You shouldn't tie yourself to someone who is not Amish."

"A tie! You're exactly right!" Hannah tore the thick ribbon that tied her apron "Just tell Mama I ripped it." She gave it to the young man.

He gave the ribbon a kiss and thanked her, tying it to one of his pipes. Colonel Bouquet called the men to order and the young piper fell in line. The sisters stood, watching where they disappeared into the horizon until the last notes of his pipes were snatched away by the wind.

Lydia rounded on her sister. "Hannah, you were foolish. He might return for you and then what will you do?"

"And what if I want him to come back?" Hannah said, defiantly. "He can always join the community."

Lydia wanted for words to scold Hannah but found them lacking. She felt the tugging of Esther using her arm like a rope to lean her small body in all directions. "I'm taking Essie home."

♥ ♥

Every day Lydia went to the post office to see if Sam's response had arrived. Evony's confession and baptism came and went and still no word from Sam until the third of August when the postman handed her a letter with Sam's familiar scrawl upon it. She smiled as she gazed at the writing, wanting to tear open the letter and read it right there, but then, wouldn't it be better to take it to her spot on the warm, sunny hills overlooking the town under her favorite little maple tree? She could take her time, letting his words write themselves upon her heart in that sharp, sloping scrawl.

"Terrible news from the territories!" the postman said to Brother Jacob.

"What is it?"

"Not in front of the women," the postman nodded over to Lydia who quickly left the diminutive shed that served as post office, hiding herself beside the window, left open in the mid-summer heat, so she could hear. She peered over the sill.

"A massacre! Over a hundred British troops dead!"

"Where?" Brother Jacob asked calmly.

"Fort Detroit."

His hand flew to his brow. "My Lord! Have they lost the fort?"

"No, it remains in British hands."

"Praise the Lord for that. When did it happen?"

"Just yesterday in the early hours of the morning. We've had a horseman through with the news; he was heading to Philadelphia."

"If we've heard, so will have they. It will make them bolder. We must prepare for an attack."

Lydia took her letter to the hill, the words she'd overheard pounding about her mind. The only tribe close enough to be a threat were the Conestoga, and they wouldn't hurt Birch Run. She'd met them, Ruth was a child of their village, her niece and brother lived here, she told herself. That was why Sam had brought Lydia to meet them, so she wouldn't fear them.

There were only a handful of them, mostly women, children, and the elderly - they were no threat. Yet her mind tried to find ways to argue her to fear. What about the Lenape? But they were so far! Too far. They were practically in Philadelphia! It wouldn't make sense for them to travel so great a distance to claim such a small prize. And had they not supported the British in the war? She needed to calm herself.

She sat in the shade of her tree, closed her eyes and took a few deep breaths. She felt the smoothness of the envelope in her hands. Sam's letter. She pictured him sitting on a log next to her, stirring a pot of rabbit stew. She opened the letter.

Lydia,

I am glad to hear from you. Your uncle and his family fare well and I am gratified to hear you do, too, but for the troubles that play on your mind. I understand your anger. There is much pretense regarding the ease of forgiveness, and sometimes it truly is easy, but it is rarely so when you've been hurt. And you have been cut deeply by this.

And, like a deep cut, it will take time to heal. It can't happen in a day or even a month. You expect too much from yourself. God understands these things take time, and He will help you heal. Forgiveness is a daily choice, not a single one. You feel the hurt, you see the cut, and it reminds you and you must choose to forgive again.

That being said, it is also your decision as to how you should act during this time of healing. You must act with your eye to the future, not to your present pain. In ten years gone by do you think you'll regret not standing with your friend? Or will you feel your rightness in your chosen actions? The town will move on - I won't tell you they'll forget about the circumstances, but they'll only talk about it in whispered tones maybe once or twice a year and never once will they recall you stood with her. Even in small towns people forget these things. But you won't forget what you do.

I can't tell you what to do - you'd probably do the opposite if I did because you're a mule-stubborn woman - but I know you have a heart of compassion and love. I think you'd regret making the choice not to stand with her. In your heart, you know she meant you no harm, that she is utterly penitent for the hurt she caused, and that you love her dearly, even if it's hard for you to feel right now. You said as much in your letter to me. So, I think you know what to do, take the step you won't regret.

Yours,

Sam

Chapter 15

By the end of the day the whole town had heard of what had been christened the Battle of Bloody Run. Late that night, Hannah crept into Lydia's room and asked, "Can I sleep with you?"

Lydia sighed and pulled back the blanket. "Here."

Hannah snuggled in beside her. "I hope my piper will be safe," she whispered.

Lydia pulled her sister closer. Hannah wrapped her arms around Lydia and nestled her head into the apron of her older sister's neck humming snatches of a tune not wholly unlike what the young man had played until she fell asleep. Lydia stared at the ceiling fearing for Sam. What would the Paxton Boys do now?

She sat down to write a letter to Sam the next morning while Hannah slept soundly, alone in Lydia's bed.

Aug. 6, 1763

Her quill paused above the paper. My dearest Sam, she wanted to write, but that was far too forward. Sam, alone, seemed wrong as well. His letter had ended in *Yours*. She heard a moaning and stirring from the bed; looking over, she saw Hannah tossing back and forth.

Lydia rushed over and shook her sister who grunted, flailing her arms out. "Hannah!" Lydia shouted.

Hannah's eyes flew open. "I was in the valley and I heard Andrew playing that song he played for us. I was running to him but I couldn't find him," she gushed. She pouted. "You shouldn't have woke me! I was almost there."

"I'm sorry, you were about to roll out of bed."

Hannah rolled on her back, her long, ash-blond hair splayed out all around her, a corona surrounding her head. "Do you think he really would join for me?"

"Hannah, you've only met him for a few minutes!"

"Yes, but you saw how he liked me." She turned over, chin balanced on her fists.

Lydia dipped a towel in the water bowl, wringing it out, purposely avoiding her sister's gaze. "He was very charming. But soldiers are often very charming." She handed Hannah the wet towel. "Don't forget your ears."

"You're just envious that he liked me and not you." Hannah scrubbed her face with the towel, then gave special attention to rubbing her ears with it.

"I thought you wanted me to treat Seth better? But, if you insist, I will set myself to a soldier."

Hannah bounced up on the bed. "No! I didn't mean that!"

"I thought not." Lydia returned to her letter.

Hannah peered over Lydia's shoulder. "Who are you writing to?"

"Just a letter to Lancaster," Lydia said, quite glad she had not decided on a salutation.

"Oh. Well, send Aunt Sarah and Uncle Zeke my love," Hannah said absently, folding her hair into a bun.

♥ ♥

A few days later, Gretel and Agatha came to visit. "I'm sorry, we've not come by sooner. Our parents wouldn't allow it." Gretel said, Agatha nodded in confirmation. "How is Evony?"

"She is well enough. Have your parents changed their minds?"

"No," Gretel said, slyly. "But we're not visiting Evony, are we Agatha?"

Agatha shook her head. "It's bad enough we can't attend the ceremony tomorrow, we couldn't bear not to help with the wedding a little bit. Is there anything we can do?"

"Hmmm... we do still need flowers. I was thinking to take my sisters this afternoon but I suppose we can all go now."

"Will Evony be coming as well?" Agatha asked, her eyes eager.

"I can ask her. I'm not certain she'll be up to it; she's grown pretty big."

"Then it won't be long now?"

"No, probably a month, if that. Michael's been working day and night on their house with Cousin Egon. He wants it to be finished before the baby is born."

"A whole house in two months?" Gretel said.

"It'd just be a small one for now. He has plans to add on to it."

"Well, ask Evony and let's go."

Lydia, her friends, and her sisters went up to the hills just outside of town to pick wildflowers. The girls made daisy chains and floral crowns for each other, including a miniature one they placed on Evony's bulging belly. Lydia braided brown-eyed-susans into Rahrah's brown hair while Hannah braided dandelions into Lydia's. They played in the fields happily, finally relaxing on the ground, watching the clouds roll by and talking as Rahrah and Essie played chase, their shrieks and giggles echoing over the hills.

"What's it feel like to be..." Gretel waved her hand abstractly.

"To tell you the truth, it's terrifying!" Evony answered. "It's so strange to have a person growing inside of you! I thought it would be simple - it always seemed simple for Mama, but then I felt it growing - truly living inside of me. And I was so scared. Scared of it. It felt so alien. Now I'm not scared of it so much, I'm scared of the birth; that I won't be able to care for it, but I feel a deep love for it. It's my baby, mine and my husband's, and I love it as I love him. I'm so thankful he chose to marry me! I can't imagine facing this alone. I still don't feel ready for it, and I'm so afraid I'll die during the birth like my mother did with me. I wasn't ready to face that and it's only a month away."

Gretel and Lydia gripped their friend's hands in support.

It distressed Lydia to think of it, that her friend might not be alive to see her own marriage, to help her with her children, to see the first snowflake of winter or watch the leaves change with the season. How could she have thought to leave her standing alone at the wedding! What if Evony died? Would she ever have forgiven herself? Leaving one of her last memories of her friend as one of abandonment and anger? Sam was right. He was always right on such things.

"Mama tells me I take after my father, that his sisters have never had any trouble with birthing babies and they have two score between them! I know we all must go through it, but don't be like me, put it off a while longer."

Agatha seemed to sense it was time to change the subject. "How is the quilt coming along, Lydia?" she asked.

"Well. I've finished most of the squares, they only want for a border and then I can begin sewing them together and quilting them."

"It's nice that Seth approves of quilts," Agatha said. "Nils only believes in plain coverlets. Quilts are too English to his family."

Lydia sighed. "I wish we could afford such things."
"I think quilts are nicer anyway," Hannah said.
"I do, too," Gretel added.

Lydia suddenly sat. "Do you hear that?"

"No," Gretel shook her head. "I don't hear anything."

Hannah understood Lydia's meaning, she shot up. "Rahrah! Essie!" she cried.

They stood, calling for the younger Fischer girls. Then Lydia saw them standing on the crest of the hill overlooking the rutted dirt road leading into Birch Run. Essie was holding a flower loosely in her fingers so that it hung almost to a pile of its plucked brethren, the wind tossed her blond bangs. Rahrah held onto her other hand. Both were silent.

Watching something.

Lydia and the other girls warily jogged up to them. "Rahrah, what do you-" the word "see?" froze in her throat.

Open-topped ox carts were passing by. Their cargo was covered by large sheets of canvas but, even then, Lydia could see patches of blood upon them. Through the rippling cloth cover she saw white arms and legs, plaid fabric stuck through the slats. The middle cart jostled from a bump in the road and a pale face turned to stare at Lydia with its glassy blue eyes, she stared back, unable to turn away. They watched in silence until the final cart passed.

Hannah fell to the ground. "My piper," she whimpered as Lydia knelt beside her.

"He might not be among them."

"No," she held up a piece of torn white cloth. "It blew up to me on the wind. He- he returned it."

"Oh, my dearest!" Lydia gathered her weeping sister up in her arms. "Evony, take the girls home." The others left the two sisters alone on the hill.

News of the battle traveled fast. By evening, rumors and conjecture were replaced by word of British victory at Bushy Run delivered by one of the Paxton Boys who took the opportunity to rail against the local tribes, demanding justice for his Scottish countrymen be taken from their red hides.

"What kind of victory is it if so many died?" Hannah bitterly spat at supper. "I hope they killed twice as many Indians!"

"Hannah! Don't say such things!" Anna Fischer admonished her daughter.

"But it's true! They're just like that Paxton man said. I hate the Indians! I hate them!"

"Not all Indians are bad," Lydia tried to defend.

Hannah stared at her sister. "No, they all are. There's no such thing as a good Indian. They are demons in human flesh. I hope those Paxton men kill them all."

"Hannah! That's enough!" Elias roared. Hannah's mouth snapped shut. "Violence begets violence and those who embrace murder for any reason only bring about the death of their own soul! You must not wish death on anyone or you have already committed murder in your heart. My dear children, we must mourn those lost in this terrible war, we must pray for their loved ones, but we cannot allow ourselves to let our sorrow turn to hatred."

"But they killed. Isn't it only just they die as well?"

"No," Egon said. "That may be what the world sees as justice, but it is not grace. And Indians deserve grace as much as any of us. Grace is the only way these wars can end, when people stop killing each other in the name of justice. Otherwise, the killing will never end."

Lydia could see the tears burning in her sister's eyes, her little pink mouth set. Hannah stood from the table and ran up the stairs, slamming her bedroom door behind her, where she stayed until the wedding the following day.

♥ ♥

"The wedding was lovely," Seth said as the crowd dwindled late into the night.

"Yes, the weather couldn't have been more agreeable," Lydia replied, picking up plates from the emptied tables.

"Was Hannah ill? Her face looked a bit puffy."

"Oh? Oh yes. She took the death of the soldiers hard."

"She's always had such a sensitive heart. I admire that about her. I know she seemed quite fond of that piper."

"Yes. I told her it was best to protect her heart and keep it within the community. But she's young. She couldn't see it would never work."

"No. It never does." Seth brushed his hand against hers. "Part of a happy marriage is the community it's built on. An outsider can never understand."

Lydia felt the conviction of her own heart in their words. It was foolish of her to allow Sam into her heart. What had she been thinking would happen? That he would join their community, become one of the Brethren? He'd never shown any inclination to it.

"What should I tell her, to help her?" Lydia asked, hoping for an answer that might soothe her own heart as well.

"That she must put her feelings aside, see them for what they are, an inclination of the heart. It's not wrong to love someone. Love is of God. But a marriage needs more than just an inclination of the heart. It needs family and friends who all support one another, it needs the same beliefs that iron may sharpen iron. The love that can only exist in marriage needs to be within the community, needs to have its home there." Seth gazed into her dark brown eyes. "That's the love I have for you, and, I hope the love you feel for me, too."

"Seth..." she said. He was right. It was an inclination of the heart. A selfish, blind inclination. Hadn't she always pictured herself as part of the village, her children playing with the children of her friends? Was not Seth the man she most wanted? And he wanted her as well - he'd put his gun away for her! But every time she thought of life with Seth, it left her troubled. "But what if I don't?"

"Don't you?"

"I don't know! I like you very much! Everything about you is what I've always wanted, and yet..."

"You aren't sure. I understand. When you think of being married, are you afraid?"

Lydia swallowed hard. "Maybe."

"I think you may just be scared of marriage. It's easy to like someone but much harder to take that first step toward marriage by sharing a bed. I wish I could make it easier, but the only way to get over that fear is to do it. Lydia, you know I care for you and I know you care for me, why don't you let me stay tonight? Help you through this fear. I know it makes you nervous, but I promise you it's not as scary as it seems."

Lydia's heart raced.

"It is only one night. If it still bothers you, we don't have to do it again, but you'll never know unless we try."

Lydia gulped. "You may stay."

Lydia found herself, once more, at the bottom of the stair, Seth's hand in hers.

"Don't look at all the stairs," Seth said. "Just focus on the one. If you'd like, I can carry you."

"No, I can do this." She stared at the first step and placed her foot on it, pushing herself up.

"That's the way," Seth encouraged her.

She took another step. It seemed easier. She focused on the next and the next and suddenly there were no more.

"You did it, Lydia! I knew you could!" He entwined his fingers in hers.

She smiled; her insides abuzz. She no longer could tell what she felt. "Thank you."

"Now, which one is your room?"

"This one."

"Take me there."

She was surprised Seth couldn't hear the pounding in her chest as she led him to the room and opened the door.

"You're wonderful, Lydia. Now let me take you the rest of the way."

He led Lydia to the bed, guiding her to her side and laying himself down on the other. She removed her shoes and stockings, as did he, and lay herself in the bed beside him, exhaling a deep breath.

"See, that's all it is," he said, smiling at her from the other side of the bed. "It's so warm we don't even need blankets. Now, we can either talk or we can sleep, whatever you'd like."

"Perhaps we might talk?" Lydia didn't think she could sleep, her heart thumping as it was.

Seth began talking, about the wedding, about his visions for their wedding, their house, their children, waxing on and on with no help from Lydia who lay there, largely frozen in place. He turned, taking her hand. "Lydia, you're such a wonderful woman. You're so, so beautiful."

His fingers found a lock of her hair come loose from her braids, and stroked it. All she could see was Sam, all she could feel was how much she wished the man next to her was him. Seth's fingers moved to her collar. Her stomach heaved. She turned away.

"Have I done something wrong?" he asked.

"Seth," she said, not looking at him. "I'm sorry. I thought, perhaps, if we tried... maybe it was as you said. I wanted so badly for it to be as you said! But it's not."

"What are you saying?"

She turned to see his bright blue eyes searching her face with concern. "Seth, my feelings for you have changed and I can pretend no longer."

Seth's aspect darkened. "For how long have you known?"

"A few months."

"Did you meet another man in Lancaster?"

"I've been courting with none other. I care for you Seth. I wish more than almost anything I could feel for you what you feel for me, but I can't. I can't make it feel right." She fought back the tears that threatened to steal her resolve. "You must forget me and find another."

Seth sat up and began putting his stockings back on. "I understand. Thank you for trying. At least I can rest easy knowing you did. I'll find another, but I won't forget you."

She heard her door close a moment later, then the door to the house, then Seth was gone.

She felt poorly for hurting Seth, but it was nothing when compared to her relief that it was finally over. Her friends were incredulous but for Agatha who only was sorry it didn't work out as hoped. Hannah, of course, refused to speak to her for a week, but it was of no matter, her mind was lost in a flurry of letters to Sam.

Dear Sam,

Men from Paxton have been through town again with a cruel preacher. They spoke of the need to revenge the deaths of Bushy Run and Bloody Run on the Indians. They claimed it was the Indians of Lancaster who went ahead and warned those at Fort Pitt of Bouquet's coming, that there was no other way they could have known. They again placed the blame on Will Sock and his brother, George.

They say, "If an Indian injures me, does it follow that I may revenge that injury on all Indians?" but that is nonsensical! They say God commands that the land given his people be rid of the heathen lest the heathen lead the people of God astray, they cite scripture from Deuteronomy and Joshua until many of the young people are confused and privately question whether they are failing to do the will of God by our pacifism.

I've asked our bishop to speak against them, but he refuses! He only will say it is imperative we stay out of matters between the English and the Indians and that I must remind those I hear speaking of violence of this thing and our history. He reminds them that the only reason our people have been allowed to exist is our oath of non-violence.

But I feel our history should make us more sympathetic to the plight of those targeted by the Paxton men, not less. Were not our people once hunted to near extinction in Europe because of what others had done decades before? Are we not still outlawed in Germany because of what others, who claimed our faith, did over one hundred years ago? People we had never met and were not related to and yet we were to pay for their sins?

How can we say it was wrong for us and then say not to intervene for others in the same circumstance? How can we sing hymns of our persecution and yet stay silent for theirs?...

My dear Lydia,

It does me good to hear you say such things. My heart is filled with sorrow for those who were killed and for those being swayed to violence and murder on both sides, for there are those trying to rally support amongst the tribes to help in the fight for Fort Pitt. But it is a lost cause. Already Indians are leaving the front lines for their homes to prepare for winter and the journey to the winter hunting grounds. The loss at Bushy Run has disheartened them, the loss of Fort Pitt could be the end of it.

I feel conflict within me as to whether I should be sad or relieved of that fact. I don't wish there to be more murder and death and only a swift end would lead to that, but such an end would mean a slow death for my kinsmen. The English will never allow us to live in peace. The settlers will forever be pushing us further and further inland at the point of a bayonet. I can only trust in God that He will not allow us to be completely razed from our land.

It is a false charge they lay at the feet of George and Will Sock, I know for they were with me the whole of the day helping teach Christy how to snare rabbits (I use their English names for your sake)...

Dear Sam,
They rang the bells in the village today for the end of the siege of Fort Pitt; they said they were being rung all the way to Philadelphia. Some of the young men here talk of chasing the rest of the Indians out of the area. I have heard terrible things from Paxton and Donegal, they talk of murder. I worry for you. I pray you will take care. I could not bear if harm came to you...

...I have heard much the same as you, but they complain Philadelphia stays their hand; that the support the tribes have from the Quakers stops them from acting. Do not worry for my sake, all will be well.
Yours,
Sam

Lydia held the letter to her chest. She knew in her heart he wasn't telling the full truth of the matter, but she couldn't be certain, from his letters, what that truth was.

Dear Sam,

Evony gave birth to a daughter yesterday morning. It was a long labor but both mother and child are well. They've named her Judith and she has a whole head of black hair already! She's such a sweet baby, quiet as a mouse. Evony is thankful for that, a first baby is hard enough, but harder still when they can't be calmed.

Have you heard the news? I suppose you must have. France and England have declared peace! The war is truly over now...

Dear Lydia,

Congratulations on the birth of your niece. Judith is a fine name. I pray for the continued health of she and your friend. I am certain you are quite the doting aunt. How is their house coming along?

Yes, I heard. I know there is much hope that when Pontiac comes to know of the treaty he will end the fighting. Without the support of the French, victory would be almost an impossibility...

...The house is coming along very well, they intend to move in next week, before the mid-October harvest. My cousin, Egon, has been so helpful with the planning and construction. It is certainly one of the finest houses in the town, far more spacious than our own. It will be wonderful for church services in the summer with its breezy design.

The ox you purchased has been a godsend! He's got the easiest temperament and it seems he never tires of the work. Egon swears he's never worked a better one. The harvest has been one of the best we've had in years. We'll have enough for the winter and more!

Are you well? I heard there was a battle in New York where many British were killed. I hope the Paxton men aren't causing you any trouble for it, but I fear they may be. I wish they would just make peace with the Indians! Surely there must be something that can be done? Some compromise that can be reached? I cannot believe that peace can only be obtained for one people through the extinction of another, though that is what some of our people suggest. Fortunately, it is very few. There must be some way that we can live together.

I am sorry to hear of Red Moon's ill health, I pray God will heal her. Please give her this dried mint for tea...

My Dear Lydia,

I am glad to hear the ox is doing well for you. In response to your question, I'm am well. Yes, the Paxton Boys have been about. I do my best to avoid them when I can, as do most of the Conestoga. Zeke's been making sure to give me a heads up when they're around so I can make myself scarce. Don't worry, they get like this after every battle or skirmish no matter the outcome. In a week or so it will all be past.

I bear sad news of Red Moon. She passed three days ago, very peacefully. She was glad to see the first of the Autumn leaves fall before she departed. With her passing, Ruth and Kwa'yo are planning to move west in the spring to be closer to their other children...

My Dear Sam,

Please give my condolences to the family. Do tell Ruth I hope to visit again before they leave...

In the final week of October, upon finishing his breakfast, Cousin Egon stretched and said, "Well, I suppose I'd best be going back to Reading now."

Anna's spoon clattered to her plate. "You can't mean today!"

"Snow's coming tonight. If I don't go today, it might be a week before I can."

"Snow? This early?" Lydia asked.

"Smelt it on the wind this morning. You can already feel a chill in the air."

"When will you go?" Hannah whined, not eager to lose her favorite cousin.

"Maybe an hour."

"Only an hour!?"

"Don't want to wait too long. The wind blows right through my buggy on the way to Lancaster."

A sudden thrill through her mind sent Lydia standing from her seat at the table, almost upsetting her plate. She had to go to Lancaster! She had to see Sam now or she might not have another chance!

"May I go with you?" Realizing how her eagerness might appear strange, she added, "I should like to help Aunt Sarah make ready for the winter."

"Of course," Egon answered. "If your parents can spare you."

Elias nodded in affirmation. "With three little ones, my brother could use the help."

"May I go, too?" Hannah asked.

"I only have room for one and she asked first," Egon said.

"Oooohh!" Hannah pouted.

"Don't whine or I won't take you next time. We'll be leaving in an hour so you'd best make yourself ready, Lydia."

Lydia did not need to be told twice; she was already up the stairs to her room before he'd finished saying her name.

Chapter 16

As they rode on, Lydia found she could not sit still. She fidgeted with her apron, with her kapp strings, with her dress, her shawl, looking here and there for nothing in particular.

"Excited to see that Indian friend of yours, are you?" Egon asked, not looking from his horse's withers.

Lydia started. Did he know? How could he? She'd always been careful with the letters, keeping them in a secret place in the barn's rafters. "What do you mean?"

"The postman mentioned a lot of letters addressed to you from a man named Sam coming from Lancaster. Reckoned he might be the reason you stopped courting with Seth. As I recall, that was the name of that Indian man who's renting from Uncle Zeke. I supposed while you were helping your aunt, you renewed the acquaintance. I told the postman not to mention it to anyone else lest it turn to gossip."

She flushed. She'd been caught. She couldn't deny it. "Don't tell my parents."

"Is there a reason I should?" Egon raised a brow at her.

She began picking at her apron again. "No. I'm not even sure if he likes me."

"As many letters as he's written you, I'd say so! Don't worry, I won't tell them. It's a far cry from two people with an inclination for each other to something I need to concern myself or your parents about. We've all had our heart's lead us to unexpected places. Your heart's free to go as it wishes; I trust you to tell them if there's ever anything to tell."

"Thank you, Egon."

"Is there anything else you'd like to say?"

Lydia thought for a moment, what could he mean? Then she realized it was Friday. Uncle Zeke would be at the public house for lunch! "You need not concern yourself with taking me to the house, the market square will do. I can walk from there."

"If you're sure," Egon said, slyly.

"Of course. You still have a long way to Reading and it's only growing colder."

"Much obliged to you for thinking of me." He leaned back on the bench seat, smiling, as if at a joke only he had heard.

The buggy slowed to a stop outside the square. Lydia gave her cousin a hug and waved goodbye as he rode off wishing her God's blessings on her endeavors. Her steps fell lightly on the ground - she might have been floating for all she felt! There was her uncle's booth up ahead.

But something was wrong. She squinted, tilting her head as though that might somehow change what she saw. That wasn't Sam at the booth but Uncle Zeke! But then, where was Sam? Perhaps he was taking lunch in the back?

"Good day, Uncle Zeke," she called, raising a hand in greeting.

Her uncle squinted, then smiled, waving. "Lydia! I didn't know you were coming! You should have written! I'd have met you."

"I would have, but I didn't know myself. Cousin Egon said a snow was coming this evening so he wanted to go before it arrived. I thought you and Aunt Sarah might be glad of help to prepare for the winter."

Uncle Zeke sniffed at the wind and surveyed the darkening clouds. "I suppose he's right. He always did have a way about the weather." He turned back to Lydia. "Of course! You're always welcome at the house. We've no end of work for you. Sarah and the girls have been busy making apple butter these past few days. Then there's the potting, the pickling, the drying - there's enough work for five of you. Of course, if you aren't too eager to see your cousins, I could use your help here."

"Certainly! What with?"

"If you could watch the booth while I nip off to eat that'd be much appreciated."

"What about Sam? Is he not here?"

"No. Hasn't been by in days. I suppose he's gone off to the western mountains. Must have known the snows were coming and wanted to get ahead of it. You know how Indians are about the weather, they can sense the change a week away."

"But he left his furs!" Lydia protested. She felt hot tears of disappointment stinging her eyes. He had to be here!

"Yes, he mentioned about that last week. That if I was inclined to, he'd leave them for me to sell when he left and I could keep twenty percent of the profit, then when he passed through in the spring, he'd collect the money."

"Did he not even say goodbye?"

"No, just wasn't here one morning about two days ago. But I suppose that's his way."

No. That wasn't his way. Maybe with Uncle Zeke but not her! He would have at least sent her a letter telling her he was leaving. He would have said goodbye! ...Wouldn't he?

If she'd known he was leaving she would have walked the ten miles herself to see him one last time, to tell him how she felt. Had he not even thought of her enough to send a letter? It didn't feel right. Nothing about this felt right.

Sam's disappearance continued to trouble her as she worked at the booth with her uncle and made apple butter with her cousins. The unsettled feeling slowly turned to dread as the evening wore on. There was something wrong. Sam had been clear he was leaving in November; that was what he'd always said.

In her heart, she knew he would never leave without saying goodbye to her. He just wouldn't. It was unthinkable! Something had to be wrong. She felt a pull at her heart as she thought it, as though telling her she was right.

She went to bed, tossing and turning under her blankets. "God, tell me, what is it? Why can't I accept he's gone? Why does it feel so wrong?"

Finally falling half-asleep and in that state of waking dreams she heard galloping hoof beats and loud screaming. "Lydia! Wake up!"

Her eyes shot open. She looked about the room for the source of the voice but found it empty. She softly padded to her aunt and uncle's room. She could see them sleeping with Phoebe cuddled up next to them. She'd probably had a nightmare early in the night. Lydia felt like Samuel, trying to find the source of the voice that had awoken him only to find all the household asleep.

"Here I am, you called me?" she muttered.

Had it been God? No, probably just her own imaginings. Suddenly, she heard a great commotion coming from her room! She rushed back to find the wind slamming against her window, causing the shutters to crash so loudly she was afraid they might break. She threw open the window, eyes shut to the onrushing gusts.

The wind stopped. She stared at the nothingness. A small breeze curled around her, tugging at her, pushing her toward the window.

She gazed out into the night. At least three inches of snow covered the ground in a peaceful white blanket, almost unbroken but for a set of rabbit tracks which led to and away from the house. By morning the ground would be covered with animal trails. Strange that a rabbit would have passed by so late. Perhaps his burrow was disturbed by a fox?

Light flakes continued to drift down, sparkling against the midnight blue of the sky. The strangely beautiful snow of a clear night. The wind pushed at her.

It was like that story Sam had told when God led him to the burnt cabins. "Do you want me to go out there?" she asked. The wind almost knocked her off her feet!

She dressed quickly and rushed from the house, following the push of the wind, not attending to where she was going at all until suddenly the wind stopped. She was next to the tavern. Howling laughter and loud Scottish accents filled the street. Why had God brought her here? This was a dangerous place for a woman like her so late at night if she was seen!

Listen... She felt the prompting in her soul. Lydia knelt down beneath the golden glow of the window.

"Ah come now, Molly! Yeh should be grateful to us for gettin' rid of that red man."

"Yeah, we sure showed 'im a thing or two!"

"You was on him punchin' an punchin' 'im in the face! Looked like a pudding when Joe got bored of 'im."

"Take a look at my knuckles if yeh don't believe me! Then Stewart took a log to 'im like a golf club!"

"Aye! We made him into a real red man!"

"Did ye take his scalp?" a woman's high voice trilled. "Or his ear lobes?"

"Nay. Slippery red devil got away from us, slid over the edge of a rock ledge. It was raining too hard, yeh couldna expect us to go down after 'im."

"But he's surely dead by now, uppiddy fur trader. If the beatin' didn't kill him, the cold surely has. I got these gloves from his camp. Probably fifty bucks worth of stuff, maybe more. If you come home with me, I'll give you a pair."

"I dinnae want Indian gloves, Joe."

"Oh, come on, Molly, just give us one little kiss!"

"Ifn' ye wan' a kiss ye shoulda brought a scalp ta shew me."

"Fine, tamorrow I'll go down and get it for yeh, providing the animals havena got to it first."

"Oh God!" Lydia gasped, tears streaming down her cheeks. In her mind, she saw the men mutilating Sam's body, cutting off his ears and scalp. She pressed her hands to her mouth to keep from throwing up. "Dear Lord, please help me find him tonight. Let me take his body to where they can never find it. My poor Sam! Give me the strength to bury him," she pleaded though her words were so thick they could scarcely be understood.

She felt something pulling at her heart, an invisible force. It was not like the wind, perhaps because she no longer required pushing forward, it was... something she could not describe, just a feeling, like a path before her. She was ready to follow.

She followed the tugging to the market and then to the edge of the woods. She could see where Wa'ya had left his marks on the trees. There was a path! It was not much more than a deer path but it shone clear in the moonlight. "Guide me, Lord," she whispered as she stepped onto the trail.

She walked on for twenty minutes, completely oblivious to the painful chill of the snow through her soaked shoes or the scratches from the branches as they caught on her frost reddened cheeks. Her bonnet was lost somewhere in the darkness to the skeletal hand of an oak and her kapp had become untied, hanging askew from a pin in her braid that was the only thing keeping it from the same fate as her bonnet. Ice hung from her nose and clung to her cheeks in lines from her tears.

She tried not to weep. He might still be alive, as unlikely as it was. That man said he'd beat his face to pudding. His handsome face! She could see it smiling in her mind, to think she might never see that face, that smile again! The thought set her to weeping again.

And what about his body? Even were he somehow miraculously alive, would it be so broken he couldn't move? Would he have to live in a chair the remainder of his days, only being moved from bed to chair and back again?

"Well, even if his face is a horror, he will still be beautiful to me. His beauty was never his face. And if all he can do is be moved from chair to bed then I shall do that for the rest of my days. If only he be alive, Father, that is enough for me. I will work for the both of us." She felt a strength growing in her breast like the glowing of a torch warming her. He wasn't dead. She would find him. God would bring her to him.

The path came to an end in the dark woods. Now where was she to go? She glanced around, nothing looked familiar. A branch snapped, her head shot in that direction but saw nothing. Sam's camp must be close by, but if she went the wrong way...

"Oh help," she whimpered. "You've brought me this far." A loud horse's whistle interrupted her prayer. "Wa'ya!" she cried. She ran to where the sound had come from.

Wa'ya stood next to a destroyed tent, still tied to a tree that shone ghostly white in the moonlight from its bark stripped trunk. "Oh Wa'ya!" She ran over to him, hugging his large head. "You poor thing, you're freezing!" She tried to undo the knot that held him to the tree, but found her frozen fingers unequal to the task.

"I need a knife," she said, digging through Sam's ruined tent. The quilt he'd purchased from her was in tatters, she grabbed it anyway, wrapping it around her shoulders. A pair of rabbit fur gloves. She hesitated. They weren't supposed to wear gloves, but if she didn't, her fingers would freeze. She slipped them on.

There! A shaping knife glinted in the moonlight. She grabbed it and ran to Wa'ya, cutting his rope. "Now, where is your master?"

She looked about the ruined camp. The fire pit had long gone cold and was coated with snow. Muddy tracks, frozen in place, littered the campsite, telling the story of a struggle. There were at least four sets, three of boots and one of moccasins. Lighting a broken lantern, she followed the trail they left, leading Wa'ya behind her.

It appeared Sam had run from them and they'd given chase. She could see where he'd slid in the mud but regained his footing, saw where one of the men fell, leaving the impression of his entire front in what was now an icy puddle. Sam must have been running fast, from the smeared prints.

Then she saw where he fell to his knees, surrounded by the boot prints. "Sam." Tears rolled down her icy cheeks. Thick ruts showed where he'd been dragged off. He wouldn't have fought back.

She followed the trail to a small clearing where deep scars marred the ground. Red ice pooled in them. She took off her glove, knelt down, and touched it. "Oh Sam." This is where it happened. Where they'd... where they'd hurt him.

The trail of red-stained mud led to an outcropping of rock. She could see in the impressions how he'd crawled on his stomach to get there. The edge was covered in blood. Lydia steeled herself to look down, knowing the sight of Sam's broken and frozen body might greet her.

But at least he would be found. She could bury him before the men came back and took his scalp. The thought of them scalping his poor body finally brought her to look.

There was nothing there but a thin layer of snow, not more than six feet down. She slid down the side of the outcropping. Where was he? He couldn't have gone far.

"Sam!" she called.

No answer.

"Sam!"

Only Wa'ya's whinny sounded in the indifferent night.

She searched the ground. There! A trail cutting through the mud. She could see the blood on the ground where he'd laboriously dragged himself forward. She followed not more than ten feet to a briar patch. The trail of blood led through a gap between the trunks of the bushes. She knelt, placing the lantern on the ground next to her. "Sam?" she called.

She peered through the bloody gap to see a pair of moccasins. It was him!

"Oh Father, give me strength, " she prayed. She grabbed Sam's ankles and drug him from the briars. Though she wasn't very big, years of farm labor made her strong. She pulled him out as easily as a stubborn pig. "Oh Sam!" she cried, looking upon his battered form.

His face was caked in mud and dried blood, eyelids blackened with bruises. His shirt had been reduced to little more than rags that stuck to his skin with dark red crusts. She watched his chest for signs of movement, but saw nothing. He couldn't be dead! He just couldn't be!

An idea came to her. She put the lantern to his mouth, careful to hold it perfectly still, her back to the blowing wind. The flame danced. A moment later it danced again. Then again! He was alive!

Lydia tried lifting him, but though she was strong, he was a full-grown man and she more than half frozen, herself.

She would never be able to get him up to the ledge, let alone onto Wa'ya. She was loathe to leave him now that she had found him, he might die in the time it took her to return.

"Wa'ya," she called.

Wa'ya strolled over to the edge. She climbed halfway up the dirt side of the outcropping, grabbing Wa'ya's rope she led him down the slope. At first tentative, he merrily jogged down the last few steps.

She searched his saddlebags as he nudged his still master. A coil of rope! That would do.

"Oh Father, please don't let me hurt him more than he's been hurt."

She lashed the rope around his wrists and took the other end over Wa'ya's saddle to form something of a crude pulley. "Steady Wa'ya," she said, patting the horse reassuringly. She pulled the rope. Sam moved forward. Wa'ya protested but did not move. Again, she pulled and slowly Sam came up over the saddle. She used the rope to secure him into place, wrapped him in the tattered quilt, and then mounted Wa'ya.

Her kapp was gone, she knew not where it had fallen off. So, to, had her hair come undone, whipping in the wind as she rode. All she knew was she had to get him home, to her home, where those Paxton Boys would never find him. She could feel Wa'ya's fatigue as they rode on, the heat and foam running in streams from his body, but he did not slow. It was as though he knew his companion teetered on the edge of mortality.

Warmed from the ride, she was more able to gently ease Sam down off Wa'ya and carry him up the stairs, one at a time, pausing to gather herself for the strain of the next. She had to be quiet. She couldn't risk waking anyone. They might insist on taking him from her, or worse, they might not allow him in! She wanted to believe in the goodness of her family, but not at the risk of Sam's life.

Lydia lay him on her bed, placing a bed warmer at his feet. Grabbing a kettle from downstairs, she filled it with water and let it heat on the stove. Pouring the water into a bowl, she began to wash Sam's injuries, letting the water loosen the bloody crust on his shirt before peeling it off, lest she tear open any wounds.

She washed his face. His nose had been badly broken. Dark lines trailed from his eyes and across the bridge of his nose, giving him a raccoon-like appearance. His cheeks were swollen and misshapen, she could feel a softness when she pressed on the bone. His lips were split and when she checked his teeth, she found the left canine and the two teeth behind it missing. Dried blood ran from his nose and mouth all the way to his chest.

His body was not much better than his face. Long bruises striped his form, in some places the skin had split from heavy impact. He was covered with cuts. Pressing his ribs as gently as she could she found far too many soft areas. His shoulder and hip had giant red and purple bruises on them, probably from where he fell.

She went through one bowl of water followed by another and another. Each crimson by the time she was through, as was the blanket under him. When he was clean, she carefully spooned warm broth into his mouth, making sure he didn't choke on it.

He was still so cold, his body ice to the touch. He needed warming or he would die! She rolled him over, removing the soaking red blanket and, seeing no other immediately available, she took her own rag quilt, still not wholly quilted yet, and wrapped him in it. Then she took off her own clothes down to her undergarments and slipped under the quilt as well, wrapping her body around him that her warmth might move from her body into his.

She rubbed his arms, his shoulders, willing heat into them. Slowly he began to shiver, then to shake, and finally his body began to warm. His eyelids fluttered open, revealing his black eyes, blacker for the red pools that flowed into the white.

"Lydia?" he said, softly. "Is this a dream?"

She shook her head. "No. Try not to move. You've been badly hurt."

He made to get up and winced, falling back to the bed. "What happened? No... I remember. Those Paxton Boys followed me to my camp. Jumped me when I went to start supper." He shook his head as if trying to forget, then gazed at her in wonderment. "How did you find me?"

She told him the whole story of God's guidance. "It wasn't really me at all, it was entirely Him leading me."

"But praise be to Him you were willing to be led. If not, I'm sure I'd be dead by now."

"Christ is the good shepherd, He will always go after the lost lamb."

"Christ." Sam smiled, revealing the gap on his left side where his teeth used to be. "I always liked Christ. I felt like I could understand Him, or maybe that He could understand me. We both are from two worlds but can never be fully part of either of them because of that. He was God but became a man and because of that He could never be fully part of heaven again, some part of Him will always be earthly, and, the same way, He couldn't be quite the same as other men because He knew heaven. Always standing as a bridge between the two worlds but never fully part of either. Like me."

He shook his head. "You know I was taken by Jesuits when I was very young, not more than five or six. I don't remember a lot about that day. My parents took me to a... well you would call it a festival but I don't know what we called it. I remember there were blue people and people with very long hair in weird styles and there was this man, I guess he was wearing a mask, it was like a face, but twisted and strange and it scared me. I remember running away into the dark. Then these men grabbed me, I remember being surrounded by them, but there were probably only three of them. I couldn't understand what they were saying. Then they took me. I don't recall much about the journey; just that it was long and I cried until my throat burned. It must have been far because I never saw people like me again."

"Sam, you can tell me in the morning. You need your rest."

"No, I want to tell you now. I want you to know. I don't want to go another minute with you not knowing who I am."

"Then tell me, I'll listen."

"They took me to their monastery and named me Sam. They said they were giving me the gift of civilization, but though they taught me to read and to write and speak the white man's languages, they treated me like a slave. I worked from well before matins to hours after compline every day, slept for a few hours and then do it all again. Every time I disobeyed, they'd beat me with the rod until I was bleeding. When I was seventeen, I finally managed to escape but I had no idea the way home. I didn't even know my real name."

"I thought if only I could find other Indians, they could help me find my people. That was when I came to the Iroquois. They had never met an Indian who looked like me before. I didn't speak a word of their language, but a few of them knew French and so we were able to communicate. They liked that I spoke the language of the white man so well, not just French and Spanish, but English which they were encountering more and more. I made a deal with them. They would teach me their languages and how to trap and I would serve as a translator for them and teach them English. They never accepted me as part of their tribe. They called me a dark-skinned white man."

"When I'd learned all I needed to, I left. I've been trapping ever since. I've never known a true home or family in the world but for my horse and the woods. Even now, if I found my tribe, I'd never be a real part of it."

Lydia tightened her hold on him. "I'll be your family, Sam. You can have your home with me."

"That's very sweet of you to say," Sam replied.

"I mean it."

"I know you do right now." His hand stuttered toward her face. He winced and brought it back down.

She took a few deep breaths; her heart was sprinting inside her chest. She took his hand in hers. "No, I mean it for always. Sam, I love you."

He closed his eyes. He was silent for so long she feared he might have fallen asleep. Then she felt his hand tighten around hers, his black eyes sought out her brown ones. "You do?"

"Yes, I do." She fought back tears as his thumb stroked the back of her hand. "I love you, Sam. I have for months. My biggest fear was that you'd leave before I could tell you."

"Lydia," his hand brushed against her cheek, she leaned into it, enjoying the warmth of it, the roughness on her soft flesh, "Can I... May I kiss you?"

Her heart was pounding as if to burst, the air felt heavy in her lungs. "Yes," she said.

He rose up, pressing his lips to hers. She pushed hers into his, feeling the roughness of the scabbed flesh from where they had split. This only made her press into them harder, remembering how she'd almost lost him. She felt his hand travel down her neck, his fingers tangling in her loose hair, felt the stutter in his motion as his body felt the pain but he ignored it, pulling her in. Her mind went black, all she could feel was his kiss, all she wanted was to be closer to him, to never part from him again.

Finally, he pulled away, kissing down her neck. Her body buzzed with each kiss. He lay his feverish brow in the crook of her neck, the tickle of his black hair thrilling through her body.

"I love you, too," he murmured, "With all that I have." A moment later, he was snoring softly, cradled in her arms.

Chapter 17

Her mind awoke to the sound of heavy footsteps and loud conversation. Something about a strange horse. There was blood on the saddle, blood in the snow below her window.

"Lydia! Are you home? Lydia!"

She heard banging at her door. It felt so far away. She was too tired for this. She nestled into Sam's body.

"Lydia... Lydia..." Sam's voice whispered in her ear. "Lydia."

Soft lips pressed the spot below her earlobe.

Her eyelids fluttered open to see Sam smiling at her. She raised herself to his lips and kissed him, again, and a third time.

He held a finger to her lips. "No more or I don't think we'll be able to stop. You don't want them to find us like this."

She nodded, though more than anything she did not want to stop. To pull away from him when he was finally in her arms, when her heart was brimming with love for him and her body entwined with his, was the hardest thing she ever had to do. As she pulled her dress on, in her heart she finally fully forgave Evony. Now she understood.

The pounding on the door grew louder.

"I'm here! I'm safe! Only give me a minute, Da!" she called. The noise stopped, replaced by low voices outside the door.

Her hair was a fright. No time to braid it or even remove all the leaves. She quickly folded it over into a bun, netting and pinning it into place. She grabbed a kapp from her drawer. It was a pity her favorite had been lost in the woods, but that was no matter. She tied and pinned the new one into place, checking herself in the mirror to be certain she looked presentable.

Lydia walked over to the bed, taking Sam's hand. "I love you, Sam," she said, kissing him, he rose up to meet her though she could feel in the tightness of his grasp the pain it caused him. Her heart ached for him.

The knocking on the door began again.

"I'm coming! Just a moment." She opened the door enough to slip through to find her parents, Michael, and Hannah on the other side.

"Lydia, why are you home?" her mother asked.

"And why is there a strange horse out front?" Michael added. "And blood on the saddle?"

"And outside your room?"

"Ma, Da, there's been some trouble..." and before she could speak another word her voice broke and every fear, every horror, every terrible moment from the night before rushed out of her in a wave. She clasped her mother, sobbing. She heard her family gasp.

"Oh no!" Hannah cried.

"Has someone died?" her father asked.

"No. Almost. Uncle Zeke's renter. The Paxton Boys... they... they beat him... they meant murder!"

"Oh, my treasure!" Anna grasped her daughter tightly.

"I found him in the woods. God showed me the way. I brought him here, where they wouldn't find him."

"Why didn't you wake us?" Elias asked. "We could have helped."

"I...I...I was afraid... you'd... you'd... because he's... he's a ..." She couldn't finish the words, only weeping more into her mother's shoulder.

"He's an Indian!" Hannah shrieked, jerking back from the gap in the door she'd peeked through. She rounded on her sister. "How dare you bring one of those red devils into the house!"

"He was hurt! He would have died!" Lydia said, her sobbing stopped but tears still running down her cheeks.

"Good. You should have let him."

"Hannah!" Elias thundered. "Outside with you!"

"Fine! I'll not be back until that- that *thing* is gone." Hannah marched down the stairs, slamming the door behind.

"You should have taken him to your uncle's. You know how Hannah feels," Lydia's father said as quietly as he could so the man in the other room wouldn't hear.

"The Paxton Boys would have heard he was there. They might have come to kill him."

"And hurt Sarah and Zeke," her mother added. "You did exactly right bringing him here. How bad are his injuries?"

"Bad. I'm not sure he can walk."

Her mother sighed as if this was the last thing she wanted to hear. "Michael, go for the doctor. Lydia, fetch a bucket of water for your guest."

As they walked down the stairs, Michael roughly took Lydia's arm. "This was damnably reckless of you, Lydia," he hissed. "Bringing a stranger into a house full of women!"

"I know him, he'd never harm any of us. He's a devout Quaker. He wouldn't hurt a soul, even to save himself. Check his knuckles if you doubt me."

"A Quaker! That's what he says, but, given an opportunity, who knows the kind of wolf that lurks inside. He's still got savage blood."

"Michael! How dare you!"

"How dare I? How dare you!" he spit on the ground and turned heel on Lydia.

By evening, the doctor had finished examining Sam. For all their attempts to beat him to death, exposure had been closer to killing Sam than any of their blows. Still, he was in no condition to be moved, he could not even stand without substantial pain. When he tried to walk, he nearly passed out.

The doctor suspected some of his bones might have been cracked, but, fortunately, the only notable breaks were in his ribs, his right hand which had been crushed under the heel of one of their boots, and his face. They would heal, in time, though his face would always carry a new asymmetry for the encounter. The doctor could only recommend they keep him in bed for a few weeks.

Lydia was moved to Hannah's room, much to Hannah's fury when she learned of it. Hannah spent the next weeks staying at Agatha's house, refusing to even see her family. The Bless family, though they praised the Fischers for their charity towards the man, as did much of the town, were only too glad to keep Hannah and the younger children at their home.

"You may stay as long as you wish; my parents would be happy to have you," Agatha offered that Sunday after services, "They are happy to have the full house and would welcome one more."

"Offer them my thanks, but I am needed at home," Lydia replied.

"They're worried for you. As am I. They just fear the same thing that happened to Aunt Ruth will happen to you."

Well, they are certainly justified in that fear! Lydia thought to herself. She'd never told Agatha what she'd seen in Conestoga. Learning her parents had lied to her, lied to the entire town for their own pride – it was too much to put on one so mild. And Agatha would feel compelled to tell what she'd learned – Agatha never could keep a secret if it violated their moral code.

They might be shunned; Ruth certainly would be. Agatha could never meet her aunt and cousins were they to be exposed. It was wrong to keep their secret, Lydia knew, but she felt terrible putting Agatha through that.

Lydia placed a hand on her friend's shoulder. "You need not worry. I will be fine. I've not even seen him since I brought him home. Ma and Da put a lock on his door."

This was the truth. For her part, Lydia was banned from caring for Sam, a punishment she felt was wholly unfair. She was an adult and, though he was an outsider, he was hardly a stranger to her; but her parents would not be moved. A lock was placed on the door that only her Da held the key for. The only time she saw Sam was the few seconds when her father and mother came in and out of the room. She tried to catch his eye and smile, but he never seemed to see her.

"Lydia! Lydia, wait!" Ald called after her as she was returning from market a few days later.

She turned to see him jogging toward her.

"Do you really have an Indian in your house?" he panted as he caught up with her.

"Yes, Ald, we do."

"Why would you do something like that? Aren't you afraid of it?"

"*His* name is Sam, and I'd be more afraid to be alone in a house with you than with he."

"But he's a heathen! You know heathen's think nothing of our moral laws."

"He's a Quaker. But even were he a heathen, it would not make me fear him. He's a good man. We'd be lucky if more men in the village were like him."

"Wait..." Ald was clearly confused. "Do you actually know him?"

"Yes. He rents space at our family booth from my uncle in Lancaster. He is a dear, dear friend and, I daresay, you would benefit from knowing him as well."

Ald shook his head. "First Seth and now an Indian. Hannah's right, you've gone crazy, Lydia."

"I can't believe you, Ald! Are you saying you would not have done the exact same thing if you heard a man was dying in the woods and would do if not for your help?"

"Well... But Lydia, he's a savage!"

"If you wouldn't think twice about my saving a man but for the color of his skin, if you would let a man die just because he's an Indian, then it is you who are crazy and savage!" She turned on her heel and strode away, leaving a flabbergasted Ald behind.

As November wore on, Lydia set herself to pickling. With her siblings gone, she had to shoulder the burden all on her own. There was cabbage, cauliflower, and the last of the peppers to pickle, kale to be dried, and apples to pick and be made into apple butter. The fire in the kitchen burned so hot at all hours, sometimes Lydia was surprised to see it was snowing.

Four weeks after arriving, Sam was able to walk and was eager to help with the chores to repay their kindness. He moved out to the barn and Hannah finally relented, moving back into her own room.

There was always a curious crowd of onlookers outside the barn now, mostly children and some of the younger teenagers. And Ald. Ald was always there. He'd originally come with Seth, but, though Seth left after a few minutes, Ald couldn't seem to stop watching.

They watched Sam milk the cows through the cracks in the barn, watched him walk the horses and carry water to the house, they watched him stir the apple butter with the great wooden paddle. "Do you want to try some?" he asked, holding out the paddle to the children. They backed away, hands behind their backs. "No? Alright then, suit yourselves." He took a fingerful for himself, tasted it, appeared to consider it for a while, frowned slightly, and stuck the paddle back in. After a few more rounds along the pot, he winced. "Hey, you." He pointed to Ald.

"Me?" Ald answered, clearly surprised.

"Yeah. You've been here every day. Ald, isn't it? Do you think you could stir for a bit? My hand's hurting bad. I'd be much obliged to you."

Stunned, Ald walked forward. Taking the paddle in hand, Sam showed him how to stir it before letting go.

"Yeah, like that. Good." Sam stepped back, watching Ald stir. Lydia observed the whole scene from a distance.

♥ ♥

"He's been a Godsend," Elias said as the family sat for supper. "Never has a cross word to say, just does the work, doesn't ask for anything. I only wish we could afford a farmhand half as good as he is."

"Yes, especially with Michael gone these evenings with his own family," Anna agreed.

Hannah scowled but said nothing. She'd been surly ever since returning home, but at least she was quiet; though she made no secret of her hatred for "That thing in the barn."

As the days became shorter, Lydia tried many times to talk to Sam. He was always polite to her, but never held conversation beyond pleasantries. At first, she'd been able to dismiss it, but now she was quite certain his coldness was intentional. Hadn't he said he loved her? If he truly did, why would he be so distant now? She often saw him with Ald about the woods with snares. Sometimes they'd come back with a hare or raccoon and Sam would help him to prepare the fur properly. So, it wasn't simply that he was being distant with everyone, only her, leaving Lydia to wonder if she'd simply dreamed it all.

"What's troubling you, my treasure?" her mother asked her as Lydia peeled potatoes for supper, or, at least, peeled the same potato down to a nub.

"Nothing, really."

"Nothing or nothing you want to talk about?"

"Nothing I want to talk about."

"You can talk to me about it or not, but I'm here to listen." She handed her daughter a new potato.

Lydia sat for a few minutes in silence. "Ma?" she ventured.

"Yes, treasure?"

"There's a man I love, and I know he loves me, but he's been so distant lately. And I wonder if I made a mistake and he doesn't love me at all."

Anna smiled. "Ah, I understand now. Sometimes men, they become preoccupied with things in their own lives and take our feelings for granted. Many even become afraid of their feelings and what they might mean. Just give him time. Once the harvest is over and winter has settled in, he'll be back around. He's always been very fond of you and Hannah."

Lydia was puzzled for a moment. Always been very fond of her and Hannah? Who did her mother mean? Of course! How could she have been so foolish! Her mother must think she meant Seth! That the mistake she made was in rejecting him! "Mother, I'm not speaking of Seth," she said, firmly.

"No, of course not. But if you are, you need not worry, I am certain he will forgive you. He cares for you very much." Anna patted Lydia's arm.

Lydia said nothing but went back to peeling potatoes.

She tried to take her mother's words to heart even if they were about a different man. Perhaps Sam was simply too busy to consider her feelings or maybe he was afraid of his own? Hadn't it taken her months to come to terms with her feelings for him? Should she not extend him the same latitude?

But every day that went by of mere passing conversation when she brought his supper broke her heart. Why was it taking so long? He'd kissed her, told her he loved her, was that not coming to terms with his feelings?

She was so preoccupied by these thoughts she didn't even notice when Ald came up beside her and Gretel as they made their way to her house after the hymn singing. "Good evening, Lydia. Evening, Gretel."

"If you're following us, go elsewhere," Gretel said. "We've important matters to discuss."

"I'm not following you, I'm going to see Sam."

"The Indian man?" Gretel was surprised. She liked Sam well enough but had never expected Ald to change his opinion, not if Seth hadn't.

"Yeah, he's going to teach me how to work leather today. He's been teaching me all kinds of things: hunting, skinning, tanning... I've never been much of a farmer, you know."

"Oh, we know."

"Yeah, so I figure I need some other skills if I ever want to support a wife and family."

"I thought you hated Indians?" Gretel mocked. "You said they were less than dogs."

"I did. A man can be wrong. And I was wrong and I'm shamed by it."

Gretel stopped short, staring at Ald in wonder. "You admit you were wrong?"

"Yeah, I was wrong. Sam's one of the best men I've ever met. Even the kids like him; he gives them apple butter and honey and plays with them."

Lydia smiled. Ever since Ald had stirred the apple butter pot for Sam, the children had lost all fear of him. Now they followed him like ducklings all across the farm, and, for his part, he certainly rewarded them for it. It was nice to see Sam so well accepted by the children of the town. Perhaps he might even decide to stay. Then they could marry and start a family.

"Hey Lydia," Seth loped up from behind them.

"Good evening, Seth," Lydia said.

"I've been hoping to talk to you for a while."

"Come on Ald, let's speed up and let them have a moment," Gretel said.

Lydia and Seth fell back.

"Do you still have that Indian working for you?" Seth asked.

"Yes," Lydia answered, a sinking feeling in her stomach. It would have been bad enough had he sought to renew his attentions, but asking about Sam with no pretense boded poorly.

"Look, Lydia, I don't want to alarm you, but I was talking to Stewart the other day. He said there was an Indian spy who was working with this bad Indian, Will Sock, to give information about Lancaster's weaknesses to the Seneca for an attack. He said they'd tried to do justice to him, but he got away. Lydia, I think he might be your Indian and, if he is, the whole town is in danger. Stewart is willing to come with some of his men and we'll chase him out of here for you. I swear, we won't hurt him, just scare him enough so he doesn't come back."

Lydia saw the butt of Seth's pistol beneath his coat. "I cannot believe you would continue to associate with Stewart and his disgusting ilk. I heard them in the tavern, myself. They were laughing and bragging about killing an Indian man to impress a woman. They were going to scalp him!"

"Likely they didn't want to scare her with the idea of an Indian attack."

Lydia met his blue eyes with her steely ones. "Tell me, Seth, why would a man who wants a woman make himself look less the hero to her?"

"I... I don't know. Lydia, just understand. I care for you. I'm afraid what this savage might do to you and your sister. He might murder you... or worse. Just because he's able to act good doesn't mean he is. What if he is a spy? What if he brings the Seneca to our town?"

"For what reason?"

"To cut Lancaster off from Philadelphia maybe. Make it easier to attack. Do you really want to take the chance? To have him and his Seneca brethren taking turns on you and Hannah and your mother? Even Rahrah and Essie? I've heard red men don't care about age. Force you into being Indian brides? All because you were foolish enough to let an Indian trick you into staying in your house! Lydia, I know you meant well, but they're demons in red flesh. They're made to take advantage of our morals with their lies. Lydia, he's tricking you and this whole town. Why can't you see?"

"Why can't she see? Why can't you with that big plank in your own eye?" Ald rounded on his cousin. "Do you even hear what you're saying? He was near beaten to death, they left him to die! Do you really leave a spy to die? No! And you know that. They did it because he was an Indian and he was successful with his sales. They were ready to scalp his dead body to get a woman's favor! And she asked for it! They robbed him, beat him, left him to die, and then they were going to mutilate his body to pay with his scalp for a lady of the night. I'd say they are the savages, not Sam. Then they lied to you about what he'd done so you'd give him up to them. Do you honestly think they won't kill him if they get the chance? That they'll just chase him out? You talk about demons lying to get in by taking advantage, well, are you sure they aren't the demons taking advantage of you? Sam's been nothing but respectable and kind so far as I've known him and Lydia's known him longer than I! And we've both known Lydia our whole lives. I should have trusted her from the start, and I trust her now. Maybe you should, too. Come on girls, let's go."

They left Seth speechless behind them.

"Ald! That was amazing!" Gretel cried, clapping her hands together. "I've never seen you stand up to Seth before!"

"Well, Seth's wrong. And I'm not going to have him hurt my friend just cause some English tell him it's right."

"Thank you, Ald," Lydia said, quietly. The trio walked on with Ald in the middle carrying on conversation with Gretel who, for once, seemed glad of it. Lydia pondered all the way home what her friends had said about Sam.

As they passed the barn, Sam waved from the door and Ald bade their pardon, though Gretel begged a few more minutes. As he and Gretel said their good nights, Lydia approached Sam. "The Paxton Boys suspect you're here. They're telling lies about you."

"Is that so?" Sam said, pointedly avoiding her gaze.

"Yes. I don't think anyone believes it, most of the people here like you. But I thought that you should know."

"Thanks for telling me. As long as the town sees it for lies, those Paxton's won't trouble us."

Lydia felt tears sting her eyes. "Sam, I'm worried for you!"

"You don't need to be. God will take care of me. Ald! Hurry and say goodbye to your girl. We don't have all night."

Ald turned toward Sam's voice, then quickly back to Gretel, giving her a short bow of the head. He ran over to Sam and they went through the barn door.

"Goodnight, Lydia," Sam said.

"Goodnight Sam." Tears rolled down her cheeks as the door shut behind him. She resolved then and there she would talk to him in the morning. She would know his true feelings even if they caused her heart to break. Better to have it break once and be done with it than to have it break a little every day.

"Can you believe he called me Ald's girl?" Gretel said, not even noticing the tear stains on her friend's face. "As if I would be courting with Ald!" She laughed, but even in the low light, Lydia could tell she'd gone beet red.

"No," Lydia agreed, only half attending to her friend's words. "No, of course not." First thing tomorrow, she would talk to him, before the milking. She would have her answer.

Chapter 18

That chill December morn, as the early morning fog hung about the fields, Lydia crunched through the frosted grass to the barn. In the distance, she could see snow coming from over the mountains. She stopped at the door, breathing in the cool mist for a few minutes as she contemplated what she would say. The idea of going back was far from her mind, but going in... *that* would be the challenge.

She heard the sound of hay bales being thrown from the loft. She closed her eyes a moment, imagining Sam throwing the hay about, favoring his left for his bad hand. She heard a low complaint from one of the cows.

"Now Gertie, be patient. I'll be down in a minute to milk you," Lydia heard Sam call from above.

She took a final breath of the cold air, watched the smoke curl around and dissipate from her mouth, and opened the barn door.

She stepped into the warm, earthy stench of the barn. "Good morning, Sam," she called.

Sam appeared at the ladder. "Good morning, Lydia. If you came for the milk, you're a bit early. I've not fed them yet."

She wasn't sure how to start. It had gone far easier in her mind. She looked to the hay bales broken upon the barn floor. "Would you mind if I helped?"

"Suit yourself." Sam hopped down from the ladder, taking an armful of hay and tossing it in Brownie's feed trough.

Lydia did the same. "Do you think the English King will accept Pontiac's suit for peace?" she asked, putting hay in Gertrude's trough.

"He'd be a fool not to. Better to end this thing quickly. The terms are the best we could hope for and they won't be as good if Pontiac suffers any further losses."

"I'm glad he ended the siege of Fort Detroit."

"It couldn't go on forever; at least he was able to make it appear as an act of good faith. Even with Devil's Hole, losing the support of the French, it's just too great a blow. Pontiac's no fool, he knows it's a lost cause."

"Sam?" Lydia stopped; she could feel her insides flopping about like land-bound fish.

"Yes?" Sam looked up from gathering the excess hay.

It was now or never. "Sam, you've been distant with me this past month. Have I done something to offend you?"

Sam sighed as though he knew this was coming. Standing to his full height, he said, "No."

"Is it about what was said the night I brought you here?"

"Yes."

She swallowed. "I meant what I said that night, I still feel the same. I love you, Sam. You said you loved me as well. Were those words your true feelings? And are they still?"

Sam's shoulders slumped; he took a deep breath. "I thought when you came to ask, I would be able to lie and tell you it was just a result of the beating; that I hadn't meant it. It would be better for both of us if I did. But I can't. Lydia, what I said was true. I love you with all that I have. If love were all there was to it, I'd marry you today. But you know it's not."

Lydia's heart knew not whether to rejoice or shatter. He did love her! But he saw it as a bad thing, something he should have lied about. "What do you mean?"

"I fear for your safety. I'm a lone Indian man with no tribe or home. I can't even offer you the protection of a tribe like Kwa'yo offered Ruth. It's not safe for you to marry an Indian man."

"Why not? I've heard of lots of Indians married to whites."

"Yes, Indian women married to white men. But white men get angry when they think Indian men are taking their women, and they'd be angrier that it was a woman as beautiful and well-mannered as you. If I had a tribe, they could offer us protection. But without one... They've already tried to murder me once; I fear they'd kill me and ruin you."

"Then why not stay here? The village is fond of you. They've seen the good man you are. They would accept you. You could make your home here with me."

"No. They wouldn't accept me, not fully, and even what part they did would only be because I'm an Acceptable Indian. They accept me because I wear plain shirts and breeches, because I keep my hair short and wear a Quaker's hat. They see me as the Iroquois did, as a dark-skinned white man. But were I to invite Kwa'yo to supper, they'd never allow it. I'd forever be denying that part of myself. And do you really think your family would support it? You heard what your sister said at the sight of me!"

"She was surprised!" Lydia defended her sister, though she knew it was undeserved. Hannah meant those things.

"She said you should have left me to die. Only your mother disagreed, and even then, more for your virtue in the rescue than her own heart."

She couldn't argue this. Her parents were kind to Sam, glad of his help, but they never saw him as more than an outsider. They'd never even considered bringing him into the order. "They have no say in who I marry. So long as you joined the Brethren, they could offer no objection."

"But Lydia, I don't intend to join the Brethren. I'm a Quaker and that's what I'll always be."

Lydia was stricken. She'd simply expected he would join. If he didn't... She wasn't baptized, she could still marry him without being shunned, but she could never be part of the community again.

Sam nodded slightly as he appraised her expression. "I see you understand why it would have been better if I lied. If you and I marry, you'll forever be an outsider. You'll never have a true home again. You'll be like me - alone."

"No, I won't. I'll have you, and you'll have me. We'll have a home together."

"You'd miss your family and friends; you'd come to resent me for taking you from them."

"We could visit them."

"Give up everything you have to be the wife of an Indian trapper, living in the woods?"

"Yes!"

Sam sighed, sadly. "You should forget me, Lydia. Marry a nice Amish man, have a mess of children, live an easy life. Once the weather clears, I'll be going west. It's too dangerous for me to remain here any longer."

Lydia took her stand, determination flashing in her eyes. "If you go, I will too."

Sam looked up at the roof. "You stubborn woman," he said quietly, not speaking particularly to her, "but I couldn't love you more for it." He met her eyes. "Just think on what I've said."

And think on it she did. For days upon days, she considered little else. It was easier without his black eyes on her to see his arguments more clearly.

What she had hoped, that he would convert to the Brethren and join the community, that they could have a little farm together, had been dashed to pieces. It had always been pure fantasy. Sam wasn't a farmer; he was a trapper. That was what he'd always been and wanted to be. It was where he found

God in his life. Could he have that same communion plowing row upon row in the summer heat? No. It wasn't him. And would she truly want him that way?

She couldn't imagine being a trapper's wife, living in the woods. She had no idea what such a life would be like. There'd be wolves and panthers. Would she have to live in a tent? Or would she have to help him build a cabin? There'd forever be blood and brains and the stench of tannin about. But Sam would be there. His arms and his lips, his warm body sleeping entwined in hers.

But was that what she wanted? Hadn't she been looking forward to her baptism? She'd been planning it for years; in the spring, after the lambs were born. She wanted the first thing she held as a clean soul to be a baby lamb. It seemed the perfect symbol of the covenant she would make. She wanted that kiss of peace on her brow, to hear that today she truly belonged to the household of the Lord.

If she went with Sam, she would never be able to truly belong to the household of her kith and kin. She would never be a member of the family, only a guest. A beloved interloper.

This was her home! These were her family! Was she really willing to give that up? There was no doubt Sam was special in her heart, that she would never forget him, but she could love another, couldn't she? She was young still, it was foolish to assume just because a person loved someone, they would have a long life together. Evony's parents hadn't even had a full year, but had her father not found another love? Could she not do the same?

If not Seth, perhaps Wendell. She'd never known a shortage of suitors. Her father would likely push for Cousin Egon if Seth were out of the picture, as they got along so well and he wasn't her first cousin, (something like second or third, she had trouble remembering) it would be allowed. It mattered little the man, so long as he was kind and she could love him.

She'd never love him as she did Sam, but she could love her husband in her own way.

She could live in a proper house and birth many children who would play with their cousins every day, growing up surrounded by friends and family until they were old enough to be baptized. It was such a bright, sunny future in her mind, filled with golden fields of yellow wheat and rocking babies and grandbabies on the front porch. Quilting and knitting with her friends until their eyes turned milky blue and their fingers knotted and they had to knit and sew by touch alone. Then finally resting with the family in the grave plots.

If she followed Sam, she'd lay far from them, alone in the wilderness. She'd never thought such a thing even mattered to her, now it seemed all she'd ever wanted!

But then she'd have to give up Sam.

It wasn't reasonable, it wasn't sensible, but the idea of giving him up - why not just contemplate cutting off an arm because she could make do with one! She prayed to God every moment to give her an answer, but how would she even know it was His answer and not just the answer she wanted? She needed help.

"Evony, do you love Michael so much you'd follow him into the wilderness?" Lydia attempted to ask casually as they stitched their quilts.

She'd decided to use Sam's ruined quilt to form the backing on hers to make it warmer. It would be perfect for Sam to sleep under on the coldest winter nights. She was sure, even if she didn't go with him, the rag quilt would, that some part of her heart would always travel with him. Gretel and Hannah looked up from their work, though Agatha kept on.

Evony tilted her head. "I don't know what you could mean. He'd never ask such a thing of me."

"But if he did?"

She thought a moment. "I suppose I would. He is the father of my child."

"But let's say before the child. Did you love him enough then?"

"I don't know. I would like to say I did, but to leave my family for the wilderness... Why are you asking such strange questions?"

"It's about Seth," Gretel whispered. "He's been forgetting our laws."

"Oh, I see. You mean the spiritual wilderness. I suppose I already made that choice." She looked to the basket with her sleeping babe in it.

"I'm not talking about Seth!" They'd never listen to her protests. "Suppose I am, how would I go about figuring out God's will in the decision?"

"Well, it's about time you saw sense," Hannah said.

"I don't know," Evony said. "Have you tried praying?"

"I've tried nothing but praying! But how can I tell what God's answer is and not just the answer I want Him to give?"

"Well, maybe that is God's answer," Gretel said.

"But what if it isn't!" Lydia moaned.

"Ask Him for a sign," Agatha said without looking up from her stitching.

"A sign?"

"Like Gideon and the fleece!" Hannah exclaimed. "That's perfect!"

"But not a fleece or Hannah will make certain it's wet and dry on the right days," Gretel said.

"Is it wrong to give God a little help? I mean, if He really didn't want it, He could always dry it out again."

"You should choose something for yourself," Agatha said. "Like an animal or a word of scripture."

"Or a flower," Evony added.

"In the middle of winter?" Hannah said. "That'd be quite a feat!"

"At least you'd know for certain the answer." Agatha smiled.

"Seems like that would be stacking the odds against a yes," Gretel said.

Agatha stopped sewing, raising her eyes to her friends. "If our God were any less, perhaps, but He made flowers bloom in the desert. He wouldn't be stopped so easily."

"Well, there are dried flowers," Hannah grumbled.

That night, sleeping with her friends in her bed, Lydia dreamt of a great yellow rose. "That's the sign," she said, waking. "God, if I'm to go with Sam, then make the yellow rose the first flower I see."

⁓⁓⁓

"It's Sam, isn't it?" Ald swung from a beam that formed the lean-to where they stored excess firewood. It wasn't even six o' clock, and yet it was dark as the night.

"What do you mean?"

"Gretel told me you'd asked for a sign about a man. She thought it was Seth, but it's Sam, isn't it? Don't worry, I won't tell."

"How did you know?"

"The way you're always looking longingly at the barn, the way he barely talks to you but he won't stop smiling for the better part of an hour after you go - honestly, you'd have to be blind to miss it."

"Seems there's a lot of blindness around," Lydia muttered.

"They don't see Sam the way we do. He's not a real person. I mean, he's human, but he's not real. In their minds, he's just a ghost. He's not a man to them so they can't see that you might be in love with him."

"Are you disappointed in me for not loving Seth the same?"

"No. Seth's chosen a dark path to walk. I wouldn't want you to follow it." He held the beam in both hands, leaning back as though he meant to sit on the air. "Truth be told, I liked you a lot, too. Hated to give the idea of you up to Seth, but I could never compete with him. He's a Garten and I'm just a Kipfer - what did I ever really have to offer a woman compared to him?"

"Quite a lot, I'd say. Sam always thought you had a strength of character, even before I saw it."

Ald grinned. "A few years ago, I would have done anything to hear you say that." He shrugged. "Sam's a good man, even if he's not one of us. I can't say I want you to marry him, but only because I know he's not going to stay. You're both my friends and I don't want to lose either of you."

"But you'd lose both of us."

Ald smirked. "At least you'd both be happy."

"I worry that I wouldn't be. It's not the life I ever imagined for myself and it's so far from everyone and everything I've ever known. I've never even been to Reading! And what if we didn't get on?"

He swung through the gap below the beam, letting go and landing in front of her. "Lydia, why do you want to stay here? Do you really want to or are you just afraid to leave?"

"Do you?"

"Yeah, I do. But you're not like me, Lydia. You're not-" He caught himself.

"I'm not what?"

"You're not like us. You know that. You don't belong here. What part of you is Amish?"

"That's a horrible thing to say!"

"And true. You know it. That's why you aren't even near crying, are you?"

"No." He was right; he could not have said a worse thing and yet she could only be mad he'd actually said it.

"You're too stubborn and independent. A little is fine, a woman should be able to make her own decisions and run a booth, but you're more than a little. I mean, you told off Seth in public. A Garten! Sure, with your pretty face, men find that attractive now, but not because they want to have a difficult woman to wive. They enjoy the fantasy of having such a stubborn woman submit to their authority. You'd hate that."

"Well, if I respected my husband..."

"Is there a single man in this town you'd respect enough to submit to without protest?"

Lydia thought for a long moment, she wanted to say her father or the bishop, but even then, if she didn't agree with them, she'd say so. She'd done so. "No, I can't think of any. Not even Sam."

Ald laughed. "I'll bet he loves that."

"He says it's one of his favorite traits."

"I imagine it would be." Ald's expression turned serious. "Lydia, you don't belong here. You know it. It's fine for Gretel and Agatha, but not for you. Even if you didn't go with Sam, you know none of the men here would ever suit you. You'd end up like your cousin, Egon."

"My father would probably marry me to Cousin Egon if he had his way. He's gotten attached to having him around."

"At least you'd be miserable together, pretending you belonged."

"I want to be angry with you, Ald," she said, defeated.

He grinned. "But you can't be. It's about time someone said it to you."

♥ ♥

Since her talk with Ald, she realized more and more how little she belonged. Had it always been this way? "Agatha, how do you feel about fully submitting to your husband?" she asked as they were quilting together one evening.

"I've never really thought about it. It's the natural way, isn't it? The woman is to submit to her husband, and her husband is to love her as Christ loved the church. Even our bodies were built to submit to him. Our job as wives is to support him."

"But what if he is wrong?"

"Then we are wrong together."

"Is it really that simple?"

"Of course. We become one flesh but he is the head. The body follows the head. If it didn't then how could it walk?"

"I wonder if I could do so?"

"Of course you could. I'm sure once you were married, you'd find it completely natural for you."

"What if I didn't?"

"Then it would be his job to help you learn, the same way you teach a child. But you won't need correction, I'm sure."

"I wish I had your confidence. There," she cut the thread. "Finished!"

"Let me see!" Agatha cried.

Lydia spread the quilt out over the bed.

"Oh! It's beautiful!" Agatha gently traced the edge of the red heart. "Where did you get the colors for those hearts?"

"Sugared blueberries and cherries."

"Hmmm... I never thought of adding sugar."

"Neither had I." Lydia noticed the piece of tatted yellow lace she'd pinned to the border in hopes she'd find a place for it. "I wish I knew what to do with this lace."

Agatha was surprised. "Where did you find lace?"

"It was my grandmother's. She brought it over from Germany."

Her friend ran it through her fingers. "Oh! It's so delicate! Here." She unpinned it and began rolling it in an odd way, flaring out the sides, adding stitches here and there. "My mother taught me how to make these when I was little." She added a few more stitches to the bottom. "There." She dropped her creation into Lydia's hand.

"It's a yellow rose!" Lydia cried. "Where should we put it?"

"You should put it between the two hearts. That would be best, I think."

Lydia nodded. "Agreed." She stitched the rose between the two hearts. *A bit obvious, don't you think, Father?* She prayed in her mind as she sewed.

"Now it's finished," Agatha said. "It's perfect, don't you think?"

Lydia nodded. "Yes, I do."

She went home that night with her stomach in knots. She knew her decision was right, but there were still two people to tell. Two people who would never understand.

She felt the smooth, worn wood of the door frame to her house. Would she ever feel it again after she left? Her house that her Da built, where she'd been born, where she'd grown up with her brothers and sisters. Where other brothers and sisters would be born that she would never know.

She looked out over the yard, past her garden, to the three crosses where Asher and two of her siblings who'd lived their whole lives before they were born were buried. Where her parents would one day lie. Would she ever visit them there? Would she ever see her brother again? Tears flowed from her eyes. How could she leave her home?

She gazed out beyond, to the barn. A light still burned in the darkness. Sam was still there. Could she bear to see that barn cold and dark? What life was there without him in it? This wasn't her home anymore. Her home was with him, wherever that might be.

She took a deep breath and opened the door. Her parents sat, her father reading from the Bible while her mother helped Rahrah with her crocheting as Hannah knit, rocking back and forth and humming a hymn while one of the barn cats batted at the yarn.

"Ma, Da? May I speak to you?" She fought to keep the tears from falling, but she could not keep the quaver from her voice.

"Of course, treasure. Hannah, could you take Rahrah to her room? It's just about her bedtime."

"Yes, Mama." Hannah put away her needles and picked up a protesting Rahrah. "Come on Rahrah, time for bed."

"But I'm not sleepy!"

"Well, I am. You know the rule, younger sisters have to go to bed before their next older sister and I'm going to bed. You wouldn't want to break such an important rule, would you?"

There were no such rules, but as far as Rahrah knew, it seemed right. She shook her head.

Hannah adjusted her hold. "You're getting big, Rahrah. Must be all that sleeping."

Lydia looked over at her sisters as Deborah wrapped her arms tightly around Hannah's neck, her legs, even bent and clinging as they were, came almost down to Hannah's knees. She was almost too big to be carried! When had she grown up so? And Hannah, she was old enough to be married! It would be her own children she was carrying soon. Lydia shut her eyes, committing the image to her memory.

"Now then, what is it you wish to talk about?" her father asked.

She took a deep breath, willing her nerves to calm. "Ma, Da, it's about Sam. He's planning to leave as soon as the weather clears."

"Oh, is he now? I suppose we should give him some provisions for the journey. I'll write your uncle to be certain he has your Indian's tent ready for him to fetch on the way through. You needn't worry, we'll make sure he's cared for." Her father turned back to his reading, flipping to the next page.

"Yes, but that's not what I meant to speak with you about. Da, when he leaves, I'm going with him. I love him and I mean to marry him."

Elias was stunned. "When did all this come about? You've barely spoken to him since you brought him to us!"

"I know it seems sudden, but I assure you, it's not. I've loved him for well over half a year now."

"And does he feel the same?"

"He does."

"Is he willing to convert?"

Lydia closed her eyes. "No."

Elias sighed, leaning back in his chair so it creaked in protest. "Lydia, I like Sam, he's a good man. A good Christian. If he were of the Brethren... I don't know how I'd feel about it. But you know your Ma and I can't support it. He's not of our faith. If you were to go ahead with this marriage, you could not be baptized, you'd have to leave the community."

"I know. I wish it weren't so, but it is."

"I agree with your Da," Anna said. "I worry it would not be a good life for you."

"It would be hard and there's no reason to believe it would work," her father added. "We wouldn't be there to help you with any of it. You'd be alone."

"I know, the thought scares me. I've considered that and more for well over a week now. I don't know how I'll live as a trapper's wife. I imagine it will be hard and cold and lonely, I don't know how we'll get by. But I know it's the right decision."

"Is Sam at all worried about what he'd be doing to you, taking you away from us?" Anna asked.

"Yes, he's expressed his fears. Were it up to him, alone, he would have left without me."

Anna nodded in understanding. "But you wouldn't let him. You didn't come to us for advice or approval. You've made up your mind."

Tears rolled down her face. "I don't belong here, Mama. You know I don't."

Anna rose and embraced her daughter. "I know, but I'd hoped."

"So did I."

"Just tell me that you've prayed on it?"

"I did, for days. I even asked for a sign to be sure He approved. An impossible sign! But the Lord provided it."

Elias shook his head. "You sound like him. Who you marry is your choice to make, you know I have no say in the matter. If I did, I could not approve it. It will be a hard life. But you have both considered it, you aren't blind to the troubles you will face, and that does give me reason to hope. Our home will always be open to you both and your children."

Lydia knocked on the barn door, panting heavily from sprinting the whole way from the house.

"Glory!" Sam shouted. "What could it be this late?" He threw open the door to reveal Lydia, clutching her chest, face flushed. "Lydia! What are you doing here? Has something happened at the house?"

She fought back the urge to leap into his arms and kiss him. "Sam, I've given what you said a lot of thought. I'm scared, I don't know what will happen and I worry I won't be up to it, but I've decided. The troubles don't matter to me, we'll face them together, if you'll have me. When you go west, I'll go with you.

Sam rolled his head from one side to the next. "Damnation Lydia!" He embraced her, kissing her.

She felt his hat roll against her ankle from where it fell. It meant nothing more than his hair was free and she ran her fingers through the short black locks.

He pulled back, looking into her large brown eyes. "Of course I'll have you!" He kissed her brow. "Since you left, hearing you say those words is all I've prayed for."

She wrapped her arms about his neck and kissed him over and over again. "When?" she managed between kisses.

"As soon as it can be arranged. I don't want to miss any more of the season if I'm going to be providing for my wife. At the end of the month, maybe?"

"I suppose I can wait that long."

Chapter 19

News of her engagement to Sam scorched through the town. By evening, everyone knew the Fischer's eldest daughter was going to marry the Indian man. There was much clucking of tongues about town, though it bothered neither the future bride nor her groom.

"How could you do this to us?!" Hannah cried at supper. "Do you know what they're saying about us around town? About our parents?!"

"No," Lydia said, cutting into her meat.

"It doesn't matter," Elias said. "We know the truth of it."

"How could you let her marry a red man?!"

"I didn't have a say in the matter. She is nineteen now, an adult in the eyes of the Lord. She has made her choice and she will have to live with it. All we can do is raise you children in our ways and hope you follow them."

"They say you must not have raised us well. First Michael and now Lydia! They say I'm probably ruined too! I've had all my friends come up to me today and tell me they aren't to be around me anymore!"

"And clearly they aren't wrong; to speak to your parents so at the supper table," Lydia shot back.

Hannah's countenance went crimson with rage, her mouth moved but no sound came out. She closed it, staring at her sister, her nostrils flaring. "You- You're no sister of mine!" With that, she spat on Lydia and stomped out of the house.

The family sat, stunned for a minute while Sam helped wipe the spit off Lydia's face.

Elias was shaking with anger. "If that's how she's going to behave, then she's welcome in my house no longer!" he roared.

"No, Da," Lydia said, looking to her beloved. She'd seen him spat on before, seen how he reacted with grace she'd never thought she could muster. Until now. She could feel in her heart the pain in her dear sister's actions. She placed a hand on her father's arm. "She's just angry. It's easy enough for me, I'll be leaving, but she has to live with the consequences of my actions. Be merciful with her."

The darkening evening sky brought with it sleet, but still no Hannah. "She must be staying with a friend," Anna said, hopefully, opening the shutters to peer once more into the darkness for her missing daughter. "It's far too late for her to be out."

Lydia turned to Sam and whispered so that her mother couldn't hear, "I'm not certain she has any left to stay with."

"I'll see if I can find her," Sam replied. Taking a woolen cloak and lantern, he stepped out into the night. Lydia waited by the window, watching as his light disappeared.

For an hour, she sat praying for the light to shine through the darkness.

"He's not returned yet?" her mother asked after having put the young ones to bed. Freezing rain pelted the roof, almost droning out Anna's question.

"No. The weather's growing worse," Lydia said, trying to keep the worry from her voice. Sam would be fine, she was certain. He'd been through far worse weather than this. But Hannah had only a wool sweater to keep her warm.

"I'll put another log on the fire."

The better part of a second hour passed as evening turned to night with no change to the shade of the sky. Lydia stared out into the dark, still watching and waiting and praying while her mother's knitting needles clicked by the seconds.

Was it her imagination? Lydia squinted. No! It was the light from a lantern, bobbing and weaving through the blackness. She flew to the door, throwing it open. "Sam!" she cried to the distant glow. "Did you find her?"

"Yes!" he called back.

Now Lydia could see the form of two people, there was Sam, soaked to the skin, and beside him, her feet bare and muddy, her face as pale as the moon but for the red of her nose, cocooned in Sam's thick wool cloak, was Hannah. Lydia ran to her room and grabbed the rag quilt, bringing it down as Sam and Hannah walked through the door.

"Oh, my poor bunny!" Anna embraced her prodigal, sopping cloak and all, her own clothes being instantly permeated by the icy water.

Hannah just stood there, giant tears streaming from her eyes. "I'm sorry, Mamma! I'm sorry! I didn't think you'd want me back."

"Of course we do! Come, my little bunny, we'll get you into some dry clothes and warm you right up." Anna led her daughter upstairs to her room.

Sam stripped off his boots and stockings, a stream of water poured from his hat as he leaned forward to do so. He took the hat off and shook it, drops of water flew everywhere. He smiled at Lydia, the gap where his missing teeth sat just barely showing.

She took the hat from his hands and kissed him on his chilled lips, letting it drop to the floor as her hands caressed his cold, clammy cheeks, his neck, wrapping around his shoulders. His hands moved to her cheeks, sliding back, under her kapp, into her hair. His fingers were like blocks of ice, but she couldn't care, only that she could feel them better as they touched her skin. After a few minutes, they separated.

"Where was she?" she asked.

"Out in the far field, under the feed shelter," Sam said, pulling off his shirt and breeches. Lydia wrapped him in the quilt.

"I'm surprised she came back with you."

"We had a long talk."

"Thank you for finding her." Lydia embraced him. "You're freezing! We need to warm you up or you'll catch your death! Why don't you stay in my room like last time? I can help warm you."

Sam chuckled. "Not a good idea. We like each other too well."

Lydia blushed. No, of course he was right. She'd had enough trouble that first morning. Now that they were engaged, the temptation would be far too great. Looking at him, naked but for his drawers and the quilt about his shoulders, was already almost more than she could stand. "Of course. But you can't stay in the barn. Take my room for the night, the fire's already lit and the bed warmed, I'll stay with Hannah whether she wishes me there or not."

They bid goodnight outside of Lydia's bedroom with a gentle kiss, then Lydia went to her sister's room, giving the door a few light raps. "Hannah, I'm coming in." She listened, but there was no response. She opened the door. There was a large lump in the center of the bed, under Hannah's quilt. It quivered slightly. Lydia sighed. It was just like when they were children and Hannah was upset.

"Go away!" the lump cried in a watery voice.

"No. Sam's using my room. I need a place to sleep."

"Use Michael's room!"

"Michael's room! There hasn't been a fire there in a week. I'll freeze!" The floor creaked as she took the few steps to the bed.

"Don't come any closer!"

"I'm not in the habit of obeying lumps." Lydia lifted the quilt and ducked underneath, seeing Hannah's back in the lamplight. "Oh, it seems there's a Hannah under here."

Hannah flipped over quickly. "Lydia!" she said, her face covered in tears. "I'm sorry! Can you ever forgive me?"

Lydia slid under the quilt and embraced her sister. "Oh Hannah, of course I can."

"How?" The wet face nuzzled into her shoulder.

"You're my dear little sister, how could I not forgive you?"

"But I was so mean!" Hannah protested.

Lydia stroked her sister's long blond hair. "You didn't mean it."

"Yes, I did!"

"Well, do you mean it now?"

"No. But I'm still not happy you're leaving me."

"I know," she rocked her. "I know. I wish I could take you with me."

"He wouldn't leave me. He gave me his cloak. He asked if he could stand under the awning with me and I told him no, so he stood in the rain. I said terrible things to him. Every time I told him to leave, all he'd say was, not without you. He stood in the freezing rain for an hour, refusing to leave me. Lydia, I could hear his teeth chattering but he wouldn't go! He just kept talking to me, until I was ready to go with him."

"That sounds like him."

"I..." she whispered so faintly Lydia could scarcely hear it, "I hope I find a husband like him, someday."

Lydia tightened her grip on her sister, kissing her brow. "I hope you do, too."

♥ ♥

A thick blanket of white covered the ground that morning of the fourteenth of December from heavy snows the night before. Even through breakfast a light snow continued to fall. "I was going to go into town today," Elias said as he finished his breakfast, "but now, I'm thinking better of it."

"What for, Da?" Lydia asked.

"I was thinking to buy a chicken for the wedding dinner and perhaps an ax as a gift for you in your new life."

Lydia hugged her father. "Oh Da! You don't have to!"

"Yes, but I want to. It'll be your last day with us and I know I can't give you a proper wedding, but I can at least give you something gladsome to remember."

Sam lay his napkin on his empty plate. "The ax will be well appreciated, Mr. Fischer."

Hannah and Lydia set to clearing the table when there was a loud banging on the door. "Mr. Fischer!" A familiar voice shouted, not even bothering to wait for the door to be opened. "Is Sam with you?"

Elias threw open the door revealing Ald, panting heavily, his chestnut hair stuck to his pale brow with sweat despite the freezing temperatures. "Yes, Ald, he's right here. What has excited you so?"

"An Indian man. Collapsed on... main road." He spoke through labored breaths. "He's bleeding bad!"

Sam was up in an instant. "Did he say anything?"

Ald held his heaving chest. "No. No one... will go near him."

Sam grabbed his hat and pulled on a cloak. Lydia put the dishes down. "I'm coming to," she said.

"I expected so." Sam tossed her a bonnet and wrapped her cloak around her shoulders while she tied the bonnet over her kapp. "Grab some rags. I'll saddle Wa'ya."

They pulled up Wa'ya's reins as they approached the main road where a crowd of people stood. From their perch, Lydia could see a brown-skinned man in a red calico shirt, his long black hair obscured the view of his face.

Sam squinted at the man. "Glory! It's Kwa'yo!" He dismounted so quickly he almost knocked Lydia off. "Kwa'yo!" he called, rushing through the crowd, arm full of bandages. Lydia followed behind him with a small bottle of whiskey.

As they broke through the people, she saw Kwa'yo's shirt, or at least the left of it, had actually been white, the red dye was coming from a hatchet buried in his right shoulder. Three arrows were embedded below that. Blood dripped from his leg, staining the ground and his moccasin.

Sam handed Lydia a knife. "Cut off his shirt. I'll do his leggings. Watch the hatchet. If it comes out there's going to be a blood bath."

"Did another tribe do this?" Lydia asked.

"No," Sam said, stonily, pulling out an arrow broken at the tip of the shaft from Kwa'yo's thigh. "These arrowheads never knew an Indian until they met Kwa'yo."

They heard a low chuckle. "You're the girl Sam brought."

"Kwa'yo!" Lydia cried.

"Kwa'yo, what happened?" Sam demanded.

Kwa'yo tried to roll over.

"No, don't!" Sam cried, his hands instinctively going up to stop him.

The injured man lay on his side. His breathing ragged. "Sam," Kwa'yo began speaking rapidly in a language Lydia did not understand, she thought she heard the word "Paxton."

Sam answered, brushing the man's hair from his paling face.

Kwa'yo spoke again, blood trickled from the side of his mouth. The words became garbled. He gazed at them both with half-closed eyes, his breath rattling. "I'm glad it is you who will send me off. Take- take care of my family." Kwa'yo's eyes rolled back into his head. His body arched and fell backward, leaning strangely on the arrow shafts.

Sam brushed his friend's eyelids closed and stood, shading his own eyes with his hand. "Lydia, come with me." His voice was thick. "Show me where the Bless family lives."

"What happened?" Lydia asked, jogging to keep up with Sam's long strides. "Who did that to him?"

"The Paxton Boys. They came at first light. They killed the elders and any man, woman, or child they could find. They cut them to pieces and burned their homes."

"What about Ruth and the children?" It was a wonder she wasn't crying. The tears refused to come. Her feelings were such a jumble of horror and sadness, and yet, they seemed strangely muted by the need to do the task at hand. Though what it was, she wasn't sure, just that it involved Ruth and her children.

"He- he distracted the Paxton Boys while they made a run for it. He told them to hide in the place where he met Ruth."

"She said Mrs. Bless found them there! She would know where it is!" Lydia began running in earnest.

Sam knocked on the door to the Bless house. The door swung open and Mr. Bless's countenance immediately darkened as he surveyed the pair. "What do you want, Red Man?"

"Who is it?" Mrs. Bless called.

"Lydia and her savage."

"Mrs. Bless!" Lydia called. "Where is the clearing you saw Ruth with the Indian at?"

Mrs. Bless came to the door wiping off her hands. "What can you mean by such a strange question?"

"Mrs. Bless," Sam said. "There's been some trouble. Ruth's husband is dead. She and her children are in danger. They were to meet him in the clearing where they first met."

"Please, Mrs. Bless, we need to find them," Lydia begged.

Mrs. Bless's countenance paled with the dawning realization. "Wait... you mean to tell me Ruth is alive?"

"Mr. Bless never told her," Sam said to Lydia.

"Never told me what? Abel, what do they mean?"

"It's not important. Go back in, Joanna," Abel Bless said.

Lydia saw Agatha creep down the stairs behind her parents.

Mrs. Bless's countenance immediately sharpened. "Abel, if Ruth is alive and you haven't told me..."

"She ran off with that Indian, Jo! She ran off to marry him!"

Mrs. Bless and her daughter's eyes grew to the size of saucers. "She wasn't kidnapped?" Jo Bless whispered in a tone far more terrifying than any Lydia had ever heard from her. "My Ruthie is alive? And you lied to me!"

"She would have shamed the family! We would have had to shun her!"

"But I would have known she was alive! I would have known she was safe and loved!"

"It was better you didn't know."

Mrs. Bless's head shook as her mouth searched for words for her husband. She turned to Sam and Lydia. "Follow me."

"Wait, I'm going with you!" her husband said.

"Haven't you done enough?" Mrs. Bless spat.

Joanna Bless led the small party through the woods. "We're almost there. Ruthie!" she called. "Ruthie!"

"Ruth!" Mr. Bless shouted. There was a rustling of bushes. "Ruth!" He began running. "Ruth! Sister!" He came to a stop with a strangled cry. "Oh God!"

"What is it, Abel?"

He turned; his visage white. "Don't come any closer, Jo. You shouldn't see this. Neither of you women."

It was too late. Lydia and Sam had already broken through the clearing to the most horrible of sights. "Oh!" Lydia cried as Sam took her in his arms, her face tucked against his chest from that bloody scene.

It didn't matter, she had seen it. Seen Ruth's body, half naked, mutilated, lying in the sanguine snow, melted from the warmth to reveal the grass beneath. Beside her, her son. The front of his hair was missing with the flesh it had rested upon. Lydia could see the white of his skull above his beautiful face, now cold and lifeless as a marble statue. And her daughter at the other edge of the clearing, prone, naked to the world, blood covering her body.

"They must have been followed," Sam said, gripping Lydia tightly to him.

"Oh Ruthie! My Ruthie!" Joanna Bless cried. Taking her shawl, she covered Ruth.

"They were just children," Abel said, gazing at the boy. He knelt down, reaching to touch him, but withdrew his hand. "Look what they did to my nephew. He was such a beautiful boy!" Tears traveled down his face and into his beard. "What was his name?"

"Timothy." Sam said.

"A good Biblical name. And the girl?"

"Ga'nígöhdáshä', it means Wisdom in the Seneca tongue."

"We'll bury them with the family. Her husband as well. All of them."

Sam let go of Lydia and went to the center of the clearing. He spoke in words Lydia could not recognize; it sounded like a prayer. "Take good care of your family, my brother," he finished.

A strange sound grabbed Lydia's attention. A faint, garbled cry, almost like a trapped kitten. "Sam, do you hear that?" They both scanned the clearing. Had the girl moved? No, she was moving! She was trying to pull herself to the woods!

"Ga'nígöhdáshä'!" Sam called, grabbing Lydia's cloak and running to her. "She's still alive!"

The moment he touched her with the cloth she turned and began screaming, even from a distance, Lydia could see the large red marks that wrapped around her throat.

"It's me! It's Sam. Your father sent me."

Still, she screamed, trying to worm her way into the forest.

Lydia rushed to Sam's side with the Blesses just behind. "Stay back! She's scared! Sam, how do I say they're gone?"

Sam said something and Lydia did her best to repeat it, though she knew it was a poor collection of syllables that resembled words in the same way a two-year old's speech did. She tried again, soothingly. Ga'nígöhdáshä' stopped screaming and regarded her quizzically.

"How do I say you're safe?" She repeated the sounds Sam made as best she could. The girl seemed to understand.

"They're gone?" she asked. Ruth had taught her their language well. She looked to Sam who she finally seemed to recognize. "Where is father? Is he coming?"

"He... he can't come for you." Sam said. "Your father sent for your Aunt Jo and Uncle Abel to care for you."

The group walked home in solemn silence; Abel cradled the body of his sister in his arms while Sam held Timothy. Jo and Lydia guided Ga'nígöhdáshä', clad only in Lydia's cloak. Lydia couldn't feel the bite of the cold as it stung her arms, it seemed as though they were walking through some horrible dream. She saw Agatha open the door, heard the words, "This is your cousin, Wisdom. She's going to be living with us from now on." But she couldn't comprehend any of it.

Sam walked her back home with Wa'ya trailing beside. When they arrived, Sam gave over the reins to Ald, telling him to ride to Lancaster and find out what news of the Conestoga. As she heard Ald's "Yah!" and the sound of Wa'ya's hooves pounding on the frozen ground, her knees buckled. Sam caught her, leading her up to her room, he helped her into bed and removed her shoes.

"Don't leave me alone," she said.

"No, I won't." Sam said, laying himself beside her. "I won't leave you." He wrapped his arms around her, pulling her tightly to him as they just lay there for the next hour, neither speaking nor moving.

"Fourteen alive!" Ald announced that evening to a town starved for news, speaking of almost nothing else that day but the fate of the poor Indian and their lost sister, Ruth. "By God's grace fourteen alive!"

"How?" Sam cried.

"God's deliverance through the blizzard! They'd been in town selling their wares and when it started snowing, they decided to stay the night with their Mennonite friends. The Paxtons attacked Conestoga before they returned."

"What's to become of them?" the bishop asked.

"They're being taken to the new workhouse next to the jail to keep them safe until the Paxton Boys have calmed down. The sheriff feels he can keep a better eye on them there."

"What of Conestoga?" Sam asked.

Ald shook his head. "All gone. Razed to the ground. Six were found dead by a Mr. Barber. Men, women, even a little boy. All of them scalped. They chopped an old man to pieces in his bed."

"Seth, what do you think about that?" Malachi said, elbowing the tall blond.

"I don't want to hear it," Seth said. "It probably wasn't the Paxton Rangers at all. It's just the Quakers trying to blame it on the Scots and protect their Indian friends. What about the Delaware? They've never liked the Conestoga! You can't tell me civilized men would chop apart an old man in his bed. That sounds like the work of savages!"

Lydia rounded on him. "Why can't you accept it was the Paxton Boys?"

"And what evidence do you have that it was besides some arrows and the word of your red man? If it were really the work of the Paxton Rangers, then why haven't they been arrested? Tell me that. No, don't bother, Indian lover. I'm leaving. I don't have time for this garbage." He stormed off.

Lydia wanted to go after him, but she felt a warm hand on her back. "Don't worry about what he thinks," Sam said.

"But he's wrong! We saw with our own eyes!"

"He'll come to know the truth soon enough. Men like them need to brag. They didn't take scalps to hide them."

"Do you think there's still danger for the Conestogas?"

"I wish I could tell you there wasn't, but they'll be mad they got so few. They might go after them again."

"What about for us?" Lydia met Sam's black eyes, finally giving voice to the thing which had haunted her since they found Ruth.

"You understand, now, why I tried to turn you away? Are you certain you still want to go through with this now that you've seen the risk you're taking? You can live the rest of your days in safety. Know I won't hold it against you if you wish to end our engagement. I can be gone and on the way to the western mountains tomorrow."

She thought for a few minutes, the images of Ruth and her children lying in the bloody snow. That could be she and her children. She didn't even want to imagine what they had done to Ruth before they killed her, what she had to endure. Did they make her watch what they did to her son and daughter? Or make them watch what they did to her? Had she heard their screams echoing in her ears as her life ebbed away? And she saw herself there in a scene so terrible it defied description, with that horrible lecherous Scotsman from the post office leering above her. Was this her future? She felt tears streaming down her cheeks. "Sam, how could I ever give you up?"

Sam wiped the tears from her cheek with his rough hand. She leaned into it, feeling his caress. "Just think about it. You can give me your answer in the morning."

Lydia found sleep difficult, tossing and turning with the horrors of the day making prey of her mind. When she finally did, she dreamt of Ruth and her children waiting in that grove for her husband, but now she was Ruth. She heard a rustle in the bushes and turned, overjoyed that her husband had finally come. But instead of Kwa'yo, a trio of Scotsmen emerged from the bushes. She couldn't understand what they were saying, but when they pointed to her daughter with lascivious gleams in their eyes, she knew. And then they came at her. She awoke screaming and slept no more that night.

All she could do was think about Ruth. If she had known how it would end, what would she have done? Would she have gone with Kwa'yo? She knew the answer as soon as she'd thought of the question.

Of course she would. She could hear Ruth's gentle voice in her mind, *"The only thing harder than the idea of life without my family was life without Kwa'yo. I simply couldn't imagine it. I would have wasted away."* She knew the risks, too, but she never regretted her choice. Even in the midst of that final hell she likely only had thoughts of love for her husband and the time they'd had together, the life they'd built.

"I have my answer," she said, walking into the barn that morning. Sam was packing his things into sacks as though he anticipated her response and was ready to leave at her word. "I'm going with you."

Sam turned his face to the rafters and mouthed two words that might have been "thank you." He turned to her. "You stubborn mule girl," he said, tenderly. "You know it will be dangerous; you could die."

"A woman who has not resigned herself to death, even a painful death, could never marry. But even if it were only a few months, I wouldn't regret it. Even if it were only a few hours, I wouldn't regret it. Even if I knew I would live one hundred years if I didn't; I'd still choose to be with you."

He didn't even speak. He just took her in his arms, kissing her with such passion as she'd never known from him. She wrapped her arms around his neck, pulling herself in, wanting to hold every moment of him as deeply as possible. She felt her knees buckle as his passion ignited her own. His embrace tightened, holding her up, lifting her to him. She wasn't sure how much time passed before his arms loosened and he lowered her back down, but the sun was shining brightly through the windows and the cows were complaining quite loudly. She nestled her head against his shoulder as he held her to his chest.

"You're certain?" he asked.

"It's one of the only things I'm certain of." She pulled herself up and kissed him as another few minutes disappeared between their lips. "I will marry you in a fortnight and then we'll be gone, far from their reach."

Chapter 20

A few days after the massacre at Conestoga, Sam received a letter from Will Sock delivered by Ald, who had twice made the journey to Lancaster for news. Sam read the letter aloud to Lydia.

"Greetings, my friend.

Thank you for your inquiries as to our health, I admit I was surprised to hear you were still in the area. My wife and I are well, she thanks you for the gloves. I do not like this workhouse they have sent us to, it is too much like being jailed for a crime others committed, but my dear wife reminds me that it is a fine new building and the brick walls keep out even the worst of the storms. Our Mennonite friends do give us cheer, bringing us food and kind words.

It has been a terrible blow to lose our dear Shebaes and poor little Christy who had barely even begun his life, as well as our other brothers and sisters. I admit, the idea of never again seeing Christy running about with his little wooden gun brings tears to my eyes. We have not heard from Kwa'yo and his family. We can only hope they escaped..." Sam's voice caught. He ran the side of his hand across his eyes.

"I don't have the heart to tell them," he said.

He continued to read. "We do not know how much longer they intend to keep us here. We do not know what we will do or where we will go. Some of the young people want to rebuild, but I fear there are not enough of us. Some want to move west to live with their kin. This is my home; I do not wish to go. Our Mennonite friends have offered that we may live with them. Many of us share their faith, but I would be sad to lose our traditions. All we can do is pray for guidance.

My wife reminds me to be thankful that the storm kept us away, that so many of us were spared because of it. Still, I fear the danger may not yet be passed. The governor has issued a proclamation for their arrest, but none have been brought in. I worry all it has done is proved to the villains that the people won't punish them for their acts. May God protect us."

Sam folded up the letter. "I fear he may be right. If they think the people agree with them, they might go after the others."

"What can the Conestoga do?" Lydia asked.

"I don't know. I wish I did. If they try to rebuild, the Paxton's may return and attack again. But to leave would mean giving up their land, the land of their ancestors. Whites will take it and they will never be able to reclaim it. It's a difficult decision to make."

Lydia thought for a minute. "I know if it were Birch Run, I would want to rebuild, even if it were just a few of us families."

"But if it were just your family, would you?"

"I don't know. I suppose all we can do is pray for them."

♥ ♥

The morning wind stung Lydia's cheeks as she walked to the barn to help Sam milk the cows. It was so cold she'd considered, for a moment, just staying in bed, wrapped in her wool blanket. But it was the twenty-seventh of December now, only two days before her wedding. In two days, she would not see the cows again, not milk them again for years, possibly not ever.

It was strange how even the most mundane chores took on such importance now that she was leaving. The idea that there would be a last time she washed the dishes, a last time she fetched water from the well or cooked corn pudding in their hearth or mended her sister's stockings made each task seem like it must be done purposefully, that she might remember it after she'd gone.

She smiled as she watched the warm pale-yellow spray of milk fill the bucket. Milking was special. Sam was awake, the rag quilt she'd given him folded neatly next to his pallet bed.

They'd offered him Michael's room, but he preferred to stay in the barn, saying he wasn't used to living with quite so many people and found it a bit too loud for his liking. She knew he had other motives; he just didn't want to frighten her family by saying them.

He was still worried that the Paxton Boy's might hear of his location and come after him. He wanted to be far from the house if that happened, Lydia knew. He wouldn't want to risk her or the family. The thought saddened her that he should even have to consider such an awful thing.

"Hannah wishes to thank you for the moccasins you made her," she said, granting Sam a quick peck as she held the sloshing buckets.

He smiled. "They'll do until spring, I imagine. Then she can get new shoes."

"I doubt we'll ever find her old ones in the fields; she said the mud swallowed them up. Poor dear."

"I'll see you inside in a few minutes." He kissed her on the head.

She left the barn, a full pail of steaming milk hanging from each hand. Two more times she would make this walk.

"Lydia." She turned to see Seth standing there. Blood spray and spatter decorated his clothing. His face was white, his head kept twitching as if he was fighting the urge to look all about him. His pistol dangled from his hand. "I didn't know where else to go."

A cold terror gripped Lydia's heart. "Seth, what is it?"

"Lydia, I've done something terrible."

"Sam!" she called, unable to hide the tremble in her voice.

"No, not him. He shouldn't have to see me."

"What is it, Lydia?" Sam came out the door. "Seth? What's happened?"

Seth only stared at the ground.

Lydia took Seth by the arm. "Come, we'll talk inside." She opened the door and checked to make sure no one was around; she didn't want him to be seen in this state. "We'll go to Da's study." She led them in to the study, seating Seth in a wooden chair by the fire. He was shaking violently, but his flesh felt warm.

Lydia realized she was still carrying one of the pails of milk and set it down next to him, seating herself by the fire.

Sam pulled up the other chair and sat across from the young man who held his pistol in a death grip. "You can let go of the gun, Seth. We aren't going to hurt you."

Seth shook his head, not wholly, it more shifted slightly than turned. "No. No."

"What happened, Seth?"

"I... There was a meeting at a pub in Paxton. We drank and talked till dawn. They were saying they wanted to kill the Indians, to cut a swath to Philadelphia and murder every Indian in their path. But I thought it was all talk! Then Stewart and the preacher came and got us, they said it was time to go. I swear I didn't know where we were going!" His gun hand started shaking.

"We broke down the doors. The sheriff just stood there. They ran, the Indians. They fled from us, scattered like bunnies. And the men went after them. The old woman fell by the back door and an older man stopped to pick her up, and then they were on them. It was like when a wolf takes a rabbit. That suddenness, that same horrible scream. Their arms bringing down the hatchets again and again. I could hear the dull thud of them cutting into their flesh. They were laughing. They cut off their scalps." His head jerked.

"When they finally moved away, I saw there were two little children as well. The woman had been holding them. All of their heads were split open, I could see inside. I heard gunshots and screams. There was blood everywhere! They chased a big man to the wall next to me. He fell to his knees begging for his life and they shot him in the chest but he didn't die. He was alive when they chopped off his hands, tried to chop off his legs. He was screaming. He begged for them to kill him. They told me to help hold him up. I did it. I took his shoulder and held him up, and then Stewart took his gun and put it in the man's mouth. And then his head was gone and all there was was blood on the wall." Seth's whole body was shaking violently.

"They were lying on the ground with their children, begging for mercy, pleading to God for mercy! And they chopped them up. All around me the thud of hatchets chopping into flesh. They cut their scalps off. A baby girl! They cut her scalp off and held it up and cheered. It was so small. Smaller than my palm. I thought I saw one or two in the corner, trying to climb up the wall to escape. I don't know if they did. I looked away, I didn't want the other men to see me looking or they might see them. But they probably did anyway. All around me people were being hacked to pieces and I just stood there. Arms, legs, feet, hands - little hands! Everywhere! I couldn't move. They killed them! *I* killed them!" His hand began shaking so violently Lydia could hear the metal parts of his pistol clacking.

"I told them you're here. They're coming!" He took his gun and stuck it in his mouth.

"Seth! No!" Lydia shrieked.

A cascade of white poured over Seth's hand. The trigger clicked and clicked again, but failed to spark.

"Hasn't there been enough blood shed today?" Sam said darkly, sitting back down and tossing the empty milk bucket away.

Seth stared at the Indian in shock. "But what about the lives of your kinsmen? Shouldn't my life atone for one of them?"

"Taking a life cannot replace the loss of a life. It is only another life gone."

Seth stared at his pistol. "I've done something unforgivable. Don't you see? I watched it happen. I helped them break down the door! I held that man up while they shot him. I told them you were here."

"Then don't add another thing to that list. There's no sin God cannot forgive. If you want to atone for your crimes then don't die for the lost, live for them!"

Seth took the pistol, poured out the powder and shot into his hand, and threw the gun in the fire. He turned to face them as fire licked at the once shining weapon. "You have to go, now! They'll be here in a few hours. I can stay, help you. Cover for you."

"I think it's best you go," Sam said.

"I'll go then. Only, take Lydia and leave."

"What's going on in here?" Elias Fischer said, throwing open the door.

"Seth!" Hannah cried. "What happened?"

"Excuse me," Seth said, passing through the family. Lydia heard the door slam and knew Seth was gone.

"Why was Seth covered in blood?" Hannah asked, wringing her hands in alarm.

"There's been another massacre," Sam said. "Seth witnessed it."

Hannah's hands flew to cover a gasp.

Elias regarded Sam grimly. "Did he take part?"

"No," Sam said. It was one of the few times Lydia had heard him lie, and to protect Seth of all people! Sam stood. "The Paxton Boys know I'm here."

"You must go, then."

"We shouldn't have to," Lydia said. "Da, they murdered twenty people - women and children! Why not have the town take a stand against them? There is a proclamation out for their arrest."

Elias's visage turned to stone. "Hannah, leave us."

Hannah scurried from the room and up the stairs.

"That is the business of the English, and not ours," Elias said.

"But Da, there are more than enough of us! We can help. Does it not affect us? Are we not called to fight injustice?"

"No, daughter. We are called to be a people set apart. We will not interfere."

"But we can stop this before any more people die!"

"Lydia! This is not up for discussion. We will not interfere. This is the bishop's word on the matter."

Lydia was stunned. "The bishop?"

"Yes. He spoke to us elders after the first killings. We all agreed that while we would take the orphan girl in, we would not involve ourselves any further in the affair. It is an English matter."

"But if we could stop it and choose not to, if by our inaction people die, isn't that tantamount to murder?"

"Daughter, you will hold your tongue! We will speak on this no more. We will help you leave, but no more than that."

She almost shook with rage. "Yes, Da."

"Go pack your things. There's not much time." He turned his back on them and walked out of the room.

"Yes, Da." She felt Sam's hand snake into hers, she let their fingers entwine. "Sam, I'm so sorry. We were supposed to be better... We should leave."

"And where would we go?" Sam asked. "They're coming from the west. There's only one road from here to Lancaster. They'll be chasing us all the way to Philadelphia if we go east and Wa'ya could never make it that far. We might try to go around them through the woods, but they might still catch us, and if they don't, there would still be the wolves, panthers, and boars to contend with."

Lydia looked down into those earnest black eyes. He was right, she could see he was right. Even were he to go alone, it would not change things. Tears welled up in her eyes. "Sam, I don't want you to die."

"Let's not talk about such things right now. There's still some time. Even if it's only for an hour, I want you as my wife. Then I can stand before them and die without regret."

Lydia wiped the tears flowing freely from her eyes. "Yes. Let's. Before it's too late."

There was a knock at the door. "Mr. Fischer, is Sam in?" Ald asked.

"He's in the study."

Ald's troubled face appeared in the door frame. "Sam, Lydia. I just saw Seth coming from here. Did something happen?" He started. "Why is there milk on the floor?"

They told him the full story.

He thought for a moment. "Well, I can bring the cart. If we use that, maybe we can get you two further along."

"The cart..." Sam's index finger moved to his lips, as if he'd just had an idea. "What if we went through them, but they didn't know?"

Ald and Lydia stared at him, perplexed.

"What do you mean?" Lydia asked.

"I have no intention of just rolling over to die if there's a way out." His fingers drummed on the back of the chair. "I think I have an idea. But it'll be risky. Ald, over here."

They spoke in hushed tones, Lydia caught snatches of their conversation. It was a mad plan, but if it worked...

Ald nodded. "Yeah, I see what you mean. I'll do it."

"You'll be risking your life."

"I don't care. It's God's for me to risk. At least if I die, it'll be for the right reasons." He thought for a moment. "Maybe if we make it look less tempting, they won't try to search the straw. But I'll need a girl for that. And a large blanket."

"It can't be Hannah, I won't have her put in danger," Lydia said.

"What about Gretel? She's braver than most of the girls I've met," Ald said. "And she's practically your sister. I know she'd do just about anything for you."

Lydia felt a pang through her heart. "She would, but can I really ask that of her? I mean, look what they did to Ruth and her daughter!"

"Well, what do you think she would say to that?"

In her mind she heard Gretel say, *Can you really not ask that of me? I'm your best friend! I'll never forgive you if you go without me!* "You're right. Let's go."

Taking Lydia's rag quilt, they knocked on Gretel's door. "Lydia, what is it?" she asked. "What's wrong?"

"Gretel, we need your help." They explained the situation and the plan to her.

"Of course I'll help!" she exclaimed. "How could you even think I wouldn't? Liesl! I'm going out for the day!"

"You're leaving me to do all the chores again?" her sister shouted from the kitchen.

"It'll be a great story for tonight, I promise!"

"It had better be worth it or I'm taking your dessert."

"Take it anyway!" She called back as she threw on her shawl and shut the door behind her.

"It will be dangerous, it's possible you might be killed, or worse," Lydia said, grasping her friend's hands.

Gretel's green eyes glinted with excitement. "Not if we do it my way. Forget the cart. You said Seth felt guilty for everything? Well, let's give him the chance to do right."

Within the hour, they took the Garten's buggy, pulled by Wa'ya and Schwartz, to the hill where Lydia's favorite tree grew and exchanged vows in front of their two friends. Sam couldn't remember the words to the Quaker vows and Lydia only knew a few lines of the Brethren's so they made their own.

"I promise to love you until I breathe my last," Sam finished, stroking Lydia's cheek.

Her hand found his and wrapped around it, she leaned into his touch.

"Which will hopefully be a long time from now," Ald said. "Let's get a move on."

Lydia and Sam carefully lay down in the back of the buggy, then Ald and Gretel threw straw on top of them and, lastly, covered them with the quilt and placed Wa'ya's saddle against Lydia's feet so it looked like an afterthought.

Ald took the driver's seat with Gretel next to him. He took a deep breath. "Alright, let's go." He hit the reins and the buggy lurched ahead, sending Sam and Lydia sliding forward and then back.

Gretel looked back. "Are you alright? Ald, watch how you're driving! You don't want to kill them, yourself."

"Do you think you could do better?"

"I'm certain of it." The argument seemed to ease the tension and Ald relaxed, driving the buggy down the road toward Lancaster.

As they rode, all Lydia could do was pray. She prayed for their safe passage, she prayed for Ald and Gretel, that no harm would come to them, even were she and Sam discovered. She prayed for her family at home, that they would understand why she could not say goodbye. She prayed for the futures of her friends and for Seth, who'd been led to such a dark place she worried if he would ever be able to find the light again.

But mostly she prayed for all those Conestoga who had died so tragically. She prayed God would welcome them into His kingdom of peace and kindness. That the children would play once more with their families. That the mothers would hold their infants, whole and gladsome in their arms. She prayed for them, each one, even those she'd never seen, that what love from their fellow man they'd not known on earth they would know in heaven. She felt tears slide down her cheeks as she prayed, but she didn't dare wipe them.

It was not long before Lydia heard a cacophony of shouts approaching. She gripped Sam's hand in hers. He leaned over, giving her a kiss. His grip tightened on her hand as the voices drew closer. Horses whinnied, hooves clopping impatiently as they were pulled to a stop. Lydia could hear their heavy breathing, smell the mustiness of the stable all around them. The buggy was surrounded.

"Who are yeh and what business do yeh have here?" a rough Scottish voice growled.

"Ald Kipfer, and I'm just taking my sweetheart for a buggy ride."

"Don't yeh know it's not safe ta be ridin'? There's Indyins about."

"Are there?" Gretel asked warily, through the straw Lydia could see she wrapped her arm around Ald's.

"Should we make him pay a toll?" one voice asked. "For our protection?"

"Nah, his kind don't have any money," another answered, "And the girl's not pretty enough to be worth the time."

"Mebbe we should see if he has anything in the back might be worth taking?"

"I'll have a look," Seth said, riding up beside. He went to the door and lifted up the corner of the quilt, just enough that he might peek under without the others seeing. His blue eyes met Lydia's and, for a moment, it seemed their entire lives passed between them, those same blue eyes that bid her safe travels as she rode off to Lancaster to sell her quilts. He turned away. "Just a bunch of straw and an old saddle." He dropped the edge of the quilt.

"Oh ho! So it's that kind of buggy ride yer plannin'! Well, yeh kids have fun. Ah! Teh be that young again!"

They rode another two miles before Ald stopped the buggy. He unharnessed Wa'ya.

"I don't know how we'll ever be able to thank you for this," Sam said, saddling his horse.

"Live a long, long life. That'll be a start," Ald said.

"Gretel! I'm going to miss you so much!" Lydia clasped her friend to her. "Thank you!"

"I'm going to miss you, too!" They separated and Gretel wiped the tears from her eyes, laughing. "Imagine how jealous Hannah, Evony, and Agatha are going to be when they find out I got to stand with you at your wedding."

Lydia laughed through her tears. "Hannah's going to be so livid. She wouldn't talk to me for a year!" She wiped her eyes. "Tell her how much I love her."

"I will." The girls embraced once more.

"Hey, you've got a long way to go," Ald said, wiping away a tear.

Lydia took his hands in hers. "Thank you, Ald, you saved our lives."

"You're welcome, Lydia. Just don't forget to name one of your sons for me." He grinned shakily.

"Take care of Gretel for me."

His smile was now truer. "You can be sure of that."

Sam offered Lydia his hand and she took it, mounting up behind him. She wrapped her arms around his waist, resting her face against her husband's back. "Thank you, Lord," she whispered as they rode off toward the western mountains.

Epilogue

Almost a decade had passed since they made their escape. The first days had been the hardest, having nothing more than the clothes on their backs, a rag quilt, and whatever they had packed in Wa'ya's saddlebags. At night they rode, relying on their activity to keep them warm. During the days, Sam would fashion a crude shelter from branches and snow and they would huddle together next to Wa'ya for warmth.

Soon, Lydia had learned how to make a fire and was helping Sam to build their shelters. It was terrible and cold, she always felt soaked through, and sometimes, a chilling, wet wind would cause her to recall those days, even now, and shiver; yet she looked back on them fondly, those first days with her husband. When they had nothing but each other and whatever God provided them from the snares and plants.

By the fifth day, they made it to the place with the burned cabins Sam had told of in his story. Here there was a well to drink from. They built a more substantial shelter around one of the old stone fireplaces and were finally able to rest in safety. Sam set his snares and soon they had plenty enough to eat and soft furs to keep them warm on the frigid nights.

It wasn't long before Lydia was asking Sam to build a cradle, but, sadly, they would know the tears of Rachel twice before it would be used for their first son, Benjamin, and then used often after. Come that first spring, they built a fine cabin for themselves, large enough for their growing family.

It now numbered six with a seventh expected in a matter of months. Sam found success as a trapper and translator, teaching Lydia the local tongues as well, at her insistence, that she might be able to conduct business with the tribes. Between them, they built up a small trading post. They were well-liked by their neighbors for their kind and humble ways.

It was almost four years before they made the journey back to the village; with Benjamin riding up front with his father and baby Ald on his mother's back. Much had happened since their leaving. The Paxton Boy's had been stopped at Philadelphia with none other than Benjamin Franklin declaring it an unforgivable affront - for what little that meant. In the end, not a single one was ever held to account for their crimes. There was much unrest in Philadelphia now, a strain of hatred for the English king coursed through the darkened alleys of the city, but such things were of little concern to those living near Lancaster.

When they approached the small hill that had once overlooked the Conestoga village, Lydia could not help but anticipate the cabins, the children as they played with their dogs, the women sitting in a circle as they wove baskets. And Kwa'yo, standing with the men, waving, ready to run up and greet them.

As they crested the hill, a large, open field with a distant farmhouse met them. They were gone. There was nothing left to say they'd ever been at all. Somewhere in her mind they'd managed to live on, as if, until the moment she saw the empty field, it wasn't truly real.

Now, all that waved to them was the wheat on the wind. But still, they were there, invisible as ghosts. Existing in that strange medium of memory that still sees what has long been lost. Sam wrapped his arm around her as she prayed for them, joining her with a prayer in their own tongue. After some time of silence, they departed toward Birch Run by way of Lancaster, for a brief visit with her aunt and uncle.

Lydia was less surprised than she thought she should have been when she arrived home to find Hannah, her three children all about her, with her husband, Seth. He had always shown a fondness for Hannah, always invited her along to any frolic, but, as Hannah explained, after the murders there was no one in town who understood him as she did. She knew the seduction of hate and its bitter fruit. What had been an inclination soon blossomed to love. But Seth never forgot, the partially melted pistol kept on the mantle to remind them both of the true ends of prejudice.

It seemed Ald and Gretel had found their pretense as sweethearts agreeable and began their courtship as soon as they returned home. She'd borne two sets of twins in as many years and their youngest, a pretty little thing they named Lydia after the bravest woman they knew. Lydia argued she should have been named for Gretel, for she sat up front and faced danger head on, while she hid in the straw. Gretel just laughed and said it would have been too confusing to have two Gretels.

Michael and Evony had struggled for some years in their marriage. It would be two years before another child was born to them, a blond-haired son. Michael gave him his name and all his love, regardless, remarking he was much like his Aunt Hannah. Their bond grew stronger and twin daughters quickly followed. Michael remarked he seemed destined to follow in the path of his father, having a house full of women. Agatha and Nils had also long since married and given her parents the house full of children they had so desperately wanted.

When Lydia inquired about Ga'nígöhdáshä, who was now called Wisdom by all but Agatha who had called her Dasha as she preferred, she was shocked to learn she'd gone off to Canada some years ago. It seemed she had never taken well to the Brethren's ways, though she was quite popular with the boys for she was very pretty. She began disappearing in the nights a year after Lydia left, sometimes not returning for days on end.

The Bless's tried to put a stop to it, but she always found a way out. Then, one day, she never returned. They received a letter from Toronto some months later. It seemed she had come upon a group of slaves fleeing in the woods some months back being led by a freedman carpenter's apprentice. For almost a year she'd been helping slaves escape across the northern border. She and the freedman, John, who gave his last name as Moses, fell in love, and, when slave hunters discovered his role, they escaped across the border as well. They were happy, though she regretted not saying goodbye and thanked them for all their care.

The years passed and Sam and Lydia's love only grew. It was not always easy, but they weathered the storms together. Then, one day, an Indian man they'd not seen before arrived at their trading post. He and Sam struck up a conversation as Wa'ya tried to grab Sam's attention.

"That's a fine horse you have there," the Indian said. "Don't see many trappers with one so nice."

"Yes, Wa'ya's a fine one, with the worst habits. Look what he did to that trough over there." Sam pointed to a water trough that had once been straight in edge but now had undulating waves chewed into it.

The Indian regarded them quizzically. "Wa'ya? That's an odd name for a horse."

"How do you mean?" Sam asked, brushing Wa'ya's insistent head aside.

"Well, doesn't it mean wolf?"

The End

Printed in Great Britain
by Amazon